WAITING TO ATTACK

"Do you know what he hit you with?" I asked.

Bettina wagged her head. "I'm not sure. It looked like some sort of pipe."

"Like a tire iron, maybe?"

Bettina shrugged. "I'm not really sure what one of those look like."

I wasn't entirely sure either, but whether Bettina's assailant was wielding a tire iron or a magic wand made a world of difference. At least it did here, in the Underworld.

"He wasn't done either," Bettina said. "He—he—was going to hit me again, in the head, but the game must have let out because people started to fill the streets. He told me that my kind needed—needed to be erased."

"Your kind? Did he—did he know you were—"

My saliva went sour and suddenly my skin felt too tight.

Demons walk among us every day. A vampire might be your neighbor; the corner store might be run by a werewolf or a troll. There is a thin veil that masks the demon differences from the human sight. That veil, combined with our human ability to unsee anything that might unsettle us, has allowed the demon race to prosper and blend into the natural world.

That veil doesn't work on me, and if Bettina's assailant was human, the veil didn't work on him either . . .

Books by Hannah Jayne

UNDER WRAPS

UNDER ATTACK

UNDER SUSPICION

Published by Kensington Publishing Corporation

UNDER SUSPICION

The Underworld Detection Agency Chronicles

▶━◆━◀

HANNAH JAYNE

KENSINGTON PUBLISHING CORP.

http://www.kensingtonbooks.com

KENSINGTON BOOKS are published by

Kensington Publishing Corp.
119 West 40th Street
New York, NY 10018

ISBN-13: 978-0-7582-5894-6
ISBN-10: 0-7582-5894-1

First Mass Market Printing: May 2012

10 9 8 7 6 5 4 3 2 1

Chapter One

You'd think by the time a guy had gained immortality, he'd tire of copying his butt on the office copy machine.

Not so.

I was pulling out the third paper jam of the morning—and tossing fistfuls of copies of a weird combination of butt cheek and hoof—when Nina poked her head in, scanning the room, and asked, "Is she gone?"

I flopped backward and blew a few strands of my hair (done up in Clairol's Red Hot) out of my eye. "Who?"

Nina shimmied into the copy room and straightened her vintage boat-necked Balenciaga dress. She had paired this little number with black-and-purple lace tights and those peekaboo booties that make me look like a poor lumberjack while it made supermodels (and vampires) look amazingly chic.

I guess living through two world wars and umpteen clothing revolutions would pique your fashion sense.

"What do you mean, who? Mrs. Henderson. This dress"—Nina did an elegant twirl—"is not only vintage, it's irreplaceable. I wore it when I nabbed a bite of John

Lennon." Nina batted her lashes and grinned, her small fangs pressing against her red lips.

I cocked an eyebrow and Nina blew out an exasperated sigh.

"Fine. It was Ringo. So, is she gone?"

Mrs. Henderson—the Underworld Detection Agency's busybody dragon and all-around most obnoxious client—and Nina have a bit of a history together. It's one that most often leaves Nina naked and hairless, with Mrs. Henderson hiccupping smoke rings and not-so-genuine apologies.

I looked down at my watch. "Oh my gosh, I'm totally late. Thanks for reminding me."

I thrust the last of the hoof-and-butt Xeroxes into Nina's hands and headed to my desk—hopping over the burnt-hole remains of a wizard, who had blown himself up, and looking away from Lorraine, UDA's resident witch and finance whiz. She tried to stop me by waving in front of my face a folder full of invoices, but I was able to dodge her, thanks in part to the seminar that HR held on "Respecting Your Coworker's Personal Space."

I flopped into my ergonomically questionable chair and blew out a deep, comforting breath, then laced my fingers over Mrs. Henderson's files. In addition to being a fire-breathing, St. John Knit–wearing dragon, Mrs. Henderson was a divorcée hell-bent on squeezing her cheating ex-husband for every last dime. As our agency detected all supernatural movement within our region, Mrs. Henderson dropped in monthly for updates and especially liked it when we were prepared for her with Mr. H's paycheck stubs and warm, fuzzy stories about his current financial woes.

Fifteen minutes later, Mr. H's statements were still undisturbed in my file folder, and Mrs. Henderson was nowhere to be found.

I buzzed the reception desk and Kale answered—I could hear the murmur of the iBud she kept continually tucked in her left ear. "Reception," she said, "what can I do you for?"

"Hey, Kale, it's Sophie. Did Mrs. Henderson call in? She's almost twenty minutes late for her appointment."

I heard Kale muss some papers on the other end of the phone and then the snap of her gum. "No, nothing. Are you sure she was scheduled today?"

"Positive. It's the fifteenth."

"Ooh, alimony pickup day. She's usually a half hour early."

"That's what I was thinking. I'll try and ring her house."

"Okay. Oh!"

I rapped my fingers on my desk, suddenly impatient. "Yes?"

"Um," Kale started to stutter and drift off, and I could almost see her biting her lower lip, curling the telephone cord around her finger.

"What about Vlad?" I asked.

Vlad was Nina's nephew—and he was a current UDA employee, leader of the San Francisco chapter of the Vampire Empowerment and Restoration Movement (VERM for short, and for annoying Vlad incessantly), and a permanent fixture on Nina's and my couch. He had the bright eyes, video game fetish, and disdain for folding clothes that most sixteen-year-olds had.

Except that he was 112.

"Do you know if he is seeing anyone?"

Kale had been in love with Vlad since he first blew into the city—moody, restless, and dressed like Count Chocula. The Vampire Empowerment and Restoration Movement required that its adherents stick to the "classic" dress code of the fearsome vampires of yesteryear (more Bela Lugosi, less Edward Cullen) and also preached a staunch code against vampire/nonvampire mixing. That left Kale—a Gestalt witch of the green order—to pine relentlessly and call me on numerous occasions to ask about Vlad's dating status.

"No, Kale, I don't think so."

She let out a loud whoosh of relief. "That's what his Facebook status said. I just wanted to make sure. Bye, Sophie!"

The hangup sounded in my ear as I pulled up Mrs. Henderson's phone number. I was in the middle of dialing when Nina stalked in, slamming the door behind her. "So what did the big lizard have to say today? She needs more money for crickets?"

I hung up the phone and rubbed my temples. "She's a dragon, not a lizard, and she still hasn't shown up. That's not like her."

Nina whipped out a nail file and gave her perfectly manicured nails the once-over. "Maybe she lit herself on fire. One can only hope. "She snorted, her smile lingering. "I want to go shopping. What do you think? Boutique in the Haight or mainstream on Market?"

I frowned. "I'm kind of worried about Mrs. Henderson."

"So send her an edible arrangement. Don't they have one with staked mice or something? Anyway, boutique or mainstream? I need your financial prowess to point me in the right retail direction."

I pulled out my calendar and flipped back a few pages. "Last week I had two missed appointments."

Nina pouted. "Are you doubting your popularity at UDA now? You know everyone here adores you and we don't even consider your . . . issue."

I felt a blush rise to my cheeks.

My "issue" was my breath. Not that it was bad (at least I don't think it is); it is that I have some. The Underworld Detection Agency not only caters to the demon community—providing transfer papers, tracking paranormal activity in the city, detecting demon activity, and protecting from demonic or human threats—it is also staffed by demons.

Except for me.

Which is why there is currently a bologna and cheese sandwich wedged between two blood bags in the office fridge and why there is a constant CAUTION: WET FLOOR sign in front of the hobgoblin receiving line (hobgoblins are constantly slobbering demons and seem to have better traction than I do).

I rolled my eyes. "I know no one cares about me being human. I've been working here forever. It's the appointments. No cancellations, no phone calls, nothing. I called the last two for follow-ups and couldn't reach anyone."

Nina shrugged. "Who cares?"

"Where do you think they're going? It's not like there is another company out there protecting demons."

"Like a demon Walmart undercutting our fees?"

I crossed my arms in front of my chest. "Yes, Nina, I'm really worried that we're losing business to Walmart."

"Bring it up with Dixon."

I gnawed my bottom lip. "I guess I could. We do have an all-staff meeting at four."

Nina's coal black eyes went wide. "I had totally forgotten about that."

"Cuts into your shopping time?"

"No." She clapped a hand to her forehead and started a rigorous massage. "Do you know how awkward that's going to be? Me and him in the same room together after what happened!"

I leaned forward. "What happened?"

"Ohmigod, you and I live together, Soph! Have you not paid any attention? *Me and Dixon?*" she enunciated. "The whole dating thing? It totally didn't end well."

"Oh, right. That's probably because it was all in your head. Nina, he's our boss. It's expected that he'd call you. And asking you to collate his copies means just that. The man needs staples."

Nina narrowed her eyes. "Oh, and I suppose you're going to tell me that him asking me to boot up his hard drive was completely innocent, too!"

I groaned.

Nina leaned over to gather her coat and enormously gaudy Betsey Johnson bag. "So you never told me. Shopping on Market or Haight?"

"I don't know. Both. I can't make a decision."

Nina raised an eyebrow and grinned salaciously. "Ain't that the truth?"

I pursed my lips and straightened the already-straight

selection of Post-it notes and general office tchotchkes on my desk. "Bite me."

Nina dumped herself into my office chair again and lolled back. She kicked her Via Spiga booties up on my desk, crossing her ankles. "Hey, I'm not judging. If I had two hot otherworldly creatures ready to duke it out to save my afterlife"—and here she splayed a single pale hand against her chest—"I'd do my damndest to keep them both around, too."

She swung out the nail file again. "So about that shopping trip . . ."

I gathered a few files from my cabinet. "Give me a half hour and I promise to be your couture mule all the way through San Francisco. Deal?"

Nina cocked her head, her long, newly colored sunshine-blond hair swishing to her elbow. "Deal."

I poked my head into the outer office, where I used to sit (back in the Pete Sampson–werewolf-boss days), and mustered up my most harmless human smile for the vampire sitting at the front desk. He was heavily interested in whatever *Cosmo* had to say, but I saw his nostril twitch. When I sucked in a breath, he stiffened.

I am pretty well used to living a vampire-filled life, but having coworkers who could smell me at fifty paces is still a little unnerving.

"Hey, Eldridge."

Eldridge Hale raised his perfectly manicured eyebrows—mine looked like mating caterpillars most often—followed by icy silvery eyes.

"Ms. Lawson."

I waggled my files. "Dixon in? I need to talk to him."

Eldridge flicked a page of his magazine, effectively

letting me know he was bored. "He's busy. You'll have plenty of time to talk to him at the staff meeting."

I straightened, clenching my jaw. "I need to talk to him now. It's official UDA business."

"Send her in, Eldridge!" Dixon Andrade's voice was spun silk even as he called from his inner office. His hearing was 100 percent killer vamp, as was his olfactory skill, which meant he got a whiff of my Lady Speed Stick as I nearly jumped out of my pants. Disembodied voices never cease to creep me out.

Though it's been over a year, I found that walking into Dixon Andrade's office still pricked a little pang of sadness in my heart and gave me a small shudder of fear. I don't think I'll ever be able to walk into this part of the UDA again and not think of Pete Sampson, not think of the day I walked in and found my desk smashed to smithereens and his office—including the steel wrist and ankle cuffs used to hold him through full-moon nights—destroyed. The worst thing about that night was that Sampson was missing, blood was spilling in the streets, and Sampson—my Sampson, who had given me my first job, took me under his wing, and brought me more morning donuts than my pants could stand—was the chief suspect.

Now Dixon was lounging behind a desk the size of a Hummer, dressed, as usual, in a top-notch Italian suit that hugged every inch of his six-foot-plus frame. He looked formidable with his dark hair slicked back, his eyebrows pinched in a cautionary scowl. And that was before he showed his fangs.

"Ms. Lawson."

"Dixon, hi. Thanks for seeing me." I flopped down in his visitor's chair and slid Mrs. Henderson's file across the desk. "Mrs. Henderson didn't show up for her appointment today, and neither did two other regulars over the last week. No answers when I call, no cancellations, nothing."

Dixon's dark brows rose, his eyes catching on something over my left shoulder. I turned and sighed.

"Hi, Vlad."

If Dixon was San Francisco chic, Vlad LaShay had all the chicness of Castle Drac, circa 1850. His black pants were a heavy wool blend, his red damask vest was resplendent, and his frilly white ascot made him look like a dork.

"Nice ascot," I said.

"Are we making the announcement first, sir?" Vlad asked, effectively ignoring me.

My ears perked. "Announcement?"

Dixon and Vlad shared a look; my head ping-ponged between them.

Finally Dixon shrugged; his broad shoulders nipped his ears. "She'll find out soon enough. Ms. Lawson, Vlad is the Underworld Detection Agency's new head of operations."

Dixon grinned and Vlad beamed.

I wasn't sure what caught me more off guard, the sight of Vlad smiling like someone who wasn't perennially sixteen and mad at the world, or the fact that Vlad, with his face full of smooth planes and soft hints of baby fat, was going to be my manager.

I scratched my head. "Come again?"

"Vlad will be replacing Mr. Turnbow. Mr. Rosenthal will be shifting from support staff to finance, and Eldridge"—Dixon gestured to the blond vamp outside—"will be the new head of internal organization."

"What happened to Mr. Turnbow? And the former head of operations?"

Dixon shrugged dismissively. "It was time for them to move on. We had a cake on Friday."

Leave it to me to miss the one day that management sprang for cake over blood bags.

"Something wrong, Ms. Lawson?"

"No," I said, swinging my head, "not at all. Congratulations, Vlad. This is a really great step for you."

"So you said something about some missed appointments?"

"You know," I answered, snatching the file from Dixon's desk, "it's really not that big a deal."

Exiting, I shut the door to Dixon's office and Eldridge looked up at me from behind his magazine, one eyebrow quirked, lip turned up and slightly parted to show off the scissor-fine edge of a fang.

"See you around, Sophie," he said.

I hopped in the elevator and mashed the UP button. My heart was thudding underneath my Nina-approved button-down blouse; pricks of sweat were breaking out all over.

"Come on, come on," I whispered to the metal box as it lurched its way up—we're thirty-six floors down—to the outer world. There was a jaunty *ding* and the doors split open to sunshine streaming through the front vestibule of the San Francisco Police Department. The squawk and buzz of department radios and telephones littered the air. That was when I smashed—chest to cardboard box—into Alex Grace.

"Hey, Lawson." Alex grabbed my arms to steady me and I wanted to crawl back against him—sans the box—and sink into those arms.

"Oh, hey, Alex. Sorry, I guess I'm just a little bit distracted."

I blinked, then looked up into those cobalt blue eyes of his. Oh yes, I was definitely distracted.

Alex Grace was heavenly. His milk-chocolate dark hair curled in run-your-fingers-through-it waves, which licked the tops of his completely kissable ears. Those searing eyes were framed by to-die-for lashes. His cheeks were tinged pink, and his lips were pressed into his trademark half smile, which was all at once genuine and cocky, with just a hint of sex appeal. A man like this was otherworldly.

And Alex had the two tiny scars just below his shoulder blades to prove it.

Alex was an earthbound angel. Fallen, if you want to be technical. But he lacked the certain technicality that made other fallen angels so annoying: *He* didn't want to kill me. Most of the time.

I tried to tear my eyes away from his beautiful, full lips—lips that I distinctly remembered kissing—and focused hard on my rogue clients; but even though we had decided to be "just friends," almost six months ago, there was still a sizzling something between me and Alex. Call it forbidden love or my addiction to Harlequin novels, but Alex Grace was not an easy man to get over.

After all, he was an angel.

"Nice box."

"Oh, this?" Alex shifted the box and I rolled up on my tiptoes and lifted the lid.

This time, my thudding heart skidded to a stop. There were books and a few wrinkled copies of *Guns & Ammo* (What? Did you think fallen angels read the Bible?), what remained of a spider plant, which Alex had brought back to life for me, overstuffed file folders, and, rolling on top, the coffee-stained *Don't Hassle Me; I'm Local* mug I got him last summer.

His eyes softened. "I didn't want you to find out this way."

I put the lid back on the box and blinked up at him. "Are you going somewhere?"

He nodded, licking his bottom lip. "I was going to tell you, but . . ." Alex shrugged and looked away in that annoying, alarming way men had when they've just told you something vague and noncommittal that could either be "I'm considering changing from boxers to briefs" or "The fate of the world hangs in the balance."

"But what?" I tried to keep my voice steady, reminding myself that a good friend doesn't let her voice go into high-pitched hypersqueak when another good friend might be leaving.

"It's not really a big deal." He shifted the box. "Can we go somewhere and talk?"

I sucked in a deep breath. "Can't we talk now? In your office?"

"My office is pretty much cleaned out, but sure."

Since fallen angel-ing didn't come with a paycheck or a 401(k), Alex spent a good chunk of his mortal life working as an FBI field detective, generally stationed in a back office at the SFPD. The vagueness of his actual job title or description allowed him to come and go as he pleased, attending to official police—or angel—business whenever necessary. And also, he really liked donuts.

I followed Alex to his office and gaped at the half-empty room. The desk, where he had worked on cases—and where I once had imagined him pulling me down into a passionate embrace—was shoved against a wall and stacked with cardboard boxes. His office chair was upended on top of them. The free 2008 Honda calendar, which had been tacked to the back wall since 2010, was missing, as was the souvenir picture of us at the Giants baseball game.

"Why is your office cleaned out?"

"It's no big deal. I just wanted to let you know I won't be around for a while."

The file in my hand was suddenly filled with cement, was a hundred-pound weight that pulled my hand down. I leaned in close to Alex, swallowing heavily to try and find the smallest bit of saliva in my Sahara-dry mouth.

"Are you going back?" I finally managed.

Alex, though earthbound and fallen, wanted to return to grace—and I wanted that for him, even though grace meant I would never see him again. But now the thought of my life without him hit me like a raw fist at the bottom of my gut.

Alex was silent for a second that lasted millennia. He put the box down gently and blew out a sigh, which held all the emotion of the last two years of our life together.

"Yes," he said slowly. "I'm going to Buffalo."

I choked on the love-soaked soliloquy I was composing in my head. The one that talked about how I would, as the Vessel of Souls and Alex's only link to the Heavenly plane, be willing to give up my life for him to return to grace. I cocked my head and felt my lip curl up into an involuntary—and undoubtedly unattractive—snarl. "What?"

"Buffalo." Alex leaned back against the wall and looked stupidly unaware of the fact that I was about to lay down my life for him, right here between the men's room and the utility closet. "Stakeout. I'll be gone for a couple of weeks. It's starting to look like the trail of the guy I was after a few years ago is fresh again, and they're shampooing the rugs here so I have to get everything out, anyway. Good timing, huh? Hey, Lawson, are you okay?"

My heart was lodged securely in my throat. Images of bloodshed, of bullets firing, of Alex's lifeless body roared through my head.

"I swear to God, I'm going to kill you Alex Grace."

Alex cocked his head. "Aw, Lawson, I'm going to miss you, too."

I let a beat pass and my annoyance die down. "You're going on a stakeout? I thought you were—you were . . ."

Alex's eyebrow arched as a hearty officer sauntered into the men's room across the hall, newspaper tucked under his arm, dark eyes intent on us.

"You were saying?"

"Have a nice trip." I could feel the scowl weighting down my lips.

Alex blew out an exasperated sigh, rolling his eyes. "Now what?" he wanted to know.

"Nothing."

Alex crossed his arms in front of his chest. "Out with

it. You can't be that pissed off about Buffalo. What is it that's making you look like someone kicked your puppy? Come on, you can't hide it. I am an angel, you know."

"Correct me if I'm wrong, but aren't your only angelic powers wolfing down a pizza in one bite—"

"And the occasional mind reading." Alex grinned salaciously and I wanted to crawl under the table. He never said it outright, but I had the overwhelming suspicion that Alex had done the occasional mind dip when my mind was . . . indisposed. Like imagining *Alex Grace greased up with coconut oil and reclining on a beach*—that kind of indisposed.

Why couldn't I fall in love with an inmate, like a normal woman?

I worked to avoid the blush that I knew was creeping over my cheeks. And here's the thing about blushing: on chestnut brunettes a bashful crimson makes a pretty glow; ditto on those sun-kissed blondes. But when you're redheaded (my *Red Hot* hair color only served to slightly mask my natural Crayola orange 'do) and have the kind of skin that people politely refer to as "porcelain" (meaning glow-in-the-dark white), a "hint of blush" equates to looking exactly like an overcooked lobster in a white button-down shirt.

"Can I go to Buffalo with you? I'm good on a stakeout. I come with my own donuts."

"Why?"

"We're having another shake-up at UDA."

Alex rifled through a box and handed me a Styrofoam cup; then he filled it from the office water jug. "Big deal. You've been through that before."

I took a gulp of water. "Yeah, but this time Vlad is my boss."

He did something between a guffaw and a choke, and water dribbled down his chin.

I narrowed my eyes. "You deserve that," I said, pointing to his wet shirt.

"Vlad? Your boss? That's priceless."

"It's not just that. In the last month alone, Dixon has replaced every higher-up with a vampire. He said a couple of people retired, but I'm not sure I believe that."

"Why? Wasn't there cake?"

"And then there's this." I handed him the file folder and he squinted at it.

"Mrs. Henderson?"

"She didn't show up for her appointment today. She *never* misses an appointment. And another couple of my clients were no-shows, too. Isn't that weird?"

Alex finished the water in one final gulp and handed the file back to me. "Not really. Why don't you just call her?"

I bit my bottom lip. "I think I'll do one better. Thanks, Alex." I spun on my heel and was halfway into the hall when I felt his hand on my shoulder.

"What are you doing?" he wanted to know.

I shrugged. "Just going to make a pit stop."

"Don't get involved, Lawson."

"Who's getting involved?" I snaked the check out of Mrs. Henderson's folder. "I'm just doing a friend a friendly favor."

Mrs. Henderson and her two obnoxious teenagers lived in a gorgeous Old Hollywood–style house in a quiet neighborhood off Nineteenth Avenue. I was pleasantly surprised when I found it on my first try. I had been there numerous times for Mrs. Henderson's Christmas parties, but generally there was an eight-foot winking Santa to guide me down the tree-lined streets.

The house, usually resplendent with an impeccably manicured lawn and showy dusting of baby pink impatiens, was hardly recognizable. The lawn was overgrown and the impatiens were leggy and capped with drooping brown blooms. I continued up the stone walk and stooped on the porch to gather up at least a week's worth of *Chronicle* newspapers and local circulars advertising great prices on everything from fertilized duck eggs to tripe.

Clamping my mouth shut against a wave of nausea, I rapped on the door, then waited. The hairs on the back of my neck slowly started to rise, as did the suspicion that I was being watched. I pressed the newspapers to my chest and slowly turned my head over my shoulder. The Hendersons' overgrown lawn and shaggy plants remained as they were and the street was empty, but I couldn't shake the creepy feeling. I stepped off the porch and glanced up and down the street. Mainly deserted, except for a few parked cars—ticketed, of course—and an old man walking a basset hound four houses down.

"I'm just jumpy," I muttered to myself. "Jumpy."

I went back up the walk and I rapped again, harder this time. The door swung open. I jumped in and spun around, catching the taillights of a car as it sped down the street. The prickly feeling was still there; so I slammed the door, then pasted on a smile, ready to greet Mrs. Henderson or one of her annoying teens.

"Thank you so much," I started to say. "Sorry, I just . . . Hello?"

There was no one in the foyer and it was dim. All the curtains were drawn and the little wedge of outside light, which came in through a small crack in the fabric, illuminated dancing dust mites.

"Mrs. Henderson? It's me, Sophie. From the UDA. You missed your appointment today. . . ." I stayed pressed up against the door, my shoulder blades wincing against the cold wood. "Is anybody home?"

My instinct told me that something was terribly wrong, that I should turn around and leave, drive straight back to the UDA.

But I was never very good at trusting my instincts.

Instead, I took tentative steps down the hallway, still clutching the newspapers, still calling into the empty house.

"I'm coming down the hall now," I announced, giving the man with a hook who was likely waiting to gut me a play-by-play. "Is anyone home?" My voice rang out hollow in the gaping hallway and I tried to think of positive things—like a surprise dragon birthday party or Care Bears.

There was a crunch underneath my foot and I let out an embarrassing yowl, dropping the newspapers in a heap and leaping backward. I clawed at my chest as my heart hammered and my sweat glands went into hyperdrive. I could feel the kinks that I dutifully blow-dried out this morning popping back. I took giant gulps of air, spinning like a maniac to catch an intruder at all sides. Nothing. I toed the newspapers and pushed last week's away, revealing a newly crushed hot pink iPod.

"Uh-oh," I murmured.

I casually kicked the iPod aside, covering it again with the newspaper. When I found the Hendersons, I'd explain it. Silently I continued down the hall into the kitchen. I stopped dead, wincing, then pressed my hand to my nose. Either someone had gotten in on the fertilized-duck-egg deal or something was rotting. I didn't want to go farther, plagued with crime scene images of dismembered bodies—their milky, staring eyes—but I had to see.

The kitchen would have looked homey under any other circumstance. There was a decorative fruit bowl on the large oak table, and a valance and chair pads all coordinated with a sea of Laura Ashley–inspired roses. I walked carefully around the tiled island. A crock, which had been stuffed with cooking utensils, was cracked and lying on its side; spatulas and slotted spoons littered the gray slate floor. There were two covered pots on the stovetop and I pushed one lid back a half inch. I tried to peer inside, but the overwhelming stench of rotting food made me gag. I rushed to the kitchen sink and heaved, feeling hot salty tears rush down my cheeks.

A cold rush of air whooshed over me and I looked up, for the first time seeing the jagged hole in the glass. The sink and the counter were littered with tiny glass pieces. I had mashed my palms into some and now the blood—searing hot—was dribbling over my wrists.

I don't know how, but suddenly I found myself outside on the Hendersons' lawn, speed dialing Alex and shifting my weight from foot to foot, silently imploring him to answer.

"Grace?" he said into the phone.

"Oh, thank God. Alex, you have to come out here. Something's wrong. Something bad happened to the Hendersons."

"Again with this? Lawson, didn't we—"

A coil of anger overtook my fear. "No, Alex. Now." I read him the address and paced nervously, trying to work the tiny shards of glass from my palm. When I saw Alex's SUV round the corner, not ten minutes later, I let out a breathy sigh and a torrent of tears. He jerked the car to a stop and I ran toward him.

"Alex!"

He got out of the car and sped toward me, his blue eyes stormy and looking me up and down. "What happened to you? Are you okay?"

I shook my bloodied palms. "Nothing. Just broken glass. We have to go in there. Mrs. Henderson could be hurt. She could be dying!"

I snatched Alex by the shirtsleeve and dragged him toward Mrs. Henderson's front door. "Something— something happened in there."

"Was there anyone inside?"

I wagged my head, using the back of my hand to swipe at tears that had suddenly started to fall. "I don't know."

"Stay here."

Alex tried to guide me back to the car; but the second he turned, I followed him. He crept up the porch and carefully pushed open the door. I ran up behind him. My breasts were just brushing against his back; my heart was thundering like a jackhammer.

"Doesn't this look suspicious?" I whispered in Alex's ear.

He held up a silencing hand and pulled his gun from the holster. I clapped a palm to my forehead, then grimaced at the sting from the broken glass. "I should have brought my gun. Or at least my Taser."

Alex gave me a cursory look. "I think you've done enough."

"What is that supposed to mean? If it weren't for me, you wouldn't be here, possibly putting both our lives in dan . . . Oh. I see what you mean."

"Stay out here." Alex gave me a gentle but firm push back.

"I'm not staying out here!" I said, pushing back against him. "The perp is probably out here just waiting to gut me!"

"Fine. Just stay quiet and close."

I clung to Alex's back as he walked silently from room to room. On the upper floor there was slightly more damage—pictures knocked from the wall, clothing torn and scattered on the floor, drawers left open.

"So? What do you think? Homicide? Special circumstances?"

Last year I had the opportunity to work with Alex to solve a case, so I was pretty well-versed in the police lingo.

Alex cocked an amused eyebrow, trying to keep the smile from his lips. "I thought we promised—no more *CSI* for you?"

I snarled, "Can we just focus on the case?"

"Okay. It's obvious that the Hendersons are not here, but it's not entirely obvious that this is a crime scene."

I stomped my foot. "Crooked pictures! Broken glass! A smashed iPod. Add it all up, Alex, it spells *duh*. What more do you need? A gallon of blood? A note from the kidnapper?"

Alex shook his head slowly, his angelic, gentlemanly way of ignoring me, and stepped around me, poking his head into a gaudy bathroom with gold fixtures and cheetah print wallpaper. Then he rested his hand on the doorknob of the only closed door in the hall. I watched as his fingers curled around the knob in slow motion. My heart lurched, lodging itself squarely in my throat. I started to shake my head.

"I don't think you should open that."

Alex's eyebrows disappeared under his bangs. "Why not? Did you hear something in there?"

I rubbed my arms, feeling the gooseflesh under my palms. "I have a bad feeling. Maybe we should wait for someone. Backup or something."

Alex rolled his eyes and nudged the door open with his shoe, poking his head in.

"What do you see? Are they—"

I couldn't finish my sentence as Alex's coughing and retching cut me off. He doubled over, stumbling backward.

"Alex!"

He snapped the door shut before I could get a look inside and I rushed over to him, helping him settle onto the carpet, clapping his back as he coughed while tears streamed over his red cheeks.

"Are you crying?" I asked, huddling down. "What did you see?"

Alex's eyes narrowed into an exasperated glare. "Couldn't you smell that?"

I looked at the closed door, my palm closing over the knob. Alex backed away and used the back of one hand to rub his damp cheeks, the other hand clasped over his nose and mouth. He nodded—a sort of "go ahead and take your life into your own hands" look in his eyes—and I wrenched the door open a half inch. I sniffed at the tiny gap, looked over my shoulder at Alex, and shrugged.

"I don't smell anything."

Hand still pressed firmly over his mouth and nose, he inclined his head and gestured for me to go in. I did, pressing the door open farther, stepping into the dim room.

"Oh God," I whispered.

The silent calm hung in the air like its own entity, oppressive and ominous. Thin shards of sunlight cut through the tears in the curtains, casting inappropriate cheery washes of light over the naked mattress, over the nightstand that was half crushed, its innards oozing out through splintered wood. My eyes immediately went to the bedclothes heaped on the floor—expensive jacquard silk and matching pillows with delicate fringe looked tramped on. These were torn and sodden with a brackish, viscous-looking liquid. The walls were stained with the same dark water; it colored the pale paint a sooty black. This time I slammed the door as I felt the bile rise in my throat.

I doubled over in the hallway and gasped, breathing in lungfuls of stale air.

"So what is that?" Alex wanted to know. "Toxic mold or something?"

I looked at him, dumbfounded, trying to work up enough saliva to unstick my jaws, to swallow down the burn in my mouth. I felt my eyes start to water, felt my nose start to run. All I could do was wag my head from side to side, my gaze fixed on the plush carpet under my feet.

"It's blood."

Alex let out something that was halfway between a snort and a chuckle. "Lawson, I may not be all that . . . local . . . but don't forget, I'm a cop. I do know what blood looks like."

"You don't know what dragon blood looks like."

Alex visibly paled and rubbed a palm over his chin.

"We have to go back in there." His cobalt eyes raked over me and then to the closed door. "Ready?" he asked.

I nodded, unable to form any words. He pushed open the door and the grim scene greeted me again: the dark spatters climbing like gnarled fingers up the walls, the cold destruction in the room. I felt my heart do a choking double thump as I scanned the scene.

"This is bad, Alex."

Alex picked his way around the broken furniture, careful not to step into the black puddles soaked into the carpet. He circled the bed, peered into the half-open closet.

"There are no bodies. Do you think maybe the Hendersons got away? From the look of the—the blood, they would have been pretty severely injured."

"No. No, they didn't get away." I gulped, toeing the discarded duvet, clamping my jaws shut against the wave of nausea that flashed when my fears were confirmed. There was more blood, the outline of broken bodies, singed into the carpet. "They were murdered."

Alex put a gentle hand on my forearm and I let him lead me downstairs and out the front door. He closed the

Hendersons' door firmly behind us and turned me to face him when we were out on the front stoop.

"I'm sorry about your friends, Lawson." He pushed a lock of hair behind my ear, his fingertips gently brushing my cheek as he did so. "Are you okay?"

I sucked in a shaky breath and pinched my eyes shut, hoping to burn the image of the Hendersons' destroyed room out of my mind. "I'm worried, Alex. This proves it. There's something going on in the Underworld."

The muscle in Alex's jaw twitched, but his eyes stayed soft, stayed focused on mine. "It doesn't prove anything. It could have been a random attack, for all we know."

"They were"—I scanned the sidewalks, dropping my voice—"demons. That would be a hell of a coincidence, don't you think?"

Alex nodded, though he didn't look convinced.

I shook my head, rubbing at the throb that had started near my temples. "And they were dragons. It's not easy to take down a dragon. Who—what—ever did this knows what he's doing. And he's strong."

"What are you going to do?"

I felt my mouth drop open. "What am I going to do? You're the police. You're a homicide detective!"

"And you work for the one entity in the entire world equipped to deal with demons."

I stared Alex down, until he blew out a sigh.

"What am I supposed to do? Call a squad in for a disappearing dragon death?"

I crossed my arms in front of my chest. "You could do worse."

"Call Dixon. Let him handle this. After what you've

been through this past year, don't you think it's time to take it easy?"

Alex tried to squeeze my shoulder in what I supposed was an attempt to be appeasing and compassionate, but I dodged him, narrowing my eyes.

"I almost got blown up by a psychotic fallen angel," I reminded.

"You almost got blown up in general."

"Which makes looking into a demon murder look like a cakewalk." I forced a Cheshire grin. "So we're on the case?"

"Let Dixon handle it," Alex repeated.

I thought of the dismissive way Dixon promised to "look into" the incident and then looked at Alex as he beelined down the front walk, stuffing his gun back into his holster. He paused at the sidewalk and looked over his shoulder. "Coming?"

I followed Alex down to his car, where he fished out a first aid box from under the seat. He carefully, tenderly picked the last bits of glass out of my palms, then swabbed the whole thing with Mercurochrome.

I squirmed. "That stings!"

"Hold still."

He fished out a roll of gauze from the kit.

"I shouldn't be letting you do this," I said finally.

"Because I'm not a doctor?"

"Because you're an idiot. *Something* is going on. It could be a band of—of Mexican drug lords or a fallen angel coming to seek her ultimate revenge or, you know, crackheads. And you didn't do a thing about it." My eyes started to sting and I sniffled furiously, willing myself not to cry. "You're going to feel so bad if they come back and gut me."

The muscle in Alex's jaw twitched and I saw he was fighting a smile. "You're just waiting for someone to get gutted, aren't you?"

I blew out a sigh. "Don't you have a stakeout to go on?"

"I'm not leaving just yet. And I'm concerned, Lawson, I am. But like I said, this"—and here he jutted his chin toward the Hendersons' very plain, very non-Underworld-looking house—"is really not police department jurisdiction." His eyes were soft, what I imagined would be bedroomy and rather sexy—were I not half covered in gauze and dried blood and just about to pee.

"So what do I do?" I asked, my voice hoarse. "Just ignore a crime scene and file it under, I don't know, weird, demonic coincidences?"

Alex wound the last bit of gauze around my left hand and then pulled it close to his lips, brushing a gentle kiss on my palm. He looked at me through lowered lashes; the blue of his eyes was intense, piercing. "I promise to look into it," he murmured, "if you promise me you won't."

I swallowed and he held my eyes.

"Promise," I said, trying to consider how to cross my fingers while Alex still held my hand.

Chapter Two

I was fishing my keys out of my shoulder bag—and cursing my apparent need to pack everything I've ever owned into eleven inches of knockoff Kate Spade—when I heard the thump from behind my locked apartment door. My hackles immediately went up. My suddenly sweaty palms worked the straps of my bag while my heart thudded into my throat and I pressed my ear to the door.

There was an audible groan. A breathy whimper.

I dumped my bag and gave the door a "hi-ya!" with my foot, splintering it open—at least, that's what I imagined I would do. Instead, I shakily retrieved the hide-a-key from the dusty top of the door frame and sank it into the lock, very slowly pushing open the door. I peered into the darkened living room, gulping heavily when my little lunatic of puppy fur and kibble breath didn't come barreling and barking to the door to greet me.

"ChaCha?" I whispered into the darkness.

The metallic stench of blood hung heavy in the air.

"Sophie?"

"Vlad?" I pressed on the light and felt my stomach churn as Vlad sprang up, shirtless, his chest alabaster pale in the now-glaring lights.

Kale sprang up from underneath him, her manicured black fingernails working furiously to button her shirt.

"Oh God. You guys! This is . . . ew!"

I tried to look away as Vlad reworked the contraption that passed for his VERM-approved seventeenth-century button fly.

"Ew, ew, EW!"

"What are you doing home?" Vlad demanded. He looked down at Kale, whose cheeks were a heady red.

"You said she was seeing Mrs. Henderson."

Kale looked up at me, dark eyes a combination of horror and embarrassment. "You were supposed to be seeing Mrs. Henderson."

I crossed my arms, and my eyes scanned the living room, littered with blood bags, a tipped glass of something sticky-looking dripping onto the carpet and—I cocked my head to listen—Barry White crooning softly on the stereo.

"Are you kidding me right now?"

Kale stood up, dressed now, eyes wide. "Please, Sophie, don't tell Lorraine about this."

I felt my left eye start to twitch.

"Just go, Kale."

Kale gathered her purse and turned to Vlad, pink lips in midpucker.

"Now," I groaned.

Kale hurried out the front door and I kicked it shut behind her and then got to work blowing out what remained of my last Pottery Barn mulberry candle.

"You were supposed to be at work," Vlad grumbled from his spot on the couch. "You're not going to tell anyone about this, are you?"

I spun to face Vlad. "First of all, it doesn't matter if I was in Timbuktu. You were schtupping Kale on the couch. *My* couch! I watch *Maury* on that couch. Now I'm going to have to burn it."

"If it helps, we hadn't actually gotten to the schtupping part."

I glared. "It doesn't."

"So . . . you're not going to say anything to anyone?"

I thought of Vlad's flock of Bela Lugosi–dressed VERM members and their anti-mixing stance while I looked at Vlad, right now more teenaged boy than broody immortal. I couldn't be entirely certain, but I'm pretty sure that trading whatever vampire's passed off as spit with the finance intern/receptionist (a witch) was probably frowned upon by the Count Chocula set.

"No, I won't say anything."

Vlad grinned, relieved, his fangs showing the slightest tinge of blood-stained pink. "Thanks."

There was an uncomfortable beat of silence. "By the way," I stated, "congratulations on your promotion. How did it go over at the staff meeting?"

Vlad beamed. "Really well. People seemed really excited—I mean, most people."

Vlad's eyes held mine and I could feel myself shrink.

"I'm really excited for you, Vlad, I am." I forced a smile almost bigger than I could stand.

"But?"

"Nothing."

Vlad's eyebrows remained high.

"You're sixteen," I finally relented.

"I died when I was sixteen." Though his voice had a determined, dark edge, there was still something in it that was soft and vulnerable—something that I wanted to nurture and protect.

"I am really proud of you, Vlad. It's just going to take a while to put two and," I said, pausing, "one hundred and twelve together, okay?"

Vlad rolled his eyes, a hint of a smile on his lips. "I know, it's the best you can do. You're only mortal."

"The expression is 'you're only human.'"

"Whatevs."

And he was back to being sixteen again.

There was a quick rap on the door and Vlad yanked it open, grinning at Will.

"Hey, mate," Will said.

Vlad sucked a leftover splatter of blood from his fingertip and pointed at me. "Sophie's over there. I need to get ready for my meeting."

Vlad disappeared into Nina's room, shutting the door softly behind him. Will looked from the door to the torn blood bags still dripping on the coffee table. The alarm was evident on his face. He held me by the shoulders and looked me up and down, finally tilting my neck. "You okay, love? Did he, uh"—Will bit his lips, trying to choose his words—"hurt you?"

Oh! My guardian angel!

I crossed my arms. "Some Guardian you are. I could have been fang food and you'd come sauntering in here asking if I was okay, love." I feigned Will's English accent.

Will narrowed his eyes. "I'm a very good Guardian,

which is why I didn't embarrass us both by rushing in here all 'good angel' on you. I knew you weren't in any real danger."

The "good angel" jab stung. While most women would adore the fact that two incredibly attractive men moved Heaven and Planet Earth (sometimes quite literally) for their personal protection, the "angel" versus "Guardian" barbs got quite old.

"Besides, I'm here for Nina."

Let's get one thing straight: I *like* Will Sherman. He's attractive in that sandy surfer with a head full of completely mussable blond-brown hair kind of way; in that sun-kissed skin, English accent, "mind the gap" sort of way. And I'll admit, in a few instances of utter weakness, I have felt a certain below-the-belly-button twinge when he smiled and his eyes did that mischievous little crinkle thing, or when he said something adorable and Englishy, like "Let's have a lag-ah and watch telly at the pub." So I *like* him, yes. He's my Guardian—and not in that "until you're eighteen" sort of way, but in an "until the balance of power has been restored between the good and the fallen, I will protect you" kind of way. Which, when you really get down to it, is hard not to like. But I don't *love* him. Which is why getting a tiny twinge of jealousy pricking at my spine was a completely unnecessary surprise.

I felt my eyebrows disappear into my bangs. "Nina? Why are you looking for Nina?"

Will held up a collection of DVDs. "I'm returning her *Entourage* set."

Again, I repeat: I don't *love* Will. So I am chalking up the cold wash of relief that flooded over me at the presentation of the *Entourage* episodes as relief that Nina's DVD collection could once again be complete, rather than the idea that my roommate was making moves on my Guardian.

"I'll be sure she gets them." I held out my hands, silently praying that Will couldn't feel the heat that wafted from me.

Will clapped his hands over the DVD spines and pushed past me. "That's okay. I'll wait." He pulled out a dining-room chair and plopped down. He kicked his feet up on the dining table and crossed his legs at the ankles, displaying his bright red-and-yellow Arsenal Football Club socks.

"Nice socks." ―

Will beamed. "Gift from Mum."

"Get your feet off my table."

"Ooh, you're snarky. So who are we after this week?"

"What?"

I followed Will's honey-colored eyes to Vlad, who had changed into a crisp white shirt, dark brocade vest, and silly-looking ascot. His black hair was slicked back in a precise hair helmet that showed off the deep widow's peak that he and Nina—and most members of the LaShay clan, I expected—shared. He had a stack of flyers under one arm and was trying to wrangle a handful of VERM protest signs in the other.

"*We* are not 'after' anyone," Vlad said, setting his signs against the table and rearranging the poof of his ascot. "We're simply planning a silent protest of Edie Havenhurst's new book, *Fendi and Fangs.*"

In one fell swoop Nina pushed through the front door, ditched her size-of-Guatemala shoulder bag and her sky-high booties and landed elegantly on the couch, her lifeless body not making a sound. She pulled up onto her knees, her grin somewhere between excited and maniacal, her coal black eyes wide.

"Ohmigod! I love *Fendi and Fangs*! I think it's even better than *Dooney, Bourke, and Buried*." Nina leaned over and pulled a worn paperback from underneath the couch cushions, holding it up like a prize. "I love, love, love Eliza Draconie. She's the reason I went blond."

Nina had taken her waist-length glossy Prell hair from her supernatural inky black to a sun-kissed California blond. Today she was wearing it in two long, skillfully mussed braids, topped off with a knitted gray beanie and a pair of heavy black-rimmed eyeglasses. Paired with the aforementioned boat-necked Balenciaga, Nina looked like a sexy Calvin Klein ad. Should I attempt the same look, I'm quite sure I would have looked like I had just walked off the set of a "Be Kind to Your Local Librarian" ad.

Nina jabbed a finger at me. "And, by the way, walking into a conversation about a book I love has totally saved your ass."

I blinked.

"Shopping!" Nina informed me.

I slapped my palm against my forehead. "Neens, I'm so sorry."

"Who's this Eliza bird?" Will wanted to know.

"Who is Eliza Draconie?" Nina's coal black eyes were as wide as saucers, and her little heart-shaped mouth was held in an astonished O. "She is only the most fashion-forward and fabulous vampire ever to live!"

I cupped my mouth with my hand and leaned toward Will. "To not live. She's—".

"I know," Will said, waving his hand at me, "undead. A vampire."

"And completely fictional," I finished.

"Maybe," Nina said, "but Edie knows what she's talking about." Nina tapped her index finger against her ruby red lips. "If I didn't know better, I'd say Edie was one of us, or is seriously entrenched."

Vlad spit out an exasperated sigh. "She is *not* one of us, nor does she have any kind of connection to the demon Underworld. She is yet another 'pop culture artist'"—he made air quotes with his pale fingers— "who is propagating this myth of the fashion-whoring vampire woman, catting around modern society and falling in love with breathers. You should be ashamed, Aunt Nina. Edie Havenhurst is setting back the female gender thousands of years."

"Back to when that ascot was in style," Nina said without looking up from her book.

Vlad glared at her and then looked back at us, his black-painted fingernails raking over his ascot. "We are simply doing a small-scale demonstration at Ms. Havenhurst's book signing tonight."

Nina was up and standing nose to nose with Vlad in half a heartbeat, and I gripped my chest. I don't care how long I've lived with a vampire—that creepy, silent, superspeed thing was going to kill me eventually.

"Edie Havenhurst is *here*? In San Francisco? Now? Ohmigod, I can't believe you didn't tell me."

Vlad grinned triumphantly and held out his protest sign to Nina. "So you're coming down?"

Nina's eyes were glassy as she tapped her fingers against her pale forearm. "I don't think I have anything to wear."

"What you have on is fine. We're not trying to stand out. Our message is." Vlad shook the sign at her and Nina glared at it as though the flimsy cardboard was doused in holy water or polyester. "Get rid of that. I'm not going on your dork march. I'm going to meet Edie Havenhurst."

Vlad let out a low growl and stomped out of the house, slamming the door behind him so hard that my requisite San Francisco dweller photo of the Golden Gate Bridge rattled in its frame. Nina, unfazed, kicked open her bedroom door, opening the gaping portal into the velvety, vampire world of vintage couture. Will and I exchanged a glance.

"Feel like watching a vampire drool?" I asked him.

"Sadly enough, I haven't anything better to do."

Chapter Three

I was white-knuckling the dashboard of Nina's little black Lexus coupe while she sped through intersections, dodging terrified-looking tourists as they clutched Nordstrom bags and hunks of sourdough bread to their chests.

"Slow down, Neens. You're the only one who's immortal here."

"Ahem," Vlad growled from the backseat.

"You know what I mean," I said without turning around.

Vlad and Will were tucked into the cramped backseat, and I could see Will's long legs trying to negotiate Vlad's collection of protest signs and VERM leaflets while he tried desperately to avoid Nina's collection of discarded drunk-on-the-go blood bags and unacceptable fashion choices.

"Did you have to bring all of this?" Will asked as he pulled a FEAR THE FANGS sign out from under one butt cheek. "I mean, aren't you VERM guys supposed to be kind of secretive?"

I watched Vlad's perfectly sculpted eyebrows come together. "The Vampire Empowerment and Restoration Movement. We don't shorten it."

Will's expression said he was waiting for more, and Vlad rolled his eyes.

"Yes, we are a rather secretive organization."

I cleared my throat. "But isn't VER—sorry, the Empowerment Movement—isn't it basically running the UDA now? I mean, you've got Eldridge and Dixon and now you."

Vlad looked positively disgusted and ignored me completely. "As I was saying, the Vampire Empowerment and Restoration Movement is a rather secretive organization. To *you* people. But there are instances—like the egregious and degrading portrayal of our kind, especially just to make a few bucks—that demand we not stay silent. As I mentioned, this will be a peaceful protest."

Will blanched. "I suppose that's good to know."

Vlad looked toward the window wistfully. "Originally we were going to have a parade."

I swung my head to gape at Vlad over the seat back. He looked slightly sheepish as he angled himself away from a lone shaft of sunlight. "That one fizzled, for obvious, we-burn-in-sunlight reasons."

Will leaned forward toward me, pressing himself into the front seat. The stubble on his chin brushed my ear, giving me a completely inappropriate little thrill.

"This bookstore we're headed to have an adult section?"

"You're disgusting," I muttered.

"I'm only human, love," Will said, winking.

I gritted my teeth, clamped my knees together, and tried to focus on the San Francisco streets racing toward us and the bits of my life flashing before my eyes. I almost took a bite of the dashboard when Nina spied a parking spot the size of a postage stamp and attempted to wedge her car into it. My heart was pinballing against my rib cage as Nina made her way into the spot, "tapping" the bumpers before and behind us because "that's what they're there for, silly." Once she had parked, Nina killed the engine and went to work smoothing her hair.

"We're here!" she crowed joyfully. "How's my hair?"

"Great."

I slammed the car door behind me and watched Vlad beeline to a group of vampires, all similarly attired as Count Chocula, all looking distressed and sullen.

Behold the bastions of Hell: a group of immortal teenagers decked out with hair gel, black nail polish, and toothy protest signs.

The VERMers were huddled together in some sort of fang-tastic motivational meeting. I half expected them to pile all their pasty hands together and then do one of those bouncy, inspirational cheerleader yells: "Vampires, vampires, vampires, YEAH!"

Will was doing an almost imperceptible bounce from foot to foot and I put my hand on his arm. "Don't worry. The VERMers talk about empowerment, but they still get their blood from bags. You should be fine." I smiled warmly.

"And I suppose you consider that the kind of pep talk that *should* be comforting?"

I rolled my eyes and yanked Will after me as I tried to keep my eye on Nina, who was elbowing her way through glamoured teenagers. The teens eyes were glazed, their breathing slow; it is this "glamour" that gives vampires their instant allure and constant access to willing necks.

I pointed to a particularly affected girl. "Remind me to get after Vlad for using glamours."

"Isn't that kind of their," Will made air quotes, "thing?"

I mimicked his quotes. "Their "thing" is like shooting fish in a barrel. Now come on."

When we finally got through the double glass doors of Java Script, the crowd was thinner, but not by much. I realized I was still gripping Will's wrist, so I let it go. My fingers brushed his and he paused; then he laced his fingers through mine and little pinpricks of heat shot through my body. The gesture might have been completely platonic and under the guise of guardianship, but there was something about the way our hands fit together that gave me pause.

"I think they've set the author up over here," Will said, letting go of my hand.

I followed him and Nina through the stacks of polished hardbacks, best sellers, and reader recommendations to a life-sized cardboard cutout of Eliza Draconie. Eliza stood one-dimensionally six feet tall, looking smug in head-to-toe leather and shoes to die for. Plumes of orange and pink smoke were painted behind her, to give the "just stepped out of a cheery, fashionable Hell" look.

If only.

Nina whipped around Eliza and stopped dead; Will and I, in turn, rammed into each other.

"*That's* Edie Havenhurst?" Nina gasped.

I don't know what I expected from a woman who spent her life writing about fictional vampire fashion-istas, but Edie Havenhurst was not it. And judging by Nina's slack-jawed expression, Edie didn't meet her expectations, either.

Edie was sitting behind a table stacked with pink-spined paperbacks that reached to her shoulders. The elegant blond waves that were a shoulder-sweeping halo in her "About the Author" picture stuck out in random arches now, with black roots giving way to brassy blond streaks that made her thick eyebrows look even darker, dwarfing her already small brown eyes. She wore no makeup, and rather than the selection of haut couture that Eliza Draconie sported, Edie Havenhurst wore a nondescript turtleneck sweater and pants suit.

"She's wearing sneakers!" Nina hissed.

Underneath the table Edie's legs were crossed at the ankles, the hem of her pants rising enough to show off thick white sport socks and those roundy boat shoes that are supposed to tone your thighs and firm your ass just by virtue of lacing them up.

"I expected Steve Maddens, at the very least." Nina shook her head disappointedly.

"Nina, if you love her books, you shouldn't—"

"Judge a book by its cover?" Will said with a satis-fied grin.

I linked arms with Nina and guided her through the crowd. "We're here. You might as well get your book signed."

We stopped in front of Edie's table and I felt Nina stiffen, heard her let out a tiny yip. Her eyes were

Disney cartoon wide, and her small chin hitched upward, with lips slightly parted. I started to panic.

I knew this look.

I *loathed* this look.

I followed Nina's laser-sharp gaze and gave a little yip myself.

He was beautiful. He was hunched over, with one perfect, large hand resting on Edie Havenhurst's shoulder. Even in this crouching state you could tell that this man was tall, commanding; he wore his confidence as well as he wore his relaxed Chinos and his smart blue button-down shirt. His eyes—an amazing cross between golden wheat and burnt sugar—were focused wholly on Nina.

The bookstore din seemed to fade and I realized I was trapped inside Nina and Mr. Perfect's lovestruck bubble. I stepped forward and gave Nina a hard, for-her-own-good shove. She pitched forward, breaking the mesmerizing stare, throwing her copy of *Fendi and Fangs* forward so that it hit poor, unsuspecting Edie smack between her too-small eyes.

While Edie rubbed vigorously at the red spot that the book had left, I noticed that her fingers were short, her nails stubby and bitten to the quick, and that I had likely lost Nina forever.

"Oh geez," I breathed out.

It wasn't that I didn't want my best friend to find true love. I did. For years I lived vicariously through Nina's never-ending parade of well-muscled party boys and San Francisco power brokers. She brought home millionaires and dukes, and they almost always left with all their blood. But when her eyes went wide and her lips pursed like that, I knew there was going to be trouble—and I was the one usually up to my neck in it.

"Oh, are you okay?" His smooth voice matched his burnt-sugar eyes.

"I'm fine." Nina's voice came out soft and breathy—like a sex kitten or Michael Jackson. "I'm Nina."

"Harley." The man held out that perfect hand and Nina grasped it; the whole exchange happened just above Edie's dark roots.

"I'm Sophie and we were just leaving." I thanked Edie for politely ignoring the Taylor Swift video going on above her, jammed Nina's now-signed copy of *Fendi and Fangs* into my purse, and pushed Nina away from the signing table.

"Harley." Nina was mouthing the word, her tongue snaking over her lips. "I think I've found my Prince Charming."

"Oh, not again," I groaned.

Before I could suck in a breath, Nina shook me off and disappeared back into the crowd of gawkers and vampire fans. She pushed her way through them with purpose and I knew—with a sickening, sinking feeling—that she was headed back toward Prince Charming, in search of her happily-ever-afterlife. The people around me seemed to close in, their voices churning around me, and I could hear the vague pulse of the VERMers' protest cries outside. I felt myself being jostled and tugged by the crowd moving toward Edie. Sweat started to bead at my hairline as panic gripped my chest.

And then there were hands on my shoulders. I sank back against a warm body and glanced up at Will, who slipped his arms around me—part Guardian, part friendly protection—and pulled me to the empty table that Alex and I had shared a day earlier. I sank down gratefully, using my fingertips to rub small circles on my temples until I could feel the tension loosen.

"I think I was about to have a panic attack," I said.

"Should we get out of here?"

I shook my head. "I can't leave without Nina. She could be in"—I paused—"love."

Will looked alarmed, leaning into me. "Is he . . . ?"

"A vampire?" I supplied. "No."

"Is that allowed?"

I shrugged as Nina wound her way through the crowd to where Will and I were stationed. Harley was walking behind her, and both were beaming wild, maniacal, puppy love grins.

"Crap," I muttered under my breath.

"Will, Sophie." Nina tore her eyes away from Harley in a way that made it obvious that it pained her to do so. She looked at Will and me. "This is Harley. Harley, my best friend, Sophie, and her friend Will. Harley is a writer."

"Like the Havenhurst bird?"

Harley raised a fawn-colored eyebrow. "Not exactly."

"Harley writes nonfiction. He's here on a publicity tour."

Without missing a beat Harley presented me with a thick hardcover book, the title *Vampires, Werewolves, and Other Things That Don't Exist* in bold red letters on the cover.

I stopped, grinned, and showed the book to Nina.

"Did you see this, Nees? It's a book about legends."

Usually the word "legend," or the indication that Nina herself is nothing more than a figment of some Hollywood film crew's imagination, made her bristle, made her tongue flick over one sharp fang as if to prove her "real-ness"—but apparently, her bubble of Harley love worked like a snuggly force field and she ignored me and the book.

I tried to hand it back to Harley with a "Wow, looks interesting," but he held up a hand and, like a benevolent ruler, shook his head.

"You take that copy for yourself. My treat."

I looked down at the book in my hand, the giant yellow ribbon marching across the bottom of the front cover boasting: FREE PROMOTIONAL COPY. DO NOT SELL.

"How nice of you. I'll treasure it always." Because it was right about the perfect thickness for spider and general bug smashing. "But we should really be heading out now."

I reached out to grab Nina's arm, but she held out her keys and dropped them in my hand. She linked arms with Harley and rubbed up against him.

"Would you mind taking the car home? Harley and I are going to have coffee. He is just so fascinating."

I could have answered, or stripped off all my clothes and tap-danced naked to a "Yankee Doodle Dandy" medley. It didn't matter. Will and I ceased to exist as Nina and Harley basked in the glow of adoration. And I'm pretty sure they were both adoring Harley.

"Harley, Harley, Harley! There you are!" A small, round, balding man was gruffly pushing people and making his way toward the café. When he saw us, he stopped, pulled out a yellowed handkerchief, and mopped his clammy brow with it. His eyes were slate gray and they were narrowed, laser sharp on Harley. As he rushed toward us, I noticed his gray suit had a weird, glossy sheen. Although perfectly tailored, it still hung oddly on the little man's potato-like body.

"Roland," Harley called out, his jovial voice cutting through the coffeehouse din. "Nina, everyone, this is my agent, Roland Townsend."

"Charmed, charmed," Roland said, without offering a hand or looking away from Harley. "I've been looking all over for you. The guys from Twentieth Century Fox want to have dinner with you."

Harley looked from Roland to Nina and grinned easily. "That sounds great. Tell them we'll do it tomorrow at Gary Danko. And add one." Harley held up an index finger and bobbed Nina gently on the nose with it. I felt my afternoon cookie lodge somewhere in my throat; judging by the disgusted snarl on his face, I knew Will felt the same.

Roland watched the exchange and continued sweating like a sponge; our proximity made me feel sticky. The handkerchief came out again and made its rounds over his bald crown.

"Plus one?" he asked, with his bushy gray eyebrows raised. "Her?" He gestured toward Nina.

Harley cocked his head, his eyes studying Nina. "Her. That is, if she'd care to join me?"

This is the point in most male-female relationships where I melt into a bowl filled with jelly and pull out all the stops in my impressive vocabulary, using homemade words like "leh" and "wah." But Nina handled everything like a pro. She cocked her head so that her hair fell over one shoulder, a few glossy strands seductively crossing her cleavage. She licked her top lip with the tip of her tongue in a way that suggested something sexily sinister and smiled coyly.

"Pick me up at seven."

Will and I were waiting on the sidewalk outside the bookstore while Nina finished up her shopping/flirting/judging of fashion-flawed writers.

"So," Will said, his hands jammed into his pockets, "that Harley guy. He's . . . one of them?"

I frowned. "One of who?"

"You know," he dropped his voice. "A demon or something."

"I don't think so. Why? Do you think so? Did you see his feet? I didn't notice if he had hooves."

Will blanched. "I'm not really into checking out a bloke's feet. I just didn't think that Nina could date someone who is . . ."

"Breathing? Alive?"

"And full of blood."

"You too?"

Will and I swung to face Nina, who was loaded down with books and steaming mad. The seduction in her eyes was gone; the sexy arch of her lip was turned into a ferocious snarl.

"Oh, here we go again," I muttered.

"Every one of you damn breathers seems to think that just because we are sustained by human blood, we're going to pounce on every person we see. Do you walk into a grocery store and tear into every box of Frosted Flakes you see? No. And neither do we. Now get in the car."

"Did she just call us Frosted Flakes?" Will whispered.

"Just get in the car," I said, knowing enough to avoid Nina's wrath.

Vlad jogged up behind us, folding himself into the car, his VERM sign nearly beheading Will and staking me.

"Protest over already?"

Vlad just shrugged and fished his iPod from his jacket pocket.

Will slid in and Nina slammed the door behind him, marching to the driver's side. "Nina seems really pissed. What was that all about?" Will asked.

Nina, my beautiful, fine-boned roommate and best friend, was tall and ballerina slim. Her normally dark hair and wide, coal black eyes, set in her flawless pale skin, gave her the look of an innocent nymph. She carried herself with an air of confidence and grace that was all at once comforting and unsettling. Though several centuries have passed, she still retained the fine manners and gentle demeanor of her French aristocratic upbringing.

When she was content, she was like Marie Antoinette with fangs.

When she was angry, entire armies died.

"Hold these." Nina dumped a stack of books onto my lap as she snapped on her blinker and pulled the car into traffic.

"Vampire-Romance Novels for Dummies? How to Write And Sell a Vampire Novel?" I read aloud. "What's all this?"

Nina grinned, fangs pressed over her lower lip. "It's brilliance is what it is. People are making millions on vampire stuff."

"And apparently, this bloke is making millions off proving that vampires don't exist," Will said, shaking the tome.

I turned around in my seat and took Harley's book from Will. "'*New York Times* best-selling author,'" I read, "'*USA Today*'s number one read. Four stars from *Newsweek.* Cavanaugh blows the fangs off vampires and vampire legends from Tinseltown to Transylvania.'"

I flipped to the back cover, where Harley, looking distinguished and all-knowing, was hunching in a cemetery, one arm draped nonchalantly over a moss-covered headstone. "Well, that's a nice touch."

"I suppose he's going to have a bit of a rude awakening at dinner tomorrow night, isn't he, then?" Will leaned into the front seat and Nina rolled her eyes, taking her annoyance out on the Lexus's gearshift. We all jerked to one side.

"Hey, Vlad, why isn't VERM—sorry," I said, catching myself, "the Vampire Empowerment Movement protesting Harley?"

Vlad shrugged, popping a single earbud from his right ear. "Why would we?"

"Because you can't be a fearsome bastion of Hell if you don't exist."

Vlad pulled his iPad out of his messenger bag. "But we're not sparkling, wearing jewelry, or falling in love with breathers. Let him think we don't exist. No skin off my nose."

"Oh." I felt oddly deflated.

"So how are you going to break the news to Harley?" Will asked.

"Harley doesn't need to know anything," Nina replied, yanking the wheel again. "So, as I was saying, vampire novels are clogging the bookshelves. They're in theatres, on TV. They're everywhere!"

"I suppose if they weren't, the VERM would have a little more time on their hands," Will said, settling back into his seat.

"Who knows better about vampires—and vampire romance," Nina continued, "than me? I'm a vampire, and, well, look at me. Romance has never been a stranger to Nina Michele LaShay." Nina held up a single finger. "The first."

"So?" I asked.

"So I am going to become the next great vampire-romance novelist!"

Nina was gesturing wildly, her joy evident, her car veering toward oncoming traffic. I grabbed the wheel and clamped my mouth shut, lest my heart leap out and flop into my lap.

"Hands on the wheel!"

"Isn't that brilliant? Me, a novelist!"

"It is brilliant," I agreed.

"Lovely. Are you going to quit your job to take on this endeavor?" Will wanted to know.

Nina snorted. "Of course not! I'm just going to write a quick little book. How hard can it be? And besides, I want to get started right away."

Nina turned to me and I glanced at her from my periphery, trying to focus on the road. My fingers inched toward the once-again abandoned steering wheel. I was certain that I would grind my molars into dust before we reached Van Ness.

"Can I use your laptop when we get home?" Nina asked.

"If we get home, you can *have* my laptop."

Chapter Four

Once we got home, and I was able to unclench my fists, I handed Nina my laptop. "Knock yourself out," I told her.

She looked over my head, a serene smile on her face. "Once my vampire novel becomes a best seller, Harley and I can go on book tours together."

"That would be nice. The author who writes about vampires that don't exist, and the vampire who loves him."

"You have no emotional depth."

I sighed while Nina tucked my Mac under her arm and pierced the blood bag she was holding, then sucked voraciously. "Thanks. Sorry about Will."

I shrugged. Though I was semi-used to Nina's driving, Will was not. He'd spent the majority of the ride with his head tucked between his knees. Before the car had even come to a complete stop, he was hightailing it across our apartment building's underground parking lot, frantically mashing the elevator's UP button.

"He'll recover."

"Uh, Soph?" Nina gulped. "You have a message."

I glanced over my shoulder to where Nina had the laptop open. The glow from the screen made her pale skin look an odd, translucent silver.

I spun the laptop to face me and read the subject line slowly. "'Someone has responded to your request from yourfamilytree.com.'" I blinked at Nina. "What should I do?"

"You should open it."

Before I could think better of it, I clicked the icon and an animated tree popped up, a single green leaf blinking jauntily begging me to Click and see who's looking for you!

My heart thundered against my chest and my stomach churned.

"Who is it?" Nina's voice was barely a whisper.

"I can't. What—what if it's him?"

I had grown up under the care of my maternal grandmother. She was the most amazing, special, intelligent woman I have ever known. Of course, when I was an overemotional preteen, she was horrendously embarrassing, odd, and loud. She wore scarves and costume jewelry that made more noise than a tambourine trio; she read palms, tea leaves, and right into my deepseated fear of forever being an outcast. She died just after I graduated college; and not too long ago, began the unsettling habit of appearing in shiny or glossy objects (cut cantaloupe was a particularly disconcerting fave), giving me advice and ominous clues about my parents and their shady past. Namely, that my mother had committed suicide to protect me.

Oh.

And also that there was a pretty good chance that my

dad was Satan. Not the "Your dad is a really bad guy—bad like the devil!" but more the "No, really, your dad is the absolute Prince of Darkness."

"Just look. You don't have to do anything about it. Don't you want to know?"

My finger hovered above the track pad and I focused on that stupid little leaf.

Nina crossed her arms in front of her chest. "Come on, Soph. What are the odds that el Diablo would sign up on Your Family Tree? I would think he'd have better things to do, you know, like Filet-O-Fish Genghis Khan or whisper in J.Lo's ear or whatever. If anything, I think this is probably a good sign."

I blew out a sigh. "You know what? You're right." I slammed the laptop shut. "It's probably just another penis ad that slipped through the Family Tree filters. I'll check it tomorrow. Right now"—I piled up Nina's selection of vampire-romance reference material—"is all about you and this amazing novel you're going to write. I'm totally supportive. I totally want you to do this."

"You're totally chickenshit." Nina smiled.

"Totally. See you in the morning."

I groaned and tried to slap the two morning DJs who cackled in my ear from my alarm clock. Instead, I knocked the picture of my grandmother and me off my nightstand and scared ChaCha half to death, causing her to spring up on her tiny little doggie legs and bark ferociously while backing herself underneath the covers.

I went to the kitchen in search of coffee, but I stopped

at the dining-room table, where Nina was slumped over. Her dark eyes were a weird combination of glassy and milky, open, but staring into nothingness. I poked her stone cold arm.

"Nina?"

Her head lolled at the sound of my voice and she blinked up at me. "Is that you, Sophie?"

I did a quick once-over, checking Nina's pale face and arms for evidence of bruising, bloodletting, or general malaise.

Nothing.

Heat started to crawl up my neck and I crouched down and shook her shoulder violently. "Nina! Are you okay? What's wrong?"

Nina pushed herself up, slowly, painfully. I clutched my thudding heart. "My God, I thought you were dead! Again."

"I might as well be," Nina said, full lips pressed into a mournful pout.

"What's going on?"

Nina blew out a tremendous sigh. "I have writer's block. It's horrendous. Awful. Crippling. I now know why authors are so tortured."

"Well, maybe I can help you. I wrote a little for my high-school newspaper."

Actually, I wrote a lot for my high-school newspaper and stashed every poignant well-worded "Letter to the Editor" in my locker, along with reams of sorrowful poetry about waxing moons, waning sunlight, and one of the guys from the New Kids on the Block. I never had the guts to submit anything. In high school, I barely had the guts to walk down the hall. I just wanted to blend in then, to quietly hide in my B.U.M. sweatshirts and stretch pants, dissolving into the spiral permed masses, but I always had the unfortunate ability to stand out.

First, on account of my fire engine red hair, which curled in all the wrong ways. Of course, that was correctable and forgettable, but my nickname—bestowed upon me by one of the prettiest, perkiest girls to ever don a Mercy High uniform—stuck. Year after year I endured the whispers, coughs, and downright shouts of "Here comes Special Sophie, the Freak of Nineteenth Street!"

It didn't matter that Nineteenth was an avenue.

I sat down across from Nina and poked her arm. "Read me what you have so far."

"That's just it!" Nina moaned. "I'm paralyzed. I haven't written a single word!"

"You have to have written something to have writer's block. Otherwise, we all have it."

It was nearly ten A.M. and the pace was humming along at UDA, but I couldn't concentrate. Each time I tried to open a new file, my mind drifted back to Mrs. Henderson, to the putrid odor and the brackish water that was seeping into her carpet and linens. Finally I pushed everything aside and knocked on Dixon's door.

"Ah, Ms. Lawson, come on in."

"Hi, Dixon. I was wondering if you had a chance to look over the information I gave you regarding the"—I paused, my stomach folding in on itself—"the incident over at the Hendersons' house."

A sympathetic look washed over Dixon's hard angles. "I did take a look at the information, Ms. Lawson." He shook his head. "Such a tragedy."

I sat down. "So what are we going to do about it? I was thinking I could go over there, maybe talk to some of the neighbors, see if they heard or saw anything—"

Dixon held up a single hand, pressing his lips into a smile that was meant to be disarming, but it came off as completely patronizing. "You don't need to worry about that."

"No, I'm happy to help. Mrs. Henderson—well, as difficult as she was, she was a very dear friend to me. I'd like to be involved in finding her—her killer."

Dixon's eyebrows rose. "Her killer?" He licked his lips, his smile inappropriately sly. "Look, Ms. Lawson, I'm aware of some of your previous endeavors, crime fighting and all"—he chuckled, a sound that sent ice water shooting through my veins—"but I sent the Investigations team over to the Henderson house myself, and they assure me that while the house was in disarray, there was absolutely no evidence of wrongdoing."

"No evidence of wrongdoing? The place was destroyed. There were windows broken and rotting food and . . . what do you think? The whole family just up and died all at once?"

Dixon remained very still, very firm. His countenance was marble solid and menacing. The slick smile was gone from his lips; they were slightly parted now, just enough to show the angled bottom of his front fangs. "The Henderson children are with their father. Now, Ms. Lawson, I'll thank you to stick to your job responsibilities, and those responsibilities only. You need to keep your nose out of things that do not involve you." Dixon jabbed a long, elegant pointer finger at me. "You are a very important part of this community, Ms. Lawson. You offer a specialized skill in the Fallen Angel Division. But if I find that you're not giving your own job responsibilities the attention they deserve, you can be replaced."

Dixon laced his fingers together and offered me a kind, milquetoast smile. "Is there anything else?"

I wanted to stand up and scream—or stake him through the heart—or remind him that I had single-handedly brought down the biggest baddie the Underworld had ever seen, but all I could do was nod mutely. The rage simmered underneath my skin.

"Thank you," I finally managed.

I was walking back to my office when Nina linked arms with me, hers ice cold and refreshing to the heat that pulsed in mine. "Someone's walking with purpose."

"Dixon," I muttered. "I told him about Mrs. Henderson and he tossed me off the case."

Nina stopped and unwound my arm from hers, crossing hers in front of her chest. "What case?"

"Not a case, per se, but something is weird there," I hissed.

"Did he say he was looking into it?"

"He said he had the Investigations team check it out, but there's something wrong, Nina. I just know it."

"What'd Alex say about it?"

I swallowed. "He said to leave it alone."

Nina raised a coy eyebrow. Her lips arced up into a "well, then, leave it alone" kind of smile.

"Something is wrong here," I repeated. "I have a hunch."

Nina pirouetted. "Is your hunch that this is the perfect lunching-with-Harley dress?"

I glanced at my watch. "It's ten-thirty in the morning."

"Is your hunch that this dress is the perfect brunching-with-Harley dress then?"

I rubbed my temples. "You know, I don't know why I even bother. When are you going for brunch?"

"We're not. At least not officially. But it behooves a woman to be prepared."

"Yes. While demons disappear, a woman should always be prepared for brunch."

Nina narrowed her eyes. "You know what? My heroine's going to be a go-get-'em crime fighter like you."

"And, like me, is everyone going to think your crime-fighting heroine is blowing things out of proportion?"

Nina pushed out her bottom lip. "No. That's not sexy. Cover for me if I'm not back from lunch in time for dinner?"

Nina left me standing alone in the UDA hallway, the fluorescent light buzzing overhead, the hum and din of demons and paper shuffling all around me. My mind went back to the squalid scene at the Henderson house, and I tried to dismiss it, tried to let my suspicions rest, let Dixon's investigative team allay them.

But something kept niggling at me.

* * *

"Alex?" I was upstairs at the police station, rapping on Alex's office door.

"You're going to have to knock a lot louder than that," someone said as they coasted by me. "He ain't here anymore."

I felt my eyebrows go up and pushed the door open an inch, poking my nose in. I snaked an arm in and flicked the light switch and then stepped in.

"Alex?"

The room was empty, every cardboard box gone. Alex's desk was still pushed against the wall, chair stacked on top, but other than that, the room was spartan. It looked as though Alex had never existed—or was never coming back.

An unexpected sob choked in my throat.

"He left? He didn't even say good-bye." I sniffled pitifully, feeling tiny and alone.

"Aren't you Sophie Lawson?"

Had there been anything in the room, I would have tumbled over it when the man spoke. Instead, I clutched my heart and stumbled backward, hyperventilating like a COPD ad.

"Oh gosh, I'm so sorry. I didn't mean to frighten you."

The man who was trying to coax me down from my near heart attack was dressed in a pristine San Francisco police uniform, which he didn't look quite old enough to wear. He had smooth, dark skin and thick eyebrows, which stood out underneath a close-cropped Caesar cut. "I'm Officer Romero. I worked with Alex a couple of times. Are you okay?"

I used the heel of my hand to wipe away my few

piteous tears. "Yeah, I just . . . um, I'm allergic to carpet and it's not been cleaned yet. How do you know my name?"

"You're the one Alex used to call when things were . . . weird, right?"

I nodded miserably. *Sophie Lawson, Call When Weird.* "Yeah."

"Then it's a good thing I found you."

"Look, I really should be heading back to work—"

"We found something."

I stopped. "Something?"

Officer Romero nodded. "They just pulled it in from the Bay."

"What is it?"

"We were hoping you could tell us."

I was following Officer Romero in his squad car, lights flashing (him), Lady Gaga blaring (me). Our little motorcade sliced through the streets, and yellow taxi-cabs and rental cars swerved to avoid us. I would have felt very presidential and important if it weren't for the cold stone sitting at the pit of my stomach.

Officer Romero had called what they pulled from the Bay "it."

When I pulled up to the docks, police barricades were already set up, and a crowd of people hunkered over them. They crowded along the sidewalks, and were rolling up on tiptoes, trying to get a better look. Phones flashed and people chatted as Officer Romero led me through the crowd. I heard the word *"chupacabra"* uttered under someone's breath. A woman, with wide brown eyes, whispered, "Tiamat" and pointed toward the dock.

Officer Romero slowed; and when I caught up to him,

he leaned into me. "We hardly had the thing out of the water before people started coming down. Everyone's got a weird idea about it. Frankly, I'm pretty sure it's just a regular man in a pretty advanced state of decomposition. He's probably been submerged for quite a while."

He shook his head and I pulled my sweater tighter across my chest.

"Let me see him."

I edged around the assembled officers and sucked in a deep breath of ocean-tinged air. Three police officers were standing in a semicircle around a body-shaped lump covered in a blue tarp and leaking seawater. Officer Romero leaned down and edged the tarp back. I saw the dark hair first, tangled with kelp and trash. The smooth arc of his neck was purpled and marred, a thin piece of plastic rope coiled around and around his throat. I saw where his lips were slightly puckered and pale, the scratches at his neck where he must have pulled at the rope. My saliva went sour and I felt that familiar sickening need to vomit. My eyes teared up, and my breathing became hoarse and ragged.

Officer Romero moved the tarp a bit more and I could see the broad, naked shoulders of the man, his lifeless limbs. My heart started a spastic palpitation as the arch of his spine gave way to coarse, sand-sprinkled fur. I knew why the police officers were shaking their heads, while the people gathered at the barricades were uttering the names of legendary creatures.

"It's a centaur," I mumbled.

There were very few centaurs registered with the UDA, and this one was curled in on itself. His human hands were bound in front of him; his flank and cloven feet were puckered with clean knife wounds and wound with thin strips of the same plastic-looking rope.

"Did you say something?" Officer Romero asked.

"Who else has seen this?"

Officer Romero opened his mouth to answer but stopped as we were both drawn to a scuffle behind the police barricades. A floodlight had gone up and a camera crew had arrived. In record time the smooth-voiced narrator was going into his spiel.

I knew that smooth voice.

Harley had one hand wrapped around a microphone, the other resting on the stooped shoulder of a woman with dark hair pulled back into a hasty ponytail, half covered by a hairnet. The camera rolled in front of them and Harley asked the woman to describe what she saw; his brows were knitted, eyes rapt.

"Es un demonio." She clawed her hands and growled, her lips curling into a fearsome snarl. *"Es un chupacabra. No lo creia, pero lo vi con mis propios ojos."*

"She says it's a *chupacabra,*" Officer Romero informed me with a disbelieving head shake. "My grandmother used to tell us the *chupacabra* would snatch us from our beds if we didn't go to sleep. I thought it was a legend."

"It is," I said, beelining toward Harley.

By the time I got to him, he was on to another woman, zeroing in on her as she used huge arm gestures. Her cheeks were flushed as she stared into the camera.

"It was Tiamat," she said, with an exaggerated shudder. "They pulled her in, and when she opened her mouth, I saw the serpent inside."

Harley had a slight, abusive smile on his face as he ping-ponged his microphone between the two women.

"No, no," the other woman shook her head, stepping in front of Harley's camera angle. *"Es un chupacabra!"* She did the growl again, and a team behind her nodded enthusiastically, backing her up with a chorus of *"Sí! Sí!"*

I yanked on Harley's sleeve. "Can I talk to you, please?"

Harley hid his annoyance at my disruption like an absolute pro; his smile never faltered even as he ushered aside his interviewees still fighting over the identity of the body on the dock.

"Sophie, right?"

"What are you doing? You're riling everybody up."

"I'm simply interviewing these bystanders."

I put my hands on my hips and cocked an eyebrow. "For your next book?"

Harley stared me down. "What does it matter? Do you have a theory on John Doe over there you'd like to kick in?" Harley's brown eyes slid over me, head to toe, and I stiffened, feeling immediately violated. "I bet you'd look great on camera."

"Aren't you interested in my best friend?"

Harley blew out a sigh and waggled the microphone in front of me. "Do you have something to add or not? This is for a major network, you know. Not cable."

"I don't care. There is nothing to see here. If you know that"—I pointed to the body that was now being moved, still under cover of the tarp—"is a regular John Doe, why are you interviewing these people?"

"I sell books, Sophie, and people like these"—he spread his arms as if he were among his brethren—

"keep the myths that I debunk alive. More myths, more books."

"More sales."

"Spoken like a true capitalist." He pressed the microphone underneath my nose. "Are you sure you don't have anything to add?"

I looked from the fallen centaur to the woman with the hairnet, wringing her hands; the woman beside her was still muttering "Tiamat" and describing the evil attributes of the sea legend.

Harley may not have had fangs, but he looked every inch the bloodsucker lurking beside them, his microphone at the ready.

"I have nothing to say to you."

I was inching through traffic and listening to Nina's cell phone ring in my ear after my run-in with Harley and the centaur. By the time a Muni bus cut me off, and a line of Art Institute students zigzagged in front of my car, Nina picked up and I screamed, "Finally!"

There was a short pause and then, "Sophie?"

"Sorry, Neens. I'm stuck in traffic and I just came from the docks."

"Trolling for dates again? Do we need to have another talk about acceptable places to meet men?"

My left eye started to twitch. "I was on the dock because the police pulled a centaur out of the Bay."

"That's weird. Centaurs are not known for their swimming prowess."

"He'd been murdered."

"Oh."

"I called Dixon. Investigations is coming out to take care of it." I shook my head, tapped my fingers on the steering wheel. "This is scaring me, Nina. First Mrs. Henderson, and now a body in the Bay?"

Nina harrumphed. "Do you know how many bodies there are in the Bay? I'm guessing thousands. That centaur could have been in there for ages and just washed up now. It's not pleasant, I'll give you that, but I don't think it's anything to worry about."

"I guess." I rested my foot on the brake, staring at the flashing lights in front of me. "You know who else I ran into? Harley."

Nina let out a pained little yip. "Harley? My Harley?"

"He's already *your* Harley?"

Nina ignored me, prattling on. "Oh my gosh, is he okay?"

"He's fine, but I can't say as much for the people he was talking to. He was here preying on their beliefs. He had an entire camera crew and was interviewing people who saw the—the body."

"*Chupacabra?* Anything that looks somewhat odd around here and it's a *chupacabra.*"

I nodded, inching my car forward as the light in front of me changed. "Yes, but . . . he was practically making fun of them. He was using them to prove his stupid debunking theories—making them look like idiots, like they all believed in these silly, made-up stories."

Nina blew out a sigh, and I imagined her on the other end of the phone, examining her manicure. "That's what he does, Sophie. He's an author. He has to interview people, has to introduce the myths so that he can debunk them. It's no big deal. It's what sells his books. Besides, half the legends that people believe in are made-up."

I wanted to zing Nina with something about her being a vampire, about her being one of the most made-up myths of all, but my mind was still churning, folding over the crumpled centaur and Harley's shiny white veneers as he listened to the women argue. Dollar signs were practically glistening in his eyes.

"He's mean, Nina. And he's wrong. There was a dead demon forty paces from him and he was interviewing some old ladies, getting them riled up about a *chupacabra* and Tiamat."

"So what do you want me to do? Drag him to the Underworld to prove that he's wrong? I'm not sure if you've recently read the UDA bylaws, but keeping the whole demon thing under wraps is really something we rely on around here."

"Doesn't it bother you at all that you're all hot and bothered by a man whose entire career centers around the idea that we don't exist?"

I could hear the rustle of cellophane as Nina unwrapped a blood bag on her end of the line. "According to him, you do exist. I don't."

I paused and Nina relented. "What are you really upset about, Sophie?"

My bottom lip pushed out and I slumped lower in the driver's seat.

"I'm not sure."

Chapter Five

I was steeling my resolve to walk into Dixon's office and demand a full-scale investigation of Mrs. Henderson's crime scene, and the body we just found, when my cell phone buzzed as I waited in the vestibule for the UDA elevator to come up.

"This is Sophie."

"Sophie? Kale."

"Hey, K—"

"Where are you? Are you on your way to the office?"

"I'm waiting for the elevator right now. Kale, what's wrong? What is that? Kale?"

When the elevator dinged thirty-five floors below the San Francisco police station, the line went dead. I banged the phone against the heel of my hand a couple of times, shrugged, and threw it in my purse, knowing I'd see Kale in a millisecond.

But I didn't.

The big metal doors slid open on the Underworld Detection Agency and it was—forgive the expression—like a ghost town. There was an ominous quiet; and though all the lights were on and business should have been in full swing, the lobby was desolate.

And then I heard the scream.

It was a high-pitched, bloodcurdling sound. It was a mixture of angst and misery, terrified and terror inducing. I clenched my hands into fists, feeling my fingernails digging little half-moons into my sweaty palms.

"Kale?" I called, my voice sounding odd and tinny in the silent room.

I took a step toward the reception desk and felt a hand grip my wrist, then yank me downward.

"Kale?"

She was huddled underneath the reception desk, a sweatshirt wrapped around her head. Pierre, our centaur filing clerk, was down there with her, sitting back on his haunches, hands pressed over his ears.

"What's going on?"

Before Kale could answer me, there was another ear-splitting scream, and then I knew.

"Banshee?" I said, grimacing.

Kale nodded and I rubbed my temples, the rhythmic drumbeat of a migraine beginning to pulse behind my eyes. "They wouldn't be so bad if they could get the screaming thing under control."

"She's waiting for you in your office," Kale said, pointing.

I nodded, then stepped out from under the desk. My ankles and knees cracked as I did so. "It's okay, everyone, you can come out."

Little by little, the UDA lobby came back to life as clients rolled out from under chairs and from behind the potted palms. Every man, woman, and beast held their hands over their ears or were sporting homemade earplugs, which may or may not have been torn from last month's *Martha Stewart Living*.

I prepared myself to meet Bettina Jacova.

She was sitting primly at the edge of my office chair. Her posture was impeccable, and her long, dark hair hung in a sheet down her back. Her hands were neatly folded in her lap and her outfit—pearls, a baby pink twinset, and a dark pink chintz skirt—stood out cheerily against her decaying gray skin.

"Hello, Bettina."

Bettina pressed her hands to the sides of her face and her mouth dropped open, ready to let out another ear-splitting howl.

"No!" I said, jumping forward and slapping my own hand against her mouth. "Sorry." I rubbed my palm against my thigh. "You'll just need not to do that here, please."

Though my new station as head of the Fallen Angel Division meant that I didn't work with the general demon population any longer, there were a few members—and demon breeds—I kept tabs on. Either because our staffers had issues (Nina, being non–fire retardant in the face of dragons) or the demons themselves had certain powers that made general fraternization difficult.

Bettina was one of those demons.

You see, Bettina Jacova is a banshee. And though people are generally aware of the banshee yell—as in, "Those kids have been screaming like banshees all day"—they fail to realize the seriousness of it. The banshee scream signifies death.

Generally, yours.

Some demons are immune, but others are not.

The UDA found it prudent not to take the chance after we lost half the finance department to our Romanian intern, who failed to mark the box "banshee—deadly" on her intake form. My magical immunity super power allowed me to work with fire-breathing dragons and Bettina with her murderous screams.

Just another perk of being the only nearly normal at the Underworld Detection Agency.

Lucky me.

I sat down across from Bettina, who eyed me nervously. I offered her my most reassuring smile, praying to Buddha, God, and Oprah that she wouldn't let loose another scream. It was hard enough to cover our clients when two of our staffers went on vacation simultaneously; should the entire group drop dead from banshee screams, well, then the Underworld Detection Agency would be in deep trouble.

"So, Bettina, how may I help you?"

"Well," Bettina started to say, kneading her fingers in her lap. "I need help. I mean, I think we all might need help."

I'll say.

"'We all,' as in all the banshees?" I mentally started to scan my inner Rolodex. From my recollection there were only six banshees total in the Greater San Francisco Bay Area. "I suppose we could get some sort of soundproofed bus for—"

"No, not just banshees." Bettina's eyes shifted uneasily. "Everyone." She paused, sucked in a sharp little breath, and cleared her throat. "Ms. Lawson, I was attacked last night."

I felt my eyebrows rise, and felt the prick of heat wash through my body. "Attacked? By whom—or what?"

Bettina's eyes started to water; her lower lip trembled. I snatched a few Kleenex from the box and pushed them into Bettina's hands. "It's okay, Bettina, you're safe here. Now, can you tell me exactly what happened?"

"Well, I was leaving my apartment. I live by the ballpark, you know. It's very loud and"—a twinge of pink bloomed in Bettina's cheeks—"there's a lot of general screams, so . . ."

So the death-signifying screams of a banshee could be drowned out before entire subsections of San Francisco mysteriously dropped dead. Smart.

"Go on."

"Well, I was going to get some groceries, and I was walking toward the bus stop. I wasn't alone, because there was a Giants game going on, so there were tons of breathers." Bettina blushed and lowered her eyes. "I'm sorry, Sophie. I meant there were lots of other people around, at first. Most of them went into the stadium so the street emptied out pretty quickly. Even so, I felt like I was being followed."

"Did you see anyone?"

"That's the thing. Before I left, I looked out the window to check the weather. I thought I saw someone on the sidewalk looking up into my window, but then the bus came and I guess he got on. I went downstairs and walked to the bus stop myself, and I got that weird feeling again."

"Like you were being watched?" I supplied, feeling the hairs on my arms prickle.

Bettina nodded. "I was walking and I looked over my shoulder, and no one was there. Then I turned back and someone hit me. Hard." Bettina's graying fingers shakily pushed aside her bangs, showing off an impressive gash just over her left eyebrow.

I sucked in a stunned breath. "Oh my. Bettina, I'm—"

"I was down on the ground, and he kicked me, too, right here." Bettina gingerly rubbed her lower belly. "I was going to scream—I would have, but he caught me by surprise—and he hit me again."

"Do you know what he hit you with?"

Bettina wagged her head. "I'm not sure. It looked like some sort of pipe."

"Like a tire iron, maybe?"

Bettina shrugged. "I'm not really sure what those look like."

I wasn't entirely certain, either, but whether Bettina's assailant was wielding a tire iron or a magic wand made a world of difference. At least it did here, in the Underworld.

"He wasn't done, either," Bettina said. "He—he was going to hit me again, in the head, but the game must have let out, because people started to fill the streets. He told me that my kind needed—needed to be erased."

"Your kind? Did he—did he know you were—"

My saliva went sour and suddenly my skin felt too tight.

Demons walk among us every day. A vampire might be your neighbor; the corner store might be run by a werewolf or a troll. There is a thin veil that masks the demon differences from the human sight. That veil, combined with our human ability to unsee anything that might unsettle us, has allowed the demon race to prosper and blend into the natural world.

That veil doesn't work on me; and if Bettina's assailant was human, the veil didn't work on him, either.

"He looked over his shoulder and ran, once the people started to come." A single fat tear rolled down her cheek and plopped onto her cheery pink skirt.

"I'm so sorry, Bettina." I patted her shoulder awkwardly and she fell into me, head buried in my shoulder, her small body shaking violently as she cried.

"I'm so scared," she whimpered. "I'm so scared."

I patted Bettina's back and let her cry; then I cocked my head and squinted as her cries gave way to a series of half-muffled screams.

I thought I heard bodies dropping in the lobby.

"Don't worry, Bettina. We're going to find out who did this to you, I promise. We'll keep you safe, too."

My heart walloped and my mouth went dry. Even as I said the words, I wondered how I was supposed to keep a killer demon safe, and who would keep *me* safe.

I escorted Bettina through the UDA lobby and stepped into the elevator with her while she whimpered, gingerly touching a tissue to her moist eyes. As we neared the first floor, I bit my lip, working out the most diplomatic way to remind Bettina to keep her mouth shut. With someone walking around beating up demons, the last thing the city needed was the entire police department dropping dead.

The elevator lurched to a stop and the doors began to open on the police department.

"Bettina, you know you need to—"

But she already had her lips clamped shut; the edges turned up in a tiny, grateful smile. She pantomimed locking her lips and tossing away the key.

"Thanks."

"So what was that all about?" Nina inclined her head toward the elevator doors when I came down again, popping a giant Hubba Bubba bubble in my face.

I don't care how long I live—and live after that— I'll never get comfortable with the weird look of vampire fangs working a piece of hot pink bubble gum.

I pinched the bridge of my nose, huffing the strawberry-scented air.

"Someone beat Bettina up."

Nina snorted. "Not a great person to hit up. Is the idiot dead now? Did she need a Certificate of Accidemal Death? I hate doing those things." She flopped her wrist around. "So much flippin' paperwork."

"No." I scanned the crowd of UDA clients lined up neatly between velvet ropes, some waiting silently, sitting on our straight-from-the-catalog office furniture, a few kids pushing around ancient toys on the IKEA kid's table. If you took away the horns, plumes of smoke, and general stench of the undead, this could have been the waiting room for any other government office.

Why would someone attack a demon?

"She didn't scream. He caught her by surprise."

Nina shrugged. "Aren't those a banshee's best screams?"

"He told her he was going to eradicate her kind."

Nina pinched her bottom lip. "What, like women?"

I shook my head. "No. Like demons."

Nina's bare shoulders quaked with a tiny shiver. "Who would want to kill demons?"

"That's what I intend to find out."

Nina crossed her arms; a single eyebrow raised. "Sleuthing?"

I rolled my eyes. "This is important."

She leaned her ear toward her shoulder and cracked her neck. "You know every time you plan to get to the bottom of something, someone gets kidnapped. Or killed."

I blinked; there was no reason to argue the truth.

"Why don't you leave this one to Dixon?" she asked, falling into step with me as I walked toward my office.

"I mentioned the missed appointments to Dixon. He barely even batted an eye. He's not going to care about Bettina."

"So what are you going to do?" Nina wanted to know. "Become the Banshee Avenger?" Her lips parted slightly, forming an O of surprise. "If so, I have a great outfit for that."

"I'm just going to look around. Maybe see if I can find any clues."

Nina crossed her arms, jutted out one hip. "Knock yourself out, Nancy Drew."

"You're not going to help me?"

"I thought you had Alex on speed dial for that?"

My stomach quivered—something between sadness and nerves—at the mention of his name. "He's not here."

Nina's eyes went wide and she sat down hard. "Heaven? Holy—"

"Buffalo."

"Crap." Nina shrugged. "Ordinarily, I would do anything for you, my breathy friend, but I have a date and you have an overactive imagination." She blew me a kiss and turned on her heel, leaving in a cloud of Chanel No. 5 and stale plasma.

"Don't choke on a blood clot!" I yelled to the back of her head.

It was half past six when I processed my last intake form. For a community that still depends heavily on divination and medieval prophecies, our computer system was surprisingly up to date. Unfortunately, that date was 1992. I was ready for chocolate pinwheels and a snuggle with my trusty pup, ChaCha, and dreaming about sinking into a mountain of sweet-scented bubbles when I walked out into the parking lot, deserted except for a couple of squad cars, an abandoned Buick, and my modest Honda Accord. I sank my key into the lock when I heard a soft cry on the wind. It was mild, but loud enough to cut through the constant city din of police sirens and honking horns of tourists, and it seemed to be coming from the alleyway that separated the police station from the rest of the looming buildings on the block. My hackles went up, prickles that started at the base of my calves and stopped at the top of my head.

I licked my suddenly dry lips and took my key into my hand, taking a tentative step toward the alley.

"Hello?" I asked. "Is someone there?"

I heard the distinctive crunch of feet on gravel and then another wince. As much as I wanted to avoid another naked Vlad-and-Kale situation, something inside me was drawn, desperate to help. Before I could think better of it, I ran into the alley. My footfalls echoed heavily between the buildings, and the limp wail, the crunching gravel, was gone.

"Hello?" I asked again.

My voice bounced off the wall and was cut off by my own scream.

Something hit me hard, cracking against the back of my head. I pitched forward, my palms and chest making contact with the damp cement. Beads of gravel dug into my skin. My knees throbbed and I tried to cry out a second time, but my breath was gone and my mouth was filled with the hot, metallic taste of blood. Someone yanked me, flipping me over so my tender skull smacked the cement. Bright white light burst in front of my eyes. I felt the urge to vomit, to cry, to wail, but my eyes began to focus. I saw my assailant above me, both hands hugging a sharpened dowel, both coming directly at my chest. There was an "oof!" and a scream, and the sharpened edge of the stake dug at my collarbone and slid over my breast.

"Run, Sophie!"

Will's English accent was hot as it sliced through me and I tried to kick away, or assumed I was kicking away. I saw him dive at my attacker, heard the hollow sound of the wood dowel clunking to the ground; then I heard footfalls—hurried, echoing, as my attacker took off across the parking lot, with Will in tow. Bitter tears flooded my eyes, stinging the shallow fresh cuts on my cheeks. I looked down to where my blouse was torn. The red angry welt puckered like pressed lips underneath my collarbone.

"Are you okay?" Will asked in a breathless pant as he jogged back to me.

I pressed the pads of my fingers against the hot tear on my skin and nodded. "I think so. What was that? Why are you here?"

Will's eyes were on my chest, on the wound. He brushed over it with his thumb and smiled up at me. "It doesn't look so bad."

"How did you know to come to—to my rescue?"

Will clasped imaginary lapels. "I'm a Guardian, love. That's what I do." He plucked a piece of gravel from my hair. "And I was having a pint across the way. Can you stand?"

He offered me a hand and I pushed myself onto shaky legs.

"Now what on earth would make you step into a dark alley at night?"

My bottom lip started to tremble and all I could manage was a pitiful shrug. "Did you see who it was?"

Will wagged his head. "Bloke was fast." He crouched, rolled the dowel toward himself, eyebrows raised. "And he tried to club you."

I took the dowel in my hand and touched the chiseled, whittled end; then I touched the purpling wound on my chest. "No, he was trying to stake me."

Chapter Six

I pushed open the door and Nina was under my nose in a heartbeat, coal black eyes wide and glistening, hands splayed.

"I smell blood," she said.

"Your hair. It's black again."

Nina pushed a glossy chunk of her back-to-black hair over her shoulder, showing off the skinny, beaded strap of her silver evening dress.

"What happened?" Her nostrils twitched. "Why are you bleeding? Will, why is Sophie bleeding?"

Will ushered me into the house. "Someone attacked her in the alley."

"At work?"

I nodded, and Nina used her forefinger and thumb to pull the neckline of my blouse aside, exposing the purpling wound. "What is that?"

"He—he tried to stake me," I said, rubbing the tender scratch.

Nina's mouth dropped open. "Like with a wooden stake?"

I nodded. "Through the heart. Will showed up just in time."

"I chased him off."

"Him who?" Nina wanted to know.

I shook my head, looking at my hands as they lay in my lap. "I don't know. I don't know why someone would attack me . . . would try to drive a stake through my heart."

"Ah, am I interrupting something?" Harley's voice was as rich and camera ready as ever as he stuck his head through our open door. His eyebrows were raised; his lips quirked into a smile that was half confused, half interested.

Heat surged across my cheeks, burning the tops of my ears. "So, yeah, steak is my heart. I love it that much."

Nina and Will exchanged glances and I shot them each a withering look. Will finally nodded and Nina murmured, "Right, steak." She pasted on a brilliant smile and glittered as brightly as the bugle beads on her Romona Keveza dress. "Harley! You're right on time."

"And you look lovely."

Nina introduced Will, and Harley nodded at me, his smile smooth, flawless. "Good to see you again, Sophie."

I clenched my molars. "Likewise."

Nina and Harley sauntered out of the apartment and Will sat down next to me. "You okay, love?"

I shrugged. "I don't like him."

"Nina's a grown-up. Like, really grown-up. And she has fangs. She can handle herself."

"I just hope she can handle him."

* * *

I woke up when I heard the lock tumble on the front door. I vaguely remembered sinking into a hot bath, and padding out to the living room in my bathrobe, where Will was watching the Discovery Channel. I remembered him handing me a hot cup of tea and a slice of toast. I must have fallen asleep, and he must have tucked the afghan around me, and muted whatever Lifetime movie I had made him watch. Despite the rash of demon abuse, despite the scratch that stung on my chest, despite my roommate waltzing in the living room, I felt oddly snuggly and cared for.

Nina leaned over the arm of the couch, teeth bared in an obnoxious grin. "See this?" She pointed to her face. "This is the face of a woman in love."

I shifted under my blanket. "Really?"

She batted her eyelashes and did an impressive pirouette, the sparkles on her dress catching the glare from Tori Spelling's *Lifetime* movie highlights. My little beaded black evening bag soared from Nina's hand.

"Thank you for letting me borrow your bag, by the way," Nina said, kicking off her three-inch heels.

I slid over on the couch and offered her half my blanket. "Tell me everything."

"First of all," Nina said, eyes narrowed, "how are you? The attack—"

I shook my head. "I'm fine. It was"—something broke inside me, turned my solid insides into quivering jelly— "not important. I'm going to talk to Dixon tomorrow."

Nina nodded knowingly, then burst into a fang-baring smile. "Harley is the man of my dreams!"

Just to clarify, Nina had lots of dreams. About a year and a half ago, her "dream" was a newly formed vampire who had lived his breathing years as a puppy police officer with the SFPD. After that, Dixon Andrade, he of large fangs and current head of the UDA, was Nina's dreamboat—until he doted more on his new power position than on Nina and her lacy Lascana lingerie. And now, apparently, there was Harley.

"He is brilliant," Nina said breathlessly, her coal black eyes glittering. "Absolutely brilliant! And he's so dedicated to his work! Did you know he is up at six-thirty every morning, writing?"

"You know what he's writing about, right?"

Nina ignored me; her bubble of love was puncture proof.

"And he is, of course, gorgeous!" She waggled her hands, spirit-finger style. "He's got these incredible eyes—they actually smolder—they *smolder*! Have you ever known someone who had smoldering eyes? And his hair is perfect—not receding at all—and he's got these incredible, huge, artistic hands. . . ." Nina hugged herself and I felt the parental need to cover ChaCha's floppy dog ears, should she start to describe whatever else about Harley might be "huge" and "artistic."

"Nina, you know he's a breather, right? Harley's alive. For the first time—I'm assuming."

Nina blinked at me, her love bubble un-burst. "Oh, Sophie, Harley is so much more than a breather." She launched herself toward me so we were nose to nose. ChaCha yipped and hopped off the couch before being the creamy filling in this roommate sandwich. "I think he might be my soul mate."

I inched back. I don't have vampire issues; I have personal-space issues. "So you told him about your . . ." I raised an inquiring eyebrow.

"About my what? My job? My roommate?"

I rolled my eyes. "Have you told your soul mate that although you're great in the 'mate' department, you're lacking a bit in the 'soul' one?"

Nina flopped back against the couch and crossed her arms in front of her chest. Her full bottom lip was pushed out in a pout. "Not exactly."

"Not exactly, like you told him you were a little older than he thought—or not exactly, like you nipped a little artery but nothing more?"

Nina gasped. "Sophie Lawson! I can't believe you would say such a thing. You know I adhere to the strictest standards of UDA-V bylaws. I signed a contract. If I eat someone without their express written consent, I lose all my benefits."

The Underworld Detection Agency not only keeps tabs on the general demon population, but we also offer such services as crossover support groups (going from dead to undead is third only to divorce and moving in terms of stress, I'm told), insurance on everything from graveyard dirt to heirloom family cauldrons, and protection benefits provided to all UDA clients that adhered to the bylaws of their particular sect. Nina, being a vampire, was classified under the UDA-V statute, and requirements for her coverage included things such as no human sacrifice, no demon sing-alongs, and absolutely no feeding on humans or "turning" anyone without their express written consent and/or prior to the mandatory 666-day waiting period. In exchange for her compliance, she could expect an eternity's worth of legal protection (from demon harassment, car accidents, or separatist issues), everlife assistance, and full-fang dental coverage. It might seem that demons are a wildly unorganized and unruly bunch, but the times we've had to "handle" demons that broke their bylaws were extremely rare.

"And besides, 'I like long walks, puppy dogs, and O-negative blood' are not the kind of things you spit out on a first date. There are rules of dating properly, you know."

I wouldn't know. Between my constant back-and-forth with Alex (or with being nearly killed or almost killed), I hadn't spent much time in the traditional dating world.

"It's really the kind of thing you ease into."

Nina hopped off the couch—her small feet making no indentation in the carpet—and I followed her to the kitchen.

"Yeah, so how did you pull off the 'I'm just a common breather' thing while on a date? What did you guys do?"

Nina raised a salacious eyebrow. Her lips curved up coyly. "Aren't you nosy?"

"Ew, no! I mean seriously, *ew.* I don't want to know what you did there. I meant, where did you go for your date?"

Nina rooted through the fridge and came out with a blood bag. She pierced the left-hand corner with one angled fang. "It was amazing. Ooh, this tastes so good. It's from a young one!"

My liver quivered. "The date?"

"Gary Danko. Have you been there?"

Gary Danko is one of the most exclusive and well-reviewed restaurants in San Francisco. While in most cities, that wouldn't mean very much, in a town like this one, where amazing food is common in restaurants from the Mission to the Marina, being "the best" was truly a compliment.

And I had never been there. I felt the corners of my lips turn down. "Tell me about it."

Nina pulled the blood bag away from her lips. "It. Was. Incredible! The ambiance is almost French—and kind of reminds me of this little tiny bistro my father used to take me to, not too far from the house. Anyway, the lighting was soft and beautiful." Nina fluttered around the kitchen. "And the food—oh, the food! It was to die for." She wiggled her eyebrows conspiratorially. "Get it?"

I crossed my arms and leaned against the kitchen counter. "You ate food?"

"Well, I had to eat a little." Nina inched her thumb and forefinger apart. "Enough to throw Harley off, at least. We ordered carpaccio, so I was able to stomach a little of that. The rest I just found ways to hide."

"You found ways to hide hunks of raw meat—"

"And truffles and caviar. That Harley knows how to order. We even had oysters! We ended off the evening with a nightcap at the Mark Hopkins. I love that place. Harley is staying there all week. They served us petit fours!"

My mouth started to water and I thought about the peanut butter and jelly sandwich I had scarfed down while sitting on the kitchen counter watching Rachael Ray make coq au vin. I was probably cutting away the tuft of green mold on my Health Nut bread while Nina was hiding two-hundred-dollar-a-scoop caviar.

"Hey. Where did you hide the food?" I wanted to know.

Nina finished her blood bag and tossed the empty into the trash. "I stuffed most of it in my purse." Another pirouette and she disappeared into her room.

I stood, openmouthed and sadly envious of my best friend. She made the most of her afterlife and I . . . Well, I had spent the last four hours of my life in a chenille bathrobe while my dog licked crumbs from my chin.

"Hey!" I said, pounding on Nina's door. "You borrowed my purse tonight!"

By eight-thirty the next morning, I had polished off my second cup of coffee and had had at least four imaginary conversations with Dixon, where he listened, rapt, to everything I had to say and declared me the head of investigating all the Underworld mishaps with a crew of shirtless men at the ready. So when Dixon actually sauntered into the agency at quarter to nine, I was shaking from a caffeine and sugar rush, and my practiced, impassioned speech sounded like "blahhhhhhh."

Dixon cocked his head and smiled serenely. "Why don't you meet me in my office and we can talk further?"

I nodded mutely and followed him. After breathing deeply and allowing my heart to return to a decaffeinated pace, I detailed last night's events to Dixon, adding extra emphasis to the near stake-to-the-heart encounter.

He furrowed his brow, and wrapped one hand around his chin. "Well, this is very disconcerting."

I gaped. "Disconcerting? Someone tried to shish kebab me outside of the San Francisco Police Department, Dixon! That's more than disconcerting, that's—that's terrifying!"

Dixon pressed his palms together, pushing his index fingers against his pursed lips. "While I don't disagree about how frightening your experience last night was, Ms. Lawson—with all due respect—in the last twelve months someone did try to set you on fire, bleed you dry, and frame you for murder."

"So what you're saying is nearly being staked through the heart pales in comparison."

Dixon gave me that thin-lipped, "if the shoe fits" look.

"Fine. My experience aside. Mrs. Henderson. The centaur. Bettina. You can't honestly tell me that all of these occurrences are just coincidence."

"Certainly not. But what I can tell you is that as we speak, there is a team of Underworld detectives working on it. So I suggest that you stick to what it is you do best, and let us handle all of this bump-in-the-night stuff." Dixon's bloodred lips cut into a sharp smile, which started out placating and ended up menacing. The prickly heat that stiffened my spine last night was back and I edged out of my chair, not blinking or breathing until I was back in the comfort of my own office. I sat in silence. My mind was buzzing like a hive of honeybees, until Kale knocked on my door and poked her head in.

"You have a visitor."

My heart did a little pitter-patter and my stomach fluttered. *Alex?* I didn't want to see him, didn't want to *want* to see him. When Will poked his head in, I was surprised that the pitter-patter didn't stop—and neither did the anxious flutter.

"What are you doing here?"

"Wanted to stop in and check on you. And I brought you these."

I felt my eyes widen, and felt a tiny prick in the back of my throat. "They're beautiful."

"Some are almond, some are plain. Those are dark chocolate." Will handed me the bouquet of Hershey bars, and my libido and stomach perked up. "Thank you." I bit my bottom lip. "Hey, I really appreciate your concern, Will, but I don't need someone looking after me."

Will sat down, kicking both feet up on my desk. "That might indeed be the case, but some nutter is out there stabbing perfectly good birds in the heart. Who's to say he won't come after me next? Safety in numbers, you know? And I can run faster than you."

"My hero." I rolled my eyes.

"So . . ." Will clapped his hands, looked around. "This is the Underworld Detection Agency."

I nodded. "It is."

Will fingered the Post-it notes lined up on my desk, and scanned my bookshelves filled with old college textbooks. "Not all that mystical, is it?"

I shrugged. "What we do isn't all that mystical."

We stared at each other for an awkward beat. "So

you're doing okay, after last night? I didn't want to leave you, but once you started snoring . . ."

I felt my cheeks redden. "Oh, thanks for the blanket, by the way."

"Did you talk to the head vamp about the whole . . ." Will made a staking motion with his left hand.

"He didn't seem all that concerned, but I am. I need to look into this."

"How about we do it over lunch?"

I cocked my head. "We?"

"I'm not working this week, and there's nothing good on telly."

"Let me just buzz Kale and have her bring over the files."

"Files?" Vlad, in all his Count Chocula glory, poked his head in my office.

"Sophie and I are doing some crime fighting."

Vlad's eyebrows went up. "Crime fighting?"

"We're just looking into some of the incidents that have happened around here. Mrs. Henderson, Bettina . . ."

Vlad stiffened and stepped into my office while I buzzed Kale.

"Front desk."

"Hey, Kale, it's Sophie. You know how I mentioned that Mrs. Henderson and a few others missed their appointments?"

"Mmm-hmm."

"Well, can you pull their files and drop them off in my office, please?"

We all stood in silence, hearing Kale pop her gum on the other end of the intercom.

"Um, now?" I asked.

I heard Kale blow out a put-upon sigh and I would have been sympathetic if a) gathering files wasn't her job and b) she hadn't been a witch who had the power to extract files from wherever they were hidden with a simple tug of the ear. And the fact that she had been oozing her near nakedness on my couch, forty-eight hours ago, also took away from my sympathy for the teen witch.

"You can drop them off in my office when you get them together."

"No problemo."

"I'd like to see those files, too," Vlad said before I had an opportunity to turn the intercom off.

"I will bring those files down to your office right now," Kale said, suddenly full of spunk and haste.

She was standing at the threshold to my office in record time, a stack of file folders pressed against her chest. Her eyes, the size of two glazed donuts, zeroed in on Vlad.

"Thanks, Kale," I said, trying to pry the files from her death grip. "Will and I are just going to look these over while we have lunch."

Vlad stiffened. "As a representative of the Vampire Empowerment and Restoration Movement, and as the new head of operations"—he puffed out his chest and smoothed his stupid damask vest—"I think I should be a part of this investigation."

Will and I shared a look.

"This could very well begin affecting vampires—if it hasn't already."

I blew out a sigh. "Fine. Kale, can I have those files?"

Kale snaked her arms around the files. "Actually, Sophie, I'm personally responsible for these files. If something were to happen to them while they were out of my care . . ."

I felt my left eye start to twitch. "Fine, you can come too."

Kale grinned and batted huge eyes at Vlad. Vlad ignored the waves of love pouring off Kale, crossed his arms, and narrowed his eyes at Will. Will just looked at me, grinning, pleased as punch and probably considering nothing more than a wad of free French fries in his future.

The whole load of us tumbled into the hallway and I bumped square into Nina, who had her shoulder bag crossed over her chest.

"Hey, what's going on here?"

"We're going to lunch," Will said.

"Of course you are," Nina replied. "Vlad?"

"Official Vampire Empowerment—"

Nina held up her hand and rolled her eyes. "Got it."

"There's been some activity in the area."

"What a surprise," Nina said, fishing in her shoulder bag and retrieving an O-positive pouch.

"Will and I are going to work on it."

Vlad cut his eyes to me. "Okay, Vlad, Kale, Will, and I are going to work on it."

"I'm just in it for the chips," Will said, shrugging.

"Want to come with us?"

"Can't." Nina tossed a lock of hair over her shoulder. "I'm working through lunch today. This book is practically writing itself." She waggled a finger a quarter-inch from my nose. "Mark my words, Soph. My new vampire romance? It's going to be huge. Don't worry, I'll totally give you a nod in the acknowledgments."

Chapter Seven

We must have looked like a motley crew walking out of the police station and down the street toward the diner: me, flaming red hair, white puffy ski jacket, and my business-on-a-budget suit; Will, looking like a cross between an Abercrombie model and David Beckam's long-lost brother; Kale, her mod teen-hates-world black-and-deep-purple ensemble thrown off by her puppy-in-love grin; and Vlad, stern-faced, slicked hair, and dressed like a Dracula reject—sans cape, though, thank God. But this being San Francisco, and veil or not, no one batted an eye as we angled our way through the secretaries in business suits and sneakers, through the kids in baggy jeans and backpacks loping around, and all the way to the Fog City Diner—aptly named as we all huddled against the frigid city summer.

I breathed deeply in the warm restaurant. My stomach rumbled as a plate of meat loaf and mashed potatoes whizzed by.

"Okay," Will said, once we were seated, "where do we start? Do we know what we're dealing with?"

I put my menu down. "Wow! You must really be into this case. Usually, Alex can't open a file without a three-course meal."

Something flashed in Will's hazel eyes and he studied the menu hard until the waitress showed up. I could see the hint of amusement playing on her matte red lips. She welcomed us, refilled our water glasses, and told us her name was Shirley. "What can I get you all?"

I quickly scanned the menu and ordered a chef's salad, with dressing on the side, and no bread; Will went for a double bacon cheeseburger, with whiskey barbecue sauce, and fries.

I smacked my menu shut. "Actually, I'll have that, instead."

Will eyed me with a wide grin. "I love a woman who can eat."

"And for the lovebirds?" Shirley grinned at Vlad—stiff, and as close to the end of the booth as possible—and Kale, snuggling up to her un-snuggable undead beau.

"Nothing for me," Vlad said, his eyes settling on Shirley. "But thank you."

Shirley's eyes slowly widened, her mouth hanging slack. "Anything," she murmured.

"Vlad," I hissed. "No glamours!"

Vlad looked at me and rolled his eyes. Shirley sucked in a deep breath, looking as though she had just awakened with a start. "Nothing for the gentleman, and you?" Her eyebrows rose expectantly.

Kale looked from Shirley to Vlad, then back again. "Clam chowder in a bread bowl."

Shirley scurried away and Kale turned to Vlad; her

cheeks were flushed, fire raging in her eyes. She looked a bit like Drew Barrymore in that old movie *Firestarter*—right at the point where whole buildings went up in flames. I nudged a glass of water across the table toward Kale, and I reveled in the fact that off duty or not, Will played a San Francisco fireman in real life.

"You were totally flirting with her," Kale said, eyes narrowed at Vlad.

Vlad shrugged. "She looked delicious." He licked his lips. "You can't blame me, baby, I'm a vampire."

I wondered quickly whether it was too late to change my order to Pepto-Bismol and soda water.

"Guys! We're here to work on Mrs. Henderson's and Bettina's cases."

Kale picked at her fingernail. "Bettina didn't look like anything was wrong with her this morning. And what's up with Mrs. Henderson?"

I opened and closed my mouth dumbly. "Didn't you hear?"

A sudden spark of interest crossed over Vlad's porcelain features. "Hear what?"

I leaned in and lowered my voice to a hoarse whisper. "Mrs. Henderson is dead. Didn't Dixon say anything?"

Kale's eyes were wide. Her hand subconsciously went for Vlad's sleeve. She pinched his shirt fabric between thumb and finger, rubbing like a child rubs a blanket for comfort. "What happened?"

I swallowed hard and looked at Will. He gave me a tiny, nearly imperceptible nod. "She was murdered."

"How do you know that?"

I pulled a lock of hair and wound it tightly against my index finger. "I went over there yesterday. No one answered the door. I went in, saw what looked like a disaster, and called Alex."

"Oh my God!" Kale's eyes were wide. "She's dead?"

I felt a lump forming in my throat and I coughed. "There was blood everywhere. It was awful. I told Dixon, and he said he would take care of it."

Vlad stiffened. "Then he must be taking care of it."

"But no one knows about it. And the centaur and now Bettina? No one knows that they should be on the alert."

Kale leaned in, brows raised, the pale blond hair on her arms standing on end. "For what? For whom?"

I bit my lip. "We don't know, exactly. Vlad, you're one of Dixon's right-hand men now. Have you heard anything? Did he call a meeting? Was he writing anything up or checking with the police?"

Vlad shrugged. "Not that I saw. But if Dixon said he was going to handle it, I'm sure he will."

I'm sure he would if the victim was a vampire, a tiny voice at the back of my skull nagged. "Let's just take a look at the files, please. Kale?"

Kale handled over her precious stack and nudged against Vlad.

"That's kind of scary," I heard her whisper to Vlad. "I don't know anyone—like us—who has ever died."

Vlad just shrugged, his brooding countenance unchanged. "Things die," he finally muttered, before huddling over his paper place mat with a black pen and doodling dark and broody things on it.

Kale alternately looked frightened and lovestruck, one hand kneading the palm of the other.

"Okay, Mrs. Henderson." Will read from the manila folder he was holding. "Filed under 'other.'"

"Yeah," I clarified, "we don't have a lot of dragon clients."

Will raised his eyebrows. "A dragon? You don't say." He studied the stack of pages that flopped out of her folder. "According to this, the bird was punctual. Never missed an appointment."

"Until last week." I nodded solemnly. "And now we know why."

Kale inched closer to Vlad. Her hands circled his bicep in a move that was part predatory, part fearful.

"Kale, you hadn't heard anything from her?" I asked. "Before this? Or maybe from the kids or husband?"

Kale's oblivious expression remained unchanged at my question.

"Do you ever get the feeling you're being watched?" Vlad asked, looking up from the doodle on his place mat.

Will snorted and turned over his coffee mug as the waitress flitted by. "You are being watched, gov."

Crimson washed over Kale's cheeks and she lowered her eyes, focusing intently on peeling a stripe of silver nail polish from her thumb.

"I don't mean from in here," Vlad said. "From out there." He inclined his dark head toward the big picture window as the fog thickened outside. "I've felt it since we went outside. Don't you feel it?"

"Don't you have super vampire sense or something?" Will asked.

"Don't you have a fire to put out?"

"Touché."

Vlad looked out the window again, and my eyes went to where he was looking. I watched cars speed through the intersection and the same group of businesspeople on their lunch break that I usually did, but gooseflesh now pricked out over my arms. I glanced over my shoulder. Though it was noon, the sky was streaked an ominous gray; the sun was choked out by ribbons of fog. People bustled by outside, looking straightforward, avoiding each other's gazes; the stores went about their business, with neon signs flashing, doors opening and closing.

Vlad gestured with his chin at my bare arms. "You feel it, too, huh?"

"I do now," I said, with a shudder.

Will picked up the next file and caught my eye. "Shall we?"

Vlad cleared his throat and sat bolt upright; his fingers were laced and sitting in front of him. He looked startlingly Dixonesque.

"So," Vlad said, "the Vampire Empowerment and Restoration Movement is concerned that whatever is happening to these demons could soon be happening to our brethren. If it hasn't already happened."

"Me too," Kale piped in. "Except about witches, too."

"Ten minutes ago you didn't believe anything was wrong with anyone."

Kale swallowed hard. "That's before we knew that anyone was dead."

Kale's plain statement struck ice at the base of my spine. "We don't even know what we're dealing with."

Vlad looked hard at me. "If we're dealing with anything at all." He shrugged while I gaped. "If Dixon had the Investigations team out, and didn't say anything to the staff, then maybe they didn't find anything."

I opened my mouth to interject, but Vlad held up a silencing hand. "We live in a big city, in a weak economic climate. Mrs. Henderson could have walked in on a burglary."

Will looked impressed. "She's a dragon, right? That's one ballsy burglar."

"Weren't you just very concerned about how this might affect your ascot-wearing buddies?"

Vlad shrugged, picked up the next file and flipped through the pages casually. "From her description, it looks like Bettina was mugged."

"Would a mugger say he was out to eradicate her kind?" I asked, crossing my arms in front of my chest.

"People do all sorts of crazy things for all sorts of crazy reasons, Sophie." Vlad grinned, fangs glowing white. "This is San Francisco. Last week Santa Claus was being walked by a dominatrix through the Mission. It wasn't even Christmas."

Will blanched and I knocked on the table. "Can we focus, please? We have a series of strange happenings that may or may not be combined. Demons who never miss appointments are missing appointments. Mrs. Henderson"—I shuddered—"murdered, and Bettina reporting an attack."

Will looked at me.

"I think all of these things seem a little too coincidental to be, you know, coincidence, don't you think?"

Kale nodded. Her large eyes let me know that she agreed with me.

"I'm not saying you're wrong. I'm just saying we shouldn't jump to conclusions."

"I didn't jump. I answered the phone. I got out of my car at the Henderson house. Lo and behold, there conclusions were. There is a full-blown Underworld attacker loose in San Francisco," I said definitively.

"As long as you're not going overboard." Vlad sighed.

"Four events. Four!" I held up my hand, wiggling four fingers. "All within a few days of each other? This is bad."

Shirley came back with our food and we stopped talking, suddenly trying to look casual in that completely suspicious way. She angled an eyebrow at us. "Can I get y'all anything else?"

I pressed my lips together and forced a smile, though my stomach quivered nervously. "No, no, I think we're okay."

The second she left, Vlad swung toward me and Will. "So there is no evidence that any vampires are in danger?"

I shook my head. "Nothing that we've seen so far, especially if these are all the files."

Will's eyes flashed and I sucked in a hard breath. "Well," I started, "someone did try to stake me."

"Stake you?" Vald's eyebrows went up.

I made the universal stabbing/staking motion and Vlad grinned. "Then it's official," he said, "this guy has no idea what a vampire looks like."

I rolled my eyes.

"Well," Vlad said, puffing out his damask vest, "please keep me abreast of the situation, particularly should something change."

He gave each of us small, curt nods and slipped out of the booth.

"You know, I should probably get back to work, too," Kale said, trying to scurry out behind him.

"Aren't these files your responsibility?" I asked.

Kale waved me off with a flick of her hand. "I trust you to get them back." She popped up onto her tiptoes to look over my head and I craned my neck to follow her gaze. Through the plate glass window I could see Vlad was already on the sidewalk, pulling up the collar of his trench coat against the light drizzle that had started. I looked at Kale's flimsy, short-sleeved T-shirt.

"You're going to get soaked to the bone. Take this." I handed her my white puffy jacket and she slipped it on, the collar swallowing her mass of dark hair.

"Looks cute on you," I said, smiling. "But you can't keep it."

Kale grinned and turned on her heel. "Thanks!"

"Such a nice work ethic with kids nowadays," Will said ruefully. "Send them out to protect something with their lives and . . ." He shrugged, cocking a boyish looking half smile.

"I think the only thing she was protecting was—"

The screeching of tires just outside the glass cut off my sentence. Will mumbled something to me, but his words were lost in the booming crush of metal and shrieks of people on the sidewalk.

"A girl's been hit," someone yelled from a booth behind us. "Somebody call 911!"

The few bites of lunch I had eaten sat in my stomach like stones. I wanted to get up and look, wanted to turn my head to glance out the plate glass window, but my whole body had gone statue-stiff. My every bone was feeling leaden. When I tried to speak, I realized my mouth was papery and dry. "Do you think . . . ?" was all I managed to get out before I felt the tears coursing down my cheeks. "Do you think-think . . . ?" I tried to start again, but another sob choked my words. They settled in the back of my throat like a solid lump. I tried to swallow, tried to steady myself, tried to get myself to move.

"The guy took off!" I heard someone yell.

"Oh my God! Oh my God!"

Will seemed to leap over the table. He gripped my arm and pulled me with him out the double doors. I think I heard him yell, "Stand back!" and "I'm an EMT!" but I felt like I had cotton in my ears—everything sounded muffled and strange.

I know I felt the cement scuffle underneath my shoes, once we made it outside. I know I felt the sting of the cold air on my exposed skin, felt chilled drops of water prick my scalp and dribble down the back of my bare neck.

"Did anyone see who it was?" a stout man in a shin-length trench coat asked the crowd.

"Does anyone know what happened?"

I looked around blankly. The slow movement, the muffled sounds—I was observing a dream. This couldn't be right.

And then I saw Kale's shoe. It was wedged under the tire of a parked car. My heart sped up and I sucked in gusts of cold air.

He missed her! I thought. *She must have lost her shoe when she jumped out of the way!* I felt a cold mist of sweat, felt the painful thud of my heart against my ribs. *She's okay.*

I pulled the shoe out and ran into the middle of the street to where a crowd had gathered.

"Will, Will, she's okay!" My mouth must have stopped in midspeech because I felt a cold lick of wind whip across my teeth.

"Kale?"

Will looked over his shoulder at me and I could see his hands. He had two fingers pressed against Kale's lovely pale neck. Her dangly purple-stoned earring was laid daintily across her cheek; it flopped out of sight when her head lolled toward the cement, listless. Her eyes were mostly closed; the heavy mascara on her lashes made a shadowed spiderwebbed pattern on her apple cheeks.

But it couldn't have been Kale.

Kale ran away and left her shoe. She left her shoe. I had it in my hand.

I had it in my hand.

In agonizing slow motion, I felt the shoe slip from my fingertips and heard the sound of it thudding on the ground; it was a weird, hollow echo. The rest of the world dropped into silence. Kale's eyelids fluttered but did not open. Will eyed me and I could see that his lips were pale and pressed together; his fire chief badge winked in the few shards of sunlight that pierced the gray, pregnant clouds. There was a smudge halfway up Will's right arm and I felt my stomach lurch.

It was blood.

Will pointed to me and I saw his lips moving, but I don't think there were any words. The rain started up again in a slow drizzle; I watched as people milled about, losing interest in the scene. They turned up their coat collars and clicked their umbrellas open. An ambulance wailed. There were fingertips on my arms and someone was pulling me backward. I stumbled over my feet, bit down hard on my lower lip but allowed myself to be led.

"She's okay," I heard myself mumble, finally able to work my mouth. "She's okay, but she lost her shoe."

I don't know how I ended up on the sidewalk, but I sat down hard on the cement. The cold, wet reality struck me and suddenly everything was loud and chaotic—the ambulance shot down the street, sirens wailing, flanked by police cars with bright lights that tore through the gray fog. People were talking; someone was crying; seabirds were squawking. Will was kneeling in front of me and I felt the warmth of his hand on my shoulder, his fingertips squeezing me gently.

"Sophie, Sophie," he was saying.

I blinked, finally registering the concern in his wide hazel eyes.

"Is she going to be okay?"

Will nodded slowly, a wet, sandy-colored lock of hair flopping over his forehead. "She'll survive, but she's going to be pretty banged up."

My heart started to thud again. The blood began to course through my veins again, and I felt a fist of anger burning low in my belly. I sprang up, fists clenched. "Who was it?"

"Who was what?" Will wanted to know.

"Who hit Kale? Did the police take him? Did they get his car?"

Will laid a tender hand on my shoulder and I winced when I saw his eyes cloud—a sure sign that something was coming that he didn't want to say—and it was likely something I didn't want to know.

"He took off, love."

"Took off? He *took off*?"

"Bloke didn't even stop."

I felt the torrent of tears again, but this time they were bitter, angry. "He didn't even stop?" It was a whisper and I felt my lower lip quiver pitifully. "How could someone do that?"

Will guided me back into the diner and into our booth. I slid in and stared down at my burger and fries, the grease from the patty congealing in a slick brown pool. I slid my plate aside and took a large gulp of ice water. "Who the hell would hit someone and just drive away? He had to know—he had to know that he hit"—I could barely form the word—"her."

"Unfortunately, hit and runs are really common in this city. Pedestrians are walking into the street—"

"You're blaming Kale?" I was incredulous.

"No!" Will held out his palm, stop sign style. "No. The only person I blame is the idiot who hit her."

Will started pulling dollars bills from his billfold.

I breathed a sigh of relief. "God, I need to get out of here."

"Do you want me to walk you back to work?"

I swung my head, trying my best to clear the hum of thoughts fogging my mind. "No. I want you to take me to the hospital. We have to make sure she's going to be okay."

Will sucked in a breath. "Okay. Let's go."

Chapter Eight

My knee was bobbing uncontrollably as I sat in the waiting room and Will was talking to the emergency staff (a perk of being an EMT/fireman) to get information on Kale. By the time he came back, I was wringing my hands.

"Did you find out anything? Is she going to be okay? Oh my gosh, oh my gosh, oh my gosh." I felt like I needed to cry—wanted to cry—but every last bit of moisture had been used up.

Will sat next to me and put his hand on my knee. I stared at it, feeling my lip quiver.

"That's not good," I said, not taking my eyes off his hand.

Will's gaze followed mine and he retracted his hand as though my knee had burned him. "No, love, it's okay. Kale's going to be fine. She's got a few broken bones and she's pretty bashed up, but she's going to come through this okay."

"Did the doctor say that?" I slid in my chair, turning

to face Will. "Did they actually use the words *she's going to be okay?*"

Will licked his lips, raking a hand through his hair. "Not those exact words. They're still running some tests, but they're pretty confident."

I nodded, unable to form words. There was a nagging pain behind my eyes—something that told me I was missing something. When Will laid his arm across my shoulders, I slumped into him, half numb, half desperate, for some kind of comfort. A tremor started from the pit of my stomach and suddenly I was shivering, clenching my teeth to keep them from chattering. My fingers fumbled for my purse; I pawed around blindly.

"What do you need?"

"My phone. My phone, please."

Will dug through my bag and handed me my phone; I mashed at the keypad.

"Nina?" he mouthed.

I shook my head, listening to the dial tone. "Alex."

I watched Will's Adam's apple bob; he looked away, taking his arm from behind my shoulders and folding his hands in his lap. As I listened to the phone ring endlessly on Alex's end, I blinked at Will, seemingly miles away now, and felt unbearably alone.

"Is she okay? Where is she? Is she okay?" Lorraine's voice was shrill and I stared up at her, squinting against the harsh yellow utility lights, almost unable to make her out.

When she came into the light, her face was gaunt; her hands were in determined little fists punching through the air. Lorraine—the UDA finance director, resident witch, and Kale's mentor—rushed down the hall like a ball of fire. Her honey-colored hair flailed behind her, and the gauzy skirts of her green dress stood out cartoonishly against the white sterile tiles of the hospital hallway.

"Will someone please tell me if Kale is all right?"

Will stood and put a calming hand on Lorraine's shoulder. "Kale is going to be okay. She's pretty banged up, but she's going to pull through just fine. She's young and strong."

"Young and strong is no match for metal and foreign-made," Lorraine said with a sniff.

I felt my eyes widen. "You know what kind of car hit Kale? How?"

Lorraine looked from me to Will. "Vlad mentioned it. Didn't you . . . Don't the police have the bastard who did this to her in custody?"

"He took off," I said, my voice sounding small.

"Took off?" Lorraine's nostrils flared and her hands once again closed into fists. A wave of static electricity shot through the air and I felt the hair on the crown of my head stand up. The steady *blips* and *beeps* of the hospital machinery cracked into a loud cackle of static. I pressed my hands to my ears.

"Calm down, Lorraine. Please, you have to try to calm down. You're going to kill everyone in here."

Will was incredulous. "That was her?"

Though Lorraine was a Gestalt witch of the green order—a faction of witches who usually did things like manipulate the seasons and specialized in herbal healing—when she got upset, her power took the form of natural devastations. Large, state-of-emergency devastations. When she caught an old boyfriend cheating (and he lied about it), the ground shook with such a fury that part of the 101 Highway crumbled in on itself and Bay Area residents spent the next six weeks ducking and covering every time a bus passed by. Reporters called it the Loma Prieta earthquake; Nina and I called it the Wrath of 'Raine.

The electricity crackled in the air.

"I talked to the police at the scene."

Lorraine looked at me and I nodded. "Will's a fireman . . . when he's not . . ." I wagged my head, unable to tack on the "saving me from imminent death" portion of his Guardian job description.

"They're doing everything to find out who did this to Kale. He's is not going to get away with it," Will assured her.

"We should talk to Vlad, too," I said, standing, beginning to pace.

"You're in luck."

Vlad was rushing down the hall toward us, with Nina in tow. She was dressed in a sparkly minidress, which showed off her long, shapely legs. Her now-black hair swirled glossily around her shoulders, dipping toward her waist. Her narrow-heeled black stilettos clicked against the tiled hallway.

"That's quite a candy striper uniform," I said to Nina.

She rolled her eyes. "I was getting ready for my date when Vlad came back to the office."

"They let you wear that to the office?" Will wanted to know, his eyes sweeping the figure-hugging sheath.

"I planned ahead," Nina said, crossing her arms.

Lorraine and I both knew that "planned ahead" meant that Nina had pulled open the file cabinet marked "Lapsed Clients" and sorted through boutique-worthy collection of vintage couture she kept there. The shoes likely came from the supply closet, which was stocked with staples, Post-it notes, and several seasons' worth of Jimmy Choos, all in Nina's delicate size 6.

"We came as soon as we heard. Is Kale okay?" Nina asked.

"She will be." My knees felt rubbery and shaky again as I thought of the screech of the tires, the horrible sound of Kale's body making contact with the steel grill of the car. I pinched my eyes closed and saw her lone shoe, wedged under that car tire, saw her head lolling listlessly to the side.

"Oh, love, you don't look so good. You should sit." Will led me to one of the cold plastic waiting-room chairs. I sank down and he handed me a bottle of water; his other hand massaged my neck. "Head between your knees, love."

I swung forward, feeling my hair sweep the ground, listening to the endless loop of him explaining what happened, hearing him reassure everyone in a flat, exhausted voice that Kale would be fine. I repeated the mantra in my head, until I was cut off by a white-coated doctor who walked up, closing a medical chart. "Kale Dubois?" He looked up expectantly.

"We're here for her. We're here for Kale," Lorraine said. "Is there news?"

"Are you family?"

"Yes," Lorraine said, her eyes cutting to all of us and daring us to object.

"Yes, family," Nina piped up.

"Sisters," I said.

"Okay, well, Ms. Dubois is going to be just fine. She

does, as I told . . ." The doctor's eyebrows rose as he looked at Will.

"Her brother," Lorraine supplied, her eyes daring anyone, again, to challenge her.

"As I told her brother earlier, Ms. Dubois has a broken femur and collarbone. Both of those have been set and should heal just fine. We—"

"So we can take her home?" Lorraine broke in.

The doctor shook his head; his eyes politely apologetic. "I'm afraid not. Though she seemed to fare quite well, Ms. Dubois was in a rather bad accident. We need to keep her here for a few days to be sure that there is nothing more seriously wrong with her."

"May we see her?" Nina asked.

The doctor seemed to be thinking. "She really does need her rest. Maybe just one or two of you, so she knows you're out here. The rest of you can come by during regular visiting hours tomorrow."

I stood up and took Lorraine's hand when I saw her eyes go wide; I saw them rimmed with tears.

"You go in, Lorraine. Tell her we're all out here pulling for her." I glanced at Vlad, held his eyes for a beat. "And Vlad should go in, too, in case she remembers anything."

Lorraine nodded and cleared her throat; then she pushed her hair back behind her ears. She pasted on a welcoming smile as she looked toward Kale's closed door, but I could feel the fear radiating from her. I wrapped my arms around her.

"It's going to be okay, Lorraine," I whispered into her hair. "I know it is."

My body quaked with Lorraine's tense energy.

"She's like a kid sister to me," Lorraine said, the single tear wobbling over her cheek. "I couldn't stand it if anything happened to her."

"Nothing will," Will said, squeezing her shoulder.

"You'll keep us posted, right?" Nina asked.

Lorraine nodded quickly. "Of course. You guys go home."

"Oh, I don't—"

"I've got you," Will said over my shoulder. "I can take you home."

I nodded dumbly, then blindly fumbled down the hall. The astringent smell of sickness and terror assaulted me the whole way down.

I slammed the car door and buckled myself into the passenger seat while Will stared straight ahead.

"You going to be okay?" he asked.

"I'm fine. It's Kale I'm worried about." I clapped my palm to my forehead. "That's right. Can you swing by the diner on the way home? We left the UDA files there."

Will double-parked in front of the diner and I jumped out, a cold mass of nerves pulsing in my gut. I tried to maintain tunnel vision and avoid the spot where Kale went down, but I had the nagging need to look. The intersection buzzed with dull regularity as a Muni bus chugged by, followed by a Subaru packed with tourists who stared wide-eyed and openmouthed, foreheads and palms pressed against the glass. I sighed: nothing, no clues, no slow-moving car plastered with bumper stickers saying MY HONOR STUDENT RAN OVER YOUR FRIEND IN THE STREET. I had my hand on the door to the Fog City

Diner, when I took one last glance back to where Will sat in the car, fiddling with the stereo. He bent low enough for me to notice a snatch of red hair on the other side of the street, a midcalf-brushing trench coat.

My heart thumped into my throat. Despite the moist, biting fog, my entire body broke out into a hot sweat. I spun on my heel and zigzagged through traffic, across the street, catching the door to Java Script as it swung closed behind the red-haired man. Vaguely I heard Will's English accent cutting through the sounds of traffic. Vaguely I heard his car door slam shut, him telling me to come back.

Java Script was warm inside and the heady smell of roasted coffee beans stung my nose. I zipped past a display of hardback best sellers and "Java Script Recommends" titles. I was looking frantically for the red-haired man.

"Hey, welcome to Java Script." A teenaged girl wearing a red apron grinned at me. "Is there something I can help you find?"

"Did you just see a man in a trench coat come in here? He had red hair like mine." I pulled a lock of my own hair to demonstrate the color. "And he would have looked"—I swallowed bitter saliva—"a little like me, too."

The girl shrugged. "Just now? The only person who came in here just now was you." She smiled and her metal braces glinted in the harsh fluorescent lights. "It's been a superslow day. But do you want me to leave a message in case someone comes in?"

The tinkling bells over the door did their thing and Will stepped inside, obviously irate. "What happened to picking something up at the diner? Next thing I know, you're sprinting through traffic."

I grabbed Will by the elbow and led him to a stack of James Patterson's *new* new releases. "Didn't you see him slip in here?"

"Who?"

I cut my eyes, left and right, then leaned in. "My father."

Will stepped back, eyebrows raised. "Suddenly dear old dad pops back on the scene and stops in for a read?"

I ran a hand through my hair. "I know he's here. At least I think he's here." I gripped at my chest. "I just kind of feel it." Bat wings fluttered in my stomach. "Do you think maybe he misses me?"

Will offered me a sympathetic—if apologetic—smile. "I'm sure any father would miss a daughter like you."

I felt a weird, unnerving sense of glee hearing that my father might miss me. That glee was only slightly doused with the unwelcome knowledge that dear old dad raked in souls by the bucketful and offered a fiery, brimstony afterlife, once all their cards were punched.

I looked over both shoulders. "Maybe he isn't looking for me. But if I'm wrong, why did you come after me? Did you come in here because you sensed I was in danger? Was your Guardian Spidey sense tingling?"

"No. My charge almost made herself into a hood ornament two hours after her friend became a hood ornament in the same intersection."

I blew out a sigh. "I'm just going to take a quick walk through the stacks and see if he's here."

"You really think ole Satan is going to be strolling through the stacks? I just kind of think, as you know, the ruler of hell, he'd have someone to pick up books for him. Or he'd Amazon it."

"I don't know. Just—"

"There's a reading going on tomorrow afternoon." The red-aproned girl walked up and shoved a flyer in each of our hands. "You guys should come. It's Harley Cavanaugh, the author of *Vampires, Werewolves, and Other Things That Don't Exist.*"

"Thanks," I said, stuffing the flyer in my purse. I put my palms on Will's firm chest. "Give me two minutes. I just want to see if he's here. I just need to know if—if it's happening again."

I spun on my heel and beelined toward the cozy-mystery section before Will could answer, before Will could say something artificially reassuring about keeping me safe and hiding my secret—as the angels liked to say—"in plain sight." I wound my way through the stacks, surprising a couple of teenagers making out in the gardening section and then running into an older man in military history. None of them were Lucas Szabo—the man who was my father, the man who left me four days after I was born.

The man who might very well be the devil.

It wasn't until recently that I found out that my family tree was "rooted in hell," as Nina liked to say. My mother, a seer and a woman who so hated her supernatural gift that she searched her entire life for a piece of normalcy, met my father, Lucas Szabo, at the University of San Francisco, where he worked teaching courses in legend and mythology. He wore cardigans and smoked a pipe and carried a leather briefcase. By all accounts he was a normal man. My mother fell deeply in love. By the time I came around, they were living in a walk-up apartment in the Hayes Valley and eating Campbell's soup and grilled cheese sandwiches. There were no vampire roommates or unexpected drop-ins by pixies and fairies. They brought me home—drooling and pink, I suspect—and slept with me as I cooed in a bassinet at the end of the bed.

Four days later my mother came home from the market to find the apartment empty, my father's closet cleaned out, and me, crying through the slats in my crib. My mother took me home to my grandmother and we settled there together.

When I was in elementary school, my grandmother told me that my mother died from a broken heart, pining for my father. I had chalked it up to the Lawson hankering for all things deep fried and chocolate dipped.

It wasn't until last year that I learned the sinister circumstances of my mother's death.

It wasn't until last year that I learned when my mother hanged herself, I was there.

Chapter Nine

"Well?" Will asked as he came up on my shoulder.

"Well, nothing," I said, backing out of the military-history book aisle. I leaned against a stack of Harley Cavanaugh's books and rubbed small circles on my temples with my index fingers. "He's not here."

I felt Will slouch next to me. He laced his fingers through my hair and gently raked through the curls. The movement sent a ticklish prickle down my spine. "Don't worry, love. It was probably just the old bloke that you saw there."

"It wasn't, Will. Believe me, I wish it were. I don't . . . I'm afraid, what if the hallucinations are starting again?"

Will turned to stare me full in the face. "The hallucinations were sent from Ophelia, and she's dead now."

"I know." I leaned in so our foreheads were almost touching. "But what if there is another angel? Alex said they might keep coming."

"I'm your Guardian and I haven't heard anything or seen anything." He shrugged. "Nothing's come over the dispatch."

I blinked. "There's some sort of Guardian dispatch?"

Will smiled. "No. Isn't it possible that you just thought you saw something?"

I blew out a sigh and stared at the toes of my shoes on the industrial-grade carpet. "I guess. I just have this feeling. . . ."

"You feel like you're missing something?"

My eyes went wide. "Then you feel it, too?"

"No, the whole ride over here you were telling me you were missing the files Kale brought over from UDA." He grinned.

"You're a gem."

"Come on, then." Will held out his hand and I took it, allowing him to lead me out of the store and across the street to the diner.

It was still warm and cozy in there and the scent of meat loaf was still heavy in the air. It turned my stomach.

"Can I help you guys?" Shirley, the waitress who waited on us earlier, rounded one of the high-backed booths. She cocked her head and smiled, pointing at me with the eraser end of her Fog City Diner pencil. "Oh, I remember you."

"You do? Great. We were here earlier."

"Right, you were with the pale kids." Her bright eyes clouded. "I'm sorry, that was your friend who got hit, right?"

"Kale, yeah. She'll be in the hospital for a while, but they think she's going to be all right." I offered a small smile, as much to convince Shirley of my statement as myself.

"That's a relief." Shirley nodded toward an empty

booth to our left. "Can I get you guys something to go, or do you need a table? We're just cutting into a Black Forest cake." Shirley waggled her eyebrows. In any other instance, I would have been knee deep in Black Forest before she had rung me up.

"No, thanks. Actually, I'm here because I ran out and left something at my table. Some file folders? There should have been three, or maybe four. Do you have them?"

Shirley tapped her pencil against her lower lip. Her eyes went to the ceiling, as if the folders were stashed up there. "I don't think so." She glanced over her shoulder at the table where we had our lunch—now occupied by a couple with bright red cheeks and matching I SURVIVED ALCATRAZ sweatshirts.

"The table's turned over a couple of times since then, but let me check with the bussers to see if they picked up anything."

"Great." I sank down on a bench, and Will paced in front of me, nose buried in a menu.

"Are you seriously going to order something?"

Will rubbed his flat belly. "I am a bit peckish. We didn't get to eat much before."

My stomach folded in on itself as the olfactory memory of those hospital smells stung my nose again. "I can't see how you can even think of food right now."

Will's eyes followed a plate of fried chicken and mashed potatoes whizzing by. "It's a gift."

"No, sorry." Shirley came back to us, shaking her head. The little jade elephants hanging off her ears were bopping against her cheeks. "No one remembers cleaning anything off that table other than the usual stuff. And none of the wait staff knew anything about any folders."

My stomach dropped to my knees. "Nothing?"

Shirley shook her head. "Nothing. Aw, don't worry." She patted my arm kindly. "I'll go get the lost-and-found bin and you both can rummage through that. If one of the customers turned them in, they'd be in there."

I felt a weak stab of hope and pumped my head. "Yeah, okay. Hey, Will . . ."

Will's head was bent; his palms were pressed against the glass of the dessert case, where fresh slices of cake were laid out. He popped up and opened his menu again, studying it. "I'll search through this display case, make sure nothing looks suspicious. You can go through that." Will nodded toward the flimsy box Shirley returned with. She grinned.

"Here you go."

I pawed through the "Remains of Vacations Past"— funky plastic sunglasses, a couple of mismatched gloves, and two full bottles of sunscreen—and sighed, pushing the box aside. I looked up to where Will stood and cocked one annoyed eyebrow at him.

"Well, at least one of us found something helpful," Will said, holding up his overloaded to-go carton, flashing a pleased grin.

Chapter Ten

A hot cucumber-melon–scented bath and half a bottle of Chardonnay later, I was home on my couch, staring at my cell phone. Alex hadn't answered when I called earlier, and I didn't bother to leave a message. Still, I hoped—it was minuscule, but it was a hope—that he would see my missed call or feel my crushed-spirit Spidey sense and come running.

No such luck.

I was about to punch the speed dial again when there was a light knock on the front door. I rolled up on my tiptoes and stared through the peephole, where Will's head, giant and misshapen, greeted me. He grinned and held up a coffee mug.

"Just need a little sugar, love."

I undid the dead bolt and the chain—you can never be too careful, even if you did live with a fashionista vampire and an eight-inch hound of Hell—and opened the door.

"Sorry it's so late. Did I wake you?"

I pulled my bathrobe tighter across my chest and

wagged my head. "No. Nina just got in. I'm too antsy to go to sleep. Any word on Kale?"

"Nothing new." Will followed me into the kitchen and I began opening cabinets. "Do you just need white sugar?"

"Please. And a tea bag, if you've got one."

I thunked half a bag of sugar on the dining-room table, where Will was making himself comfortable, and glared at him. "You came over for some sugar and a tea bag."

"I fancied a cup of tea."

"Can I get you some hot water, too?"

Will leaned back in his chair and grinned. "That would be capital."

I put the kettle on the stove and set out a cup for myself, plus a plastic bear filled with honey.

"So what's the fits about, then?"

"Fits?"

Will squirmed in his chair. "You said you were antsy, right?"

"Oh, fits. Yeah. I just"—I used my fingernail to dislodge a prehistoric piece of Hang Chow fried rice stuck to the table's fake wood veneer—"I feel like I'm forgetting something."

"Didn't we have this conversation? You said you were forgetting something. I told you it was the files, and you showered me with thanks and biscuits?"

"Where are the files, then?"

"Where are my biscuits, then?"

"Anyway," I said, my patience wearing thin, "I know that what happened to Kale wasn't a coincidence. I know that this wasn't just some guy tearing through an intersection. Ditto with Bettina"—I swallowed thinly—"and Mrs. Henderson."

"And you." Will reached out toward me, his finger tracing what still remained of the bruise and scratch on my collarbone.

Whether it was his gentle touch or the tenderness of the injury, I wasn't sure, but my skin immediately broke out into a sheath of gooseflesh, every fiber of my being on high alert.

"You're worried," he commented.

I gave him my "duh" look and poured boiling water from the kettle.

"But you know you've got your Guardian right there across the hall." Will patted his chest smugly.

"And you're going to defend me with what? You don't even own a tea bag."

Will cocked an eyebrow. "With all due respect, Miss Ungrateful, I wasn't planning on killing anyone with a tea bag. And you certainly didn't mind my interference during your run-in with the idiot vampire slayer."

I chuckled despite myself. "Imagine someone thinking I'm a vampire."

"Well, you could use a bit of sun, love."

I shot Will a withering look. "Tanning advice from the sun-kissed Brit."

Will rolled his eyes and dunked his tea bag, then squeezed it against the side of his mug. "Anyway, who said I wasn't going to outsmart your projected assailant?" He tapped a finger to his temple. "Brain can be stronger than brawn."

"And you're all brain?"

"Cunning, even." Will sat back in his chair and sipped

his tea. "So cunning that I have an entire cupboard full of tea and yet here I am, drinking yours."

"Well, now that you've said that, I feel ever so foolish." I batted my eyelashes and sipped my tea.

"So tell me what you're so worried about."

"I'm not that worried," I said.

"So you shredded that napkin for the sadistic pleasure?"

I looked down at the heap of napkin shreds and sighed. "I think there might be another fallen angel."

"Do you think another one is possible?"

I shrugged. "Why not? There was Ophelia, and then Adam and his band of goons. Why wouldn't there be another fallen angel taking their place?"

Will was playing with the handle of his mug and avoided my gaze.

"What aren't you telling me, Will? What do you know?"

"I was just thinking . . ." His words trailed off.

"What were you thinking?"

"Maybe it's not *another* angel after you. Maybe it's the one that's always around."

I spat my tea in a mammoth shower. "Alex? You can't be serious!"

"Look"—Will's hazel eyes glittered, the light from our chandelier catching the gold flecks in them—"you said yourself that fallen angels are unrepentant. You said yourself that they would keep coming until the Vessel of Souls is theirs, right?"

I rubbed a napkin shred between my forefinger and thumb. "That's what Alex told me. But he was helping me. He was protecting me from Ophelia."

"Or he was protecting the Vessel *from* Ophelia."

"I don't believe you."

"Hey, you're the one who said there is something more to all this demon-gone-missing stuff." He sipped his tea, looking at me over the brim. "No need to shoot the ruggedly good-looking messenger."

I chewed my bottom lip, considering. "Yeah, but if this was about me, why mess with my demons?" I forced a chuckle and then stopped. "My demons." My heart did a double thump. "All the missing demons are my clients."

"And?"

"And maybe someone is trying to distract me, to get me focused on something else."

Will bobbed his head. "Okay, I'll bite. Now what about Kale?"

"She works with me."

"Directly?"

"No, she's in finance. But she's out at the front desk a lot and—and we're friends."

Suddenly the hot honeyed tea burned in my stomach. My saliva went bitter and my throat felt dry.

"Sophie?"

"It was me, Will."

"What, now?"

"The person who hit Kale. He thought he was hitting me." I slammed my palm to my forehead. "Oh God. I set her up. She was wearing my coat. I *told her* to wear my coat. Think about it. We're about the same size, and in my jacket—especially with the collar cocked up like I had it—Kale would have looked like any other townie heading across the street. If whoever did this watched us walk into the diner, he must have thought that he was hitting me. Oh God. Oh God. Ohgodohgod." I rested my forehead on the table. "It's happening again. Alex said it was just a matter of time before another group of angels found out about me, and now they have."

Will rested his chin on the table so he could look at me. "We're not sure of that, love."

"Not sure?" I sprang up. "Someone tried to *kill me,* Will. They tried to smear me on the asphalt—only it wasn't me." I pinched the bridge of my nose. "I should never have let Kale wear my jacket. I should have known better! Of course it was personal. Of course it was! I'm Sophie Lawson—supernatural Vessel of Souls— and everyone wants to kill me." I felt my eyes tear. "You've got to get out of here, Will. You're not safe. You're not safe around me. No one is." My voice had reached a high-pitched squeak, and the sob that I re- fused to release ached in my chest.

Will stood up and wrapped his arms around me, and I fell into his hug, slumped against his chest.

"Anyone around me is going to be in danger," I said. "I can't do that to my friends."

Whitesnake's "Here I Go Again" thundered through my head, my own personal hair band soundtrack. I sniffed. My miserable existence didn't even warrant Bon Jovi.

Will gently rested his chin on the top of my head. "Well, you're stuck with me, love. Protecting you is exactly what I'm here for."

He pressed his lips into my hair, and I couldn't hold back the sob any longer. I pinched my eyes shut and felt the tears rush over my cheeks. My mind filled with pictures of the intersection, of Kale, crumpled and battered, her head resting in Will's hands.

That was supposed to be me.

"We have to find out who's doing this, Will," I said. "We have to find out before anyone else gets hurt." I pulled away from Will. "Mrs. Henderson, Bettina—and now Kale!"

"Do you think they mistook her for the dragon and the—what's the bird again?"

I frowned. "A banshee. And I don't see how they would. Bettina was leaving her apartment. It's across town, by the ballpark. And she looks nothing like me."

Will nodded thoughtfully as though this all made perfect sense. "Right. No one would mistake you for a banshee."

I knew he was playing with me, but he pulled me back toward his chest, enfolding me in his arms. I felt remarkably, unexpectedly safe. His heart thumping against my chest was a comfort, as were the little puffs of his moist breath against the part in my hair. Standing there wrapped in Will's arms, I almost felt safe. Almost allowed myself to feel comfortable. But somewhere in the back of my mind, I thought of Kale, and Bettina— and Alex.

I stepped away, completely out of Will's reach this time. "You should probably go."

Will's hand was on the doorknob when the car alarm went off. Its wailing siren was insistent and annoying, and the side of Will's lip curled in disgust.

"Did you know in Australia that's the sound the tropical birds make?" He shook his head. "I don't see why people don't do away with those bloody things. No one listens to them, anyway."

I clenched my teeth together in a forced smile and grabbed my purse from the peg by the door. "That one's mine."

Will cocked an eyebrow.

"I parked on the street. There was parking right out front and I was a little too creeped out for the underground."

Will opened the door and ushered me out. "Let's go turn it off."

I stepped out into the hallway, a sudden prick of fear sending gooseflesh all over. "Do you think it's something bad?"

Will snorted. "It's a car alarm, love. A heavy breeze probably came by and set the thing off."

I pushed through the vestibule door, with keys in hand, trying to soak in Will's nonchalance. "You're probably right."

"Maybe someone thought your car was a werewolf," Will said, grinning.

I rolled my eyes at his stab at humor.

Though my rent includes an underground parking space, the cavernous darkness of the parking garage gives me the heebie-jeebies. So on the rare occasion that I can find aboveground parking in my zip code, it's too good to pass up. Today the parking gods and Gavin Newsom must have been smiling down on me because I caught a cherry spot almost directly across the street. Sure, I had to shoehorn my little Accord into the space and make a forty-seven-point turn in the process, but kicking open the car door and having sunlight—or the

graying drizzle that passed for sunlight in San Francisco—
was wonderful.

I really wish I had given the underground spot a
second thought.

"Oh no."

I didn't realize I was standing in the middle of the
street until a Muni bus came barreling past me. The
driver was laying on the horn that wailed like a dying
duck. I jumped out of the way and tried to press myself
flat against my car door, but my car door wasn't flat.

Also, it wasn't attached to my car.

I felt my lower lip start to wobble; I felt the moist heat
of tears behind my eyes. The hood of my car was bashed
so solidly that the metal roof undulated like hard green
ocean waves. Every window was smashed out and the
car seemed to sink under its own destitution. I sniffed,
trying to blink away tears, but I was still able to see that
every single tire had been slashed repeatedly until the
rubber flopped out in jaunty ribbons. I took a second
step closer and felt the crunch of a car window underneath my sneaker. I tried to take a step closer, to run my
hands over the puckered metal, but something was pinning me back. When I turned to look, I realized that a
hunk of headlight—the size of my fist—had snagged my
shoelace. I shook it off and rounded the car, somehow
hoping the damage might not be so severe on the sidewalk side.

That *so* wasn't the case.

"Wow, lady, looks like you really pissed someone
off," a kid said as he wandered by. His baggy pants
pooled at the ankles and he walked with the kind of

exaggerated limp that was meant to call up images of Snoop Dogg and original gangsters. Instead, he just looked like he was trying to keep his pants up.

A low whistle from the other side of the car caught my attention. I peered through the broken-out passenger-side window and met Will's gaze as he smiled at me through the driver's-side window.

"Good thing your car alarm went off," he told me.

"Oh God, Will. What am I going to do?"

"You've got insurance, don't you?"

I sighed and leaned against the battered car door as Will came around to join me. "Yeah, but this car was new. Or sort of new. And now I have to report once again that my car got mysteriously bashed in."

"Did they take anything?"

I yanked on the door handle and the door swung open easily, leaving a confetti-like spray of broken glass in its wake. I was about to slide into the car when Will grabbed me by the shoulder, slipped out of his sweatshirt, and laid it on the car seat.

"There's glass everywhere. You don't want your arse to look like—"

"My tires?" We shared a small smile and I crawled onto Will's sweatshirt, taking inventory of my front seat.

"Bad news," I said, pushing my head out. "They got my *American Idol* CD."

I could see the smile in Will's eyes. "That's rather good news, actually."

I turned in my seat—the selection of broken window glass crunching loudly underneath me—and felt my eyes go wide. "Wow."

Scrawled on the inside of the battered windshield was the word *freak*.

I swallowed slowly, my own saliva choking me, crawling up the back of my neck. "I have to get out of here." I pushed past Will and edged out of the car. I stumbled on the sidewalk and doubled over, taking little short breaths of cold night air.

From the corner of my eye I saw Will's head disappear into the cab of the car; he pulled out again, looking slightly confused. I expected at some point I should fill him in on me and why a five-letter word would spur me to nausea.

Though I comfortably live with a vampire, have spent a good chunk of time talking to my dead grandmother through a hunk of fruit, and share an office wall with a hobgoblin who has to use a slobber tray, the freak thing is something that, to this day, still cuts to the spine.

Like every other teenager in the world, I had only wanted two things: to be popular or to be invisible. The invisibility thing was pretty much a lock all through junior high. I never made many friends and the school bus (thankfully) dropped me off a full seven blocks from the little stuccoed house that I shared with my grandmother and the four-foot-high neon hand that flashed PALM READING . . . PALM READING . . . PALM READING through the front window.

Without knowing about my grandmother's occupation, and every day, clad in a rotating collection of Guess? jeans and oversized B.U.M. sweatshirts, I looked just like any other anonymous mid-1990s high schooler.

Until they came to my house.

They were the popular girls who had scrunchies that matched everything they owned, and they drove enviable cars, like the Geo Storm. On one Saturday in May they thought it would be hilarious to have their futures foretold. Of all the days of the year for the Psychic Friends Network to go on hiatus.

The knock came at three o'clock in the afternoon, and my world went crashing down two days later. On Monday morning, at nine o'clock sharp, "Special Sophie, the Freak of Nineteenth Street" was born, illustrated, and pasted to my locker.

From then on, it was stupid mentions of my crystal ball and a constant inner begging to suddenly get powers—preferably, powers that could blow up perky blond cheerleaders who had smooth ponytails and grandmothers who baked banana bread rather than herbal elixirs.

I was leaning against what would have to pass as my new car door when Will came around the side.

"They know who I am," I whispered, starting to cry.

"That doesn't matter," Will said, his accent warm and familiar, "because they will never get to you. Not as long as I'm around."

I wanted to believe him. Wanted to put my hand in his and snuggle up on the couch, putting all of this behind me.

"It's only going to get worse, Will. It's only going to get worse, and no one is listening to me."

Will held me closer and I sank into his arms. I felt my body curve into his. He pushed a thick lock of hair behind my ear and kissed the lobe gently.

"I'm listening to you," he whispered, "and I promise to keep you safe, Sophie Lawson."

Chapter Eleven

I woke up jittery and exhausted, having tossed and turned all night. Images of Kale, of the concrete, of her lolling head, haunted my dreams. I forewent my usual morning jaunt to Philz Coffee and headed into the agency early. We were packed, and the entire waiting room buzzed with a kind of nervous energy. But everything seemed to drop into an awkward silence when I stepped onto the floor. I paused, and clients turned to gape at me—the flat, cold-as-stone eyes of zombies; the sharp, narrowed eyes of vampires. They all seemed to zero in and though I desperately tried to tell myself I was imagining it, I couldn't quite get over the strange chill of the room.

I shrugged out of my jacket and smiled, anyway, beckoning the first person over.

"I can help who's next in line."

Several pairs of eyes (and the occasional single) raked over me, but no one moved. I stepped forward, inclining my head toward the person at the front of the line.

"I can help you right now."

She was a behemoth of a woman, with a blunt-cut black pageboy and eyes that took up the better half of her face. Her pale lips were quirked in the kind of smile that is meant to be friendly, but it oozed avoidance.

"That's okay," she said to me. Her head snapped back to bore through the back of the person in front of her. "They're almost through here."

I craned my neck and eyed Nina, who was doing her best to cut off the woman in front of her, who continually kept thrusting photos of her newest grand-demon at her while Nina processed her paperwork.

"I think it's going to be a while," I said in what I thought was a friendly tone.

"No, thank you." Blunt-cut black pageboy kept her eyes fixed; her knuckles turned white as she gripped her paperwork.

"Okay." I shuffled back to the person behind her, and wished I had kept my jacket on when I realized it was Windigo, a recent Canadian immigrant, with a stack of papers the thickness of my right thigh. Each time he shifted, a waft of frigid air floated from him.

"Hi, Windy. I'm Sophie Lawson. I can process your paperwork if you'll follow me, please." I reached out for the stack and Windy blinked at me, a pointed tongue darting out of his ice-tinged mouth as he licked his bottom lip. He didn't move to hand me his paperwork, and I dropped my hand to my side, frowning.

"I thought you only handled fallen angels now," he said, his voice an icy rasp.

"Oh, well, that's true. I do do fallen angels, but I still work with the generals. Especially when there's a line this long. So, are you ready?"

Windy shifted, taking a small, unsure step toward me. He seemed to think better of it, and then stepped back in line. "I think I'll wait."

I stepped closer to Windy, who immediately stiffened and rose to his full height, which was at least two heads taller than I am. His decrepit skin seemed to crack as he did so.

"Is there some reason you don't want me to help you?"

I saw him considering—the smoky haze in his eyes studying me, as if assessing the challenge. The man was a pointy-toothed man-eater whose breath froze human hearts solid, and *he* was assessing all five feet two inches of *me:* fiery red hair, T-shirt with barely faded ketchup stain, oblivious expression (I'm assuming) on my red-cheeked face.

"Look, Sophie," Windy said, leaning close, "it's not that I don't appreciate your willingness to help. It's just that"—his eyes cut left and right, his voice dropped to an even lower, even chillier octave—"everyone knows that lately any one of us you come into contact with . . . well . . . dies." He looked immediately apologetic. "Or at least gets really hurt."

I felt my mouth drop open and stumbled backward, taking stock of the line of demons—man-eaters, night stalkers, shape-shifters—all avoiding my stare, all frightened of me.

"Is that true? Do you all feel this way?"

No one answered me, but Windy finally nodded, looking half apologetic, half matter-of-fact. "No one wants to take the risk." His eyes went from my toes to my face. "Not for someone like you, anyway."

Someone like me.

"Human?"

I watched the deceased remains of Windy's Adam's apple bob in his throat as he swallowed heavily.

"Okay."

I turned around and headed toward my office, not bothering to turn my eyes from the private pixies in the hallway, not needing to avoid Lorraine and her ever-present stack of questionable invoices, because they all avoided me.

I swung into my office with a plan to take a heavy breather and talk myself out of a panic attack. Instead, I opened the door, stepped inside, and felt my mouth drop wide open.

"What the hell happened here?"

Though my desk and obsessive-compulsive straight lines of Post-it notes and pencils remained untouched, I couldn't say the same for the rest of the office. The walls and carpet showed great rectangular lines of fresh paint and cleanliness, where file cabinets had been removed, and my ever-present spider plant was set gently on the floor, along with a stack of general office tchotchkes. Joining this disarray was a photo of my grandmother and me that usually lived on top of a book-case normally stuffed with tomes on UDA standard operating procedures, *The Modern Classification of Demons, Monsters, and the Undead for Insurance and Appraisal Purposes*, stacks of life/afterlife insurance forms, and a tattered copy of *What Color Is Your Parachute?* The last book remained, but nothing else.

I didn't know why, but I knew Dixon was behind this. Dixon, or at very least the newly formed fanged triumvirate that was Dixon, Vlad, and Eldridge, top-seated vampire representatives of UDA, VERM, and . . . *Queer Eye for the (Undead) Straight Guy.* White-hot anger roiled through my veins, and I felt my hands automatically roll into fists so tight that my fingernails bored into my palms, cutting through the skin.

I made a beeline to Dixon's office and didn't even slow when Eldridge tried to feed me some crap about Dixon being a busy man and me needing an appointment. I breezed past him and kicked open Dixon's office door, not even stopping to shiver when a series of pale-faced vampires stared up at me, surprised and hunger evident on their faces.

"Where are my files?"

Dixon, chilled as a pre–global warming iceberg, knitted his hands and looked up at me. His brown eyes were wide and open; his mouth pushed up into a calm smile. "Well, Ms. Lawson, what an unexpected surprise. Gentlemen, this is Sophie Lawson, the acting head of our newly established Fallen Angel Division here at the Underworld Detection Agency."

I felt a snarl tug at my lip. "Acting head?"

Dixon tipped his head from side to side, but made no move to explain. "As you can see here, Ms. Lawson, I'm kind of in the middle of something. Is this something that Eldridge can help you with?"

I finally scanned the faces of the assembled—there were four men, all vampires—sitting around Dixon's desk. Two I recognized as Dixon's new promotions, one was Vlad, and the third, brand-new.

"What's going on here?" I asked, unease walking up my spine.

"Board meeting," Dixon answered breezily. "Now what did you need?"

"My files," I said, suddenly uncertain, my anger turning to suspicion.

"We've simply lightened your load," Vlad piped up. "Some of our clientele were looking for a change, a provider a little more in line with their needs. We thought it would also be a great opportunity for you to begin expanding your division." Vlad's answer smacked with scripted practice, and his lips curved into that same stupid serene smile that Dixon wore like a mask. "Do you have a problem with that?"

Unable to form a cohesive thought—or a witty response—I turned on my heel and sped back to my office, my mind ticking. I was there for a millisecond before Nina sauntered in, completely oblivious to the spring-cleaning that had cleared out my office, unaware of the gales of pissed-off heat that wafted off me.

"What do you think of Athena Bushant?" she asked.

I pinched the bridge of my nose, willing the thundering headache that was starting behind my eyes to hold off. "What's an Athena Bushant?"

Nina rolled her eyes and flopped her head back, as if I'd just asked her to ride shotgun in a primer-colored Pinto. "Not what. *Who.* Athena Bushant." She thrust out her chest and stepped forward, arms splayed, superstar style.

I shrugged. "Is she new?"

"I am Athena Bushant. Actually, Athena is me. Athena Bushant is my pen name. What do you think? Perfect, right? Just the right combination of mystery and wisdom. And it'll look great on a dust jacket. I've already come up with my bio. Listen to this."

"Nina, I don't have time for this right now. Look at

my office." I spun around, with excess room to do so—now that more than half my file cabinets were gone.

"I think it looks great. Now listen. 'Athena Bushant holds a master's degree in the mystical arts from Oxford University. When not sailing—'"

"Does Oxford even have a department of mystical arts? Does any school other than Hogwarts?"

"It's called artistic license."

"Nina, listen. Dixon, Vlad, and the rest of the Fang Gang board members have moved all my files out. They're taking over more than half my cases because I'm apparently not"—I made air quotes—"in line with my clients. I basically have nothing to do but twiddle my thumbs all day."

"Consider yourself lucky. Do you know how hard it is to have a full-time job *and* be a novelist?"

I put my hands on my hips. "Do you even know where your office is?"

Nina growled at me. "Funny." She looked around, dark eyes raking over my pillaged space. "Sophie, you're overreacting. So Dixon came in and handed a few of your cases over."

"He's edging me out, Nina, I know he is."

"He already fired you once."

"Thanks for never letting me forget that."

"What I'm saying is, if he wanted you out, he would fire you. He did it before, and he'll do it again." Nina held up her hands when I tried to protest. "But it's probably not that. The economy is bad everywhere. There's a mass exodus out of the city. Everyone's work-load is getting cut."

"Is yours?"

"No, but I've got the novel." She flopped her hands around. "I think I'm getting carpal tunnel syndrome."

"Is that even possible? Ugh!" I pinched the bridge of my nose and closed my eyes. "I need some answers. I need help."

Nina slid her arm across my shoulders and pulled me to her in a marble-cold embrace. "Okay, sorry. What can I do to help, Soph?"

"Aren't you even the slightest bit concerned about any of this? Mrs. Henderson—she was murdered, Neens. And Bettina, and the centaur." I swallowed a desperate sob as images burned into my brain.

"I'm immortal."

"Unless someone knows how to hurt you."

Nina nibbled her bottom lip as if considering. "Okay. So?"

"So I need you to check up on Dixon."

"Why me?"

"Because Dixon can smell me a mile away. I just need you to tail him a little bit, find out what's going on. Everyone on management is a vampire. Are they trying to take over?"

Nina cocked her head. "You realize I'm a vampire, right?"

"But you're not one of *those* vampires."

"Okay. I'll do it. I'll tail Dixon. I'll see if I can find his file folder marked 'Dixon's Evil Plan.'"

"That's all I ask."

Nina's dark eyes glittered. "I think my vampire romance is going to have a mystery in it, too." She tapped a perfectly manicured fingernail against her chin; then she pulled her literary-minded half glasses from her sweater pocket and cleared her throat as she began to free associate.

"Cecila LeChambray stared at the mysterious stranger before her. Something about the darkness in his eyes cut her like . . . like . . ." She scanned my office; then her eyes settled on mine, expectant.

I flopped back into my desk chair, my forehead thunking against the cold wood of my nearly naked desk. "I can't help with your fiction career right now, Neens. My nonfiction life is out of control."

I heard Nina spin, and heard her voice dropping as she walked down the hall.

"Cecilia's best friend, Stephanie Littleman, was of no help at all. An overanxious mortal, she had trouble with looking a gift horse in the mouth. . . ."

I spent the rest of my workday holed up in my office, determined that neither a vampire management team nor clients who didn't want me around were going to push me out of the Underworld Detection Agency. By the time the clock rolled around to five, I had organized everything that remained in my office by color and subject, created a master list of "Things That Could Be Responsible for the Underworld Killings" and hung up on Alex's voice mail six times. Finally I resigned myself and headed out the door, aiming only for a bottle of wine and a good, long session with my down comforter and pillow.

The next morning I woke up to ChaCha's kibble breath pouring over my face and what passed for sunlight during a San Francisco summer pressing through my window. I growled at the red numbers on my alarm clock—10:52—and rolled out of bed and into a pair of sweats, which were either clean or stained consistently enough to look clean. I was lying on the couch balancing a mammoth bowl of Lucky Charms (I'm donut free, remember?) and watching a string of Disney TV shows when Nina plowed through the front door and gaped at me, eyes wide.

"Don't tell me you're wearing that," Nina said.

"Okay," I said, mouth filled with cereal, "I won't."

Nina snatched the remote and clicked off *Hannah Montana* smack in the middle of a song about ice cream.

"Hey! I was watching that."

"Oh, thank God."

I shot a narrow-eyed stare over my shoulder, where I found Vlad perched at the dining-room table, eyebrows raised over the top of his open laptop screen. "That ice-cream girl was giving me a toothache."

I pointed my spoon at him. "When did you get here?"

Vlad gave me his disenfranchised-youth grunt. "I've been here."

God, I hated that supersilent vampire thing.

"I'm buying you a bell," I said.

Nina raked a hand through her glossy black hair and gave me a parental "I'm not angry, just disappointed" look. "Did you forget what today is?" she asked.

I shifted my cereal bowl, chasing a slew of marshmallows with my spoon. I took a heaping bite. "It's Saturday."

Nina looked at me expectantly.

"Saturday, the seventeenth?" I asked. "Wait, did I forget our anniversary?" I chuckled, then choked on a particularly substantial marshmallow.

Nina's face remained stony. "It's Saturday, the seventeenth, and my beau—and possible future after-life mate—"

I raised my eyebrows at her, and Nina waved a hand.

"No one lives forever, Soph." She stuck out a fat lower lip. "Harley is reading from his book today, and you promised you'd be there. You promised you'd come and support me."

"I did?"

Nina nodded. "You did."

"I don't remember that."

Nina shoved a single suede pump underneath one of my butt cheeks. "You were just about to get in the shower and wear that cute cashmere twinset that I bought for you, right?"

She bared a fang, and I snarled.

"You don't scare me, Nina."

She bared another fang, and I lumbered off the couch, shoving a final enormous scoop of the cereal into my mouth, watching in dismay as a shower of crumbs slid from my lap/dining tray. I turned around quickly, fairly sure my blush was visible from the back of my head, too.

"And hurry up! I told Harley we'd be there early to help him set up!"

After the shortest shower in the history of man or vampire, I shimmied into my birthday twinset and a pair of regular jeans, which had somehow turned into skinny jeans. (Maybe I should give up donuts *and* marshmallow pinwheels?) I was yanking on a sock and fumbling for a pair of boots that matched *each other,* when Nina came in and silently glared at me, hands on hips, lips pursed.

Though she was my best friend, and by far the most gentle pointy-toothed afterlifer I'd ever met, there is just something about a vampire staring you down that sends shivers up the spine, and made me suddenly have to pee.

I didn't dare.

Instead, I pasted on a smile and beelined for my shoulder bag. "Ready to go!" I sang.

"In the car!" Nina bellowed.

Nina and I hurried toward the door, but Vlad stayed put. His dark eyes were intent on his computer screen; its light reflected eerily off his pale features. A series of gunshots, screams, and something that sounded squishy exploded from the computer's speakers. He grinned.

"Shut it, Vlad. We're going."

Vlad looked over his screen, and Nina pointed a finger at him. "And don't even think about protesting this one."

Vlad rolled his eyes and clicked his laptop shut, grumbling and sighing the whole time.

Note to self: Find teenaged vampire summer camp. Stat.

I was waiting for Nina to grab Vlad by the ear, but she didn't. We both went out behind Nina, who marched purposefully down the hall. Will popped his head out as we passed his door.

"What's going on here?"

"We're going to see Nina's new boyfriend," I whispered. "Shh, she's scary."

Vlad must have heard my whisper because he spun around. He and Will shared one of those exceptionally manly head nods—you know, the one that basically says, "Hey, dude, I see you and acknowledge you without showing any actual emotion."

"You're all going?" Will asked.

My left eye twitched and I dropped my voice to a barely audible whisper. "Nina's making us."

Will grinned; then he disappeared into his apartment and returned a millisecond later, sliding a red Adidas jacket over his football jersey. "Then she won't mind me coming along."

We made it down to Java Script with the minimum of issues, and with my spine almost completely intact. The four of us huddled and squirmed in Nina's Lexus as she vaulted through intersections. Her pale hand blared the horn as she yelled out admonishments and quirky warnings about tearing out people's throats.

"She's charming," Will said, his smile hinting on crazy.

"Shh," I hissed. "She can hear you."

Nina slammed on the brakes and we all catapulted toward the dashboard, where my heart now rested. She turned to us and batted her lashes. "Okay, guys, listen up. Harley is a professional, and there are going to be all sorts of media types and likely some other big-name writers. These will be my peers."

Will opened his mouth to say something, but I pinned him with a glare that threatened "Say anything and I'll literally kill you."

"I'll need you"—Nina craned her head over her shoulder and eyed Vlad, her coal black eyes stern—"to be on your best 'I'm a real boy' behavior. No protests, no VERM, no glamouring any breathers. Understand?"

Vlad rolled his eyes and continued hunching in the backseat, resentment emanating from him. "Yes, ma'am."

I fished a tube of ChapStick out of my bag. "So I guess you'll just want me to keep these guys in line while you woo Harley, right?"

"I do not woo. And yes, you will be in charge of the KISS Army back there."

I raised my eyebrows at Vlad and Will, who shrugged as Nina continued her tirade while using a traffic island as a bumper. "And I expect you to act as my best friend and wingwoman."

I snorted. "Your wingwoman?"

Nina glared and the tops of my ears went hot.

"Maybe I can hand out some bookmarks or something," I said with a hollow smile.

I was still shaking and praying that my small intestine would dislodge itself from my rib cage, when Nina's black Lexus jumped the curb and came to a neat rest, directly in front of Java Script's double glass doors.

Nina kicked the car into park and clapped her hands delightedly. "We're here!" She turned to look at us, a smattering of pale faces holding down our lunches after "Nina LaShay's Wild Ride," I suspected.

"Ready, everyone? Big smiles!"

Will and Vlad un-pretzeled themselves and filed into Java Script. I was taking up the rear, but Nina stopped me before I could step over the threshold. Her dark eyes clouded, and her heart-shaped mouth started twitching, showing off one angular fang. She poked at my chest.

"All ready, Soph?"

I followed her finger down and fought the urge to

giggle. The remains of something unnaturally blue had trailed between my breasts, leaving a cheerful line across the pale yellow knit of my shirt to my belly button.

"It's not that bad," I said. "I can just button up the sweater." I hurriedly did the buttons and frowned at the way they pulled and gaped across my belly. "I guess it shrank in the wash."

"You have to change your shirt."

I held up my ultrasmall purse. "Into what? Does this purse look like I can carry a wardrobe?"

Nina pointed to the trunk of the car. "Take your pick and meet me inside." She dropped her keys into my palm.

My good sense told me to take the car and flee back to the comfort of ChaCha, my couch, and what remained in the Lucky Charms box.

But I knew better.

I rummaged through Nina's trunk, pushing aside Vlad's VERM posters and his duct tape, three seasons' worth of brown boots, and enough bronzer to turn Nina into a member of the Jackson 5. I finally found the clothing spilling out of a Louis Vuitton duffel over the wheel well. I pawed through the things on top: a delicate lace camisole, a few cute tees large enough to fit over my head, and some random shoes. I hunkered deeper into the trunk and gave the bag a yank to get a better look inside, but it was caught on something. One more yank and the bag came flying out—a metal pipe jarred loose and hit the pavement with a loud *plink!*

I stared down incredulously at the metal pipe. It started to wobble slowly into the street as if showing itself from every angle. I stepped closer, crouching to grab the pipe and return it to the trunk, when I saw the smear on the end. It was just a tinge, easy enough to miss if someone had run a rag hastily over the pipe in an attempt to clean it, but it was there. A dark, rust-colored smear of blood. And pinned to it were a few straggly strands of graying hair.

Suddenly my skin felt too tight. I looked at the pipe and then through the big glass doors of Java Script, where Nina was grinning broadly. Her fangs were hidden behind glossy, cherry red lips as she clung to Harley, her eyes glued to his winsome smile. Vlad stood behind them both, flanked by two Vampire Empowerment henchmen. The trio was almost unnoticed in the shadows, but Vlad stood out, his shoulders hunched, his lips held in a disgusted sneer as his eyes cut across the assembled crowd. He glanced out and caught me staring, standing openmouthed with the trunk open, the Louis Vuitton in my hand, the soiled pipe at my feet. I swallowed hard, broke his gaze, and tossed everything back into the trunk.

Chapter Twelve

I snapped the trunk shut, slid into a sweater I pulled from the bag, and used the sleeve to dab at the sweat that now dotted my forehead and upper lip. I was two feet into Java Script when Nina's laser gaze burned through me. She yanked me by the sleeve, pressed her ice-cold lips to my ear and whispered, "That looks so much better."

She tugged me to where Harley stood, uneasily smiling at Will and Vlad; the silent air that hung among them uncomfortable. I looked over my shoulder to where Vlad's buddies had been lurking, but they weren't there.

"Hey, have you seen—"

"And look who else came out to see you!" Nina's eyes were glossy and gleeful; she linked arms with Harley, who looked handsome in a brown corduroy jacket and slacks. Nina pinned us all with a warning glare. For the first time in my life, I felt a tiny niggle of fear.

Could Vlad?
Could she?

"I told them all that they didn't have to come here, but they wouldn't stay away!" she gushed, a perfectly convincing lie.

No, not Nina. I kept wringing my hands in an attempt to bring some blood into them; they were as icy as Nina's. Images kept slipping through my brain: Mrs. Henderson's ruined house, the fear in Bettina's eyes.

The pipe was hidden under a stack of VERM propaganda.

The Vampire Empowerment and Restoration Movement. Vlad.

I worried my lower lip. *Has VERM moved on from picketing and protesting to . . . cleaning up?*

"Sophie?" Nina was asking.

"Yes, vampires, no," I said, forming sentences that would make my high-school English teacher weep.

Harley looked at the group of us and smiled softly. "Thank you so much. It really means a lot that you came here to hear my talk. I hope you enjoy it."

"They all read your book. My copy. But they're all going to buy their own. And the Kindle version, too." Nina looked at each of us, smiling politely, the edge of one sharp fang just visible against her pink lips.

"Loved it," Vlad said.

"Going to buy a copy for my mum," Will reported.

"Sophie?" Nina prodded.

There was a table heaving under the weight of Harley's books, and I eyed the cover, the faded images of vampires, werewolves, witches, and ghosts covered with big red X's. I felt a snarl growing.

"Yeah," I said, "I've been sleeping with Nina's

copy underneath my pillow. She doesn't sleep so much, you know."

Harley looked adoringly at Nina. "I know, she's such a night owl."

"You don't know the half of it," Will said.

Java Script was starting to fill up and Harley ushered us to our seats—a few reserved folding chairs in the front row.

"You're not planning on throwing your panties up there, are you?" I asked Nina, nudging my head toward Harley's vacant podium.

Nina waggled her eyebrows. "Who said I'm wearing any panties?"

I shuddered, then rolled around in my chair and was half relieved, half terrified, to see Vlad and his cronies sitting in the back row. Their arms were crossed, and their faces were drawn and stern.

"Hey, Neens, has Vlad borrowed your car recently?"

Nina snarled. "He better not have. He still has a nineteenth-century driver's license. Buggy certified."

Just then, Roland Townsend, Harley's sweaty little agent, took his spot behind the podium. His bushy eyebrows were just barely visible over the wooden rim. He cleared his throat, then fished another yellowed handkerchief from his suit pocket and mopped his brow.

"Ladies and gentlemen," he addressed the crowd. "Ladies and gentlemen, please may I have your attention? Please?"

The slight din of conversation in the room quieted and Roland cleared his throat again.

"How many of you believe in ghosts?"

A few people in the small crowd raised their hands

halfheartedly; others didn't even bother looking up from their iPads.

"Okay," Roland continued. "How many of you believe in the afterlife? Heaven? Hell? Spirits who walk the earth even after their corporeal being is physically dead?"

I cut my eyes to Nina, who stayed rapt. I stared at Will, then, who rolled his eyes and flashed me his "*Can you believe this guy?*" half smile

"Well, ladies and gentlemen, you know my client Harley Cavanaugh from his previous best sellers. The book that stayed on the *New York Times* Best Seller list for a record thirteen weeks, *Ghost Hoaxes* and its follow-up—also a best seller—*Haunted Hoaxes*. Now Harley Cavanaugh comes to you with his soon-to-be best seller, the book that blows the pearly gates off the myths of angels, demons, vampires, and the like. Ladies and gentlemen, please welcome Harley Cavanaugh to San Francisco and Java Script!"

There was a small smattering of applause as Harley came out from behind a maroon curtain with a hand-written EMPLOYEES ONLY sign safety pinned to it. He was grinning wildly, hands splayed, apparently under the guise that the group of us, two homeless guys, and a couple of tourists who recently walked in were his very adoring public. I decided that a latte and a donut (hey, dire times, okay?) would make this situation more palatable. When I turned toward the aisle behind me, however, I was shocked to see that every folding chair was taken, and there were several people—people who looked like they knew where they were and had actually intended to be here—standing in the aisles, grinning, and clutching copies of Harley's book.

"Christ," I mumbled, sinking back into my chair.

"We've all heard of ESP. Heck, every one of us has probably had a premonition that turned out to be true. Am I right?"

I craned my head to see delighted heads bobbing all around me.

"And does that mean each and every one of us here is psychic? Of course not! There is a sixth sense, indeed—but it's not the one you've been fed through movies and tall tales and so-called 'true accounts' of run-ins with Big Foot, Dracula, angels, and ghosts. But don't get me wrong. All of these *things* exist. As do aliens, and unicorns, and mermaids, and—and—"

"Leprechauns!" someone from the audience supplied.

"Witches!" Another hoot from behind me.

The energy in the room was heavy, tinged with electricity as people shouted out their mythological creatures. Though people were smiling, nibbling cookies, and pawing through Harley's books, the reading started to feel a lot less jovial and a lot more like a hate rally.

I leaned over to Nina. "I don't think we should be here," I whispered.

Nina waved me off, her eyes intense, focused on Harley.

"Right!" Harley said, quieting the crowd, hands up, preacher style. "All of these things do exist." He took a long pause, his eyes glittering as he scanned the crowd. Finally he pressed his index finger to his temple. "In the mind!"

I gaped at the eruption of applause and felt physically ill when I saw Nina, next to me, her small hands clapping away.

"You can't be serious," I hissed at her.

"Shhhh," she said emphatically, not taking her eyes off Harley.

I sat through another forty-five minutes of Harley's "patented technology" and "psychological studies" that proved the nonexistence of half the demon population. Half the demon population that I had the privilege of validating week after week at the Underworld Detection Agency. He blew the cover off trolls—blaming the Brothers Grimm and the occasional land baron for creating the "silly little bridge dwellers."

Naturally, he forgot to mention that trolls are not silly. As a matter of fact, they pride themselves on their intelligence (hence the constant questioning). Unfortunately, they do not pride themselves on bathing (hence the putrid stench of blue cheese and feet whenever one strolled by). He said that werewolves were nothing more than a Hollywood mock-up of an old Native American legend; ditto for witches (but they were the progeny of Disney); and my personal favorite, vampires.

I stiffened and glanced at Nina, who sat back in her chair coolly, as if about to witness a chat about organic gardening rather than her lover bash her existence.

"Now, we've all noticed the proliferation of vampires in the last five years. Vampire books, vampire movies, and, of course, vampire sightings."

Nina's attention remained fixated on Harley. Her

pallid glow was obvious in the fluorescent Java Script light.

"Now, we all know vampires don't glitter."

Applause.

"Or fly."

Applause.

"Or exist."

Huge, hooting applause as though Harley had just made the revelation of a lifetime or had just moon-walked across Market Street. Harley sat back and basked in the cacophony of crowd adoration. His research may have been flawed, but his crowd control was not. He had the stage presence, the somewhat serious lip purses, and the easy stance of someone who knew exactly how to be the apple of his public's eye. Even Will sat rapt, and Vlad and his cronies, though struggling to look cool and nonchalant, were clearly at attention.

"We know that the so-called vampire—or night walker, as you'll often hear them referred—"

And I just have to break in here, because as someone really, really well-versed on what it is that vampires do (and more so, what they like to be called), I feel it's important. Night walker falls with frightening speed immediately down to the bottom of the list. Just above pointy-toothed bloodsucker and Nosferatu. And for good reason, too. Vampires no longer spend their nights "walking," pacing, prowling, whatever. It's modern times and all the vamps I know have gotten with the program and either spend their evenings holed up playing Bloodsport and protesting various improper vampire images (Vlad), or boogying away at the latest vamp hot spot (Nina); this week it's an underground club in the Haight called AB Negative.

Harley continued strutting around the makeshift stage as though he was about to heal the lame and blow the cover off Kim Kardashian's week-long marriage once and for all. He dashed ideas of zombie takeovers, mutant fish, and the Rapture.

"And don't even get me started on the succubae!" he declared, laughing as though we were all having a friendly Carrie Bradshaw–style chat over brunch and our Manolos.

I edged the tiny spiral-bound notebook I kept in my purse out and balanced it on my lap. The notebook was a nod to Alex and the police officers who always carried a little leather-bound one to jot down clues and pertinent information. Mine had fluffy clouds and glittery pink kittens, but it was still able to carry the badass clues that a seasoned crime fighter like me could include.

Sophie Lawson, Undercover PI, All-Around Badass.

I opened to a blank page and listed all the myths that Harley debunked in his sermon—vampires, werewolves, succubae—then drifted off as he went off on a tangent about losing his luggage outside Transylvania. I tried to poke Nina with my pen when Harley said something about graveyard dirt in the overhead compartment (hello, cliché?), but she was still rapt, back arched, chest pressed forward, lips glossed and pursed, like she was hearing the Word of God or the sound of the Red Cross collection bus pulling up.

Java Script erupted into a chorus of applause and I was snapped back to Harley, grinning wildly; his mousy agent, Roland, doing the same, yellowed hankie hanging out of his breast pocket.

"He's brilliant, don't you think?" Nina said, clapping spastically. "Just so brilliant!"

I leaned over and lowered my voice. "Nina, you realize that we've sat here for"—I checked my watch—"over an hour while your new boyfriend reported on how you— you, Nina—could not possibly exist. How can you call a guy like that brilliant? I mean, he's close-minded, and small-thinking, and—and—"

"So beautiful."

Nina's dark eyes were fixed on Harley as he leaned over, shirtsleeves pushed up to his elbows, signing book after book. He nodded and grinned at the crowd. If I weren't relatively certain that he was a grade-A magicless breather, I would have thought there was some sort of glamour going on.

"I have to get out of here," I muttered.

I filtered through the people and pushed open the double glass doors out front, breathing in deep lungfuls of Muni scented air. I could see Nina through the window, buzzing around Harley; the book that turned her existence into a joke was clutched to her chest. Suddenly I wanted to cry.

"You okay, love?" Will asked, letting the door snap shut behind him.

"Don't you think this is ridiculous?"

"What? That people would line up to meet an author? A little bit, but, you know, to each his own fancy, right?"

"Not that people want to meet a writer, but that they want to meet *this* writer. This guy's a quack. His debunking is as serious as—as—"

"Most people's proof that there is a fourth element?"

I crossed my arms and slumped against the building. "I guess."

"You've got to admit, the guy found a niche. He's got to be making millions. Not a single person has walked out of the store without a copy of that thing. And I heard they're talking about giving him his own show."

I blinked. "They're giving Harley Cavanaugh a reality show?"

Will shrugged. "Why not?" He nodded toward the twelve-foot-high poster of *Vampires, Werewolves, and Other Things That Don't Exist.* "He's debunked all the city myths. You have to admit, that's kind of interesting."

"He debunked the haunting of the abandoned army hospital in the Presidio. Big whoop. I could have done that. Ditto the whole thing about the Lincoln High rape and murder."

"You have to admit the reports of people hearing toilet paper rolls unrolling by themselves is enough to give anyone the willies."

I stomped my foot. "No one haunts a bathroom! And people are considering this guy a guru because he does some higher math and determines that vampires can't exist? If vampires can't exist, then who's paying half my rent, huh? Tell me that Johnny DeBunkerpants!"

"Sophie, calm down. You're attracting attention. And that's not easy to do in this city."

"And werewolves? Werewolves can't exist because they would need a retro virus to fully rewrite their DNA? Oh, really? Then I spent the last five years chaining up, what, a hirsute who just happened to look fabulous in Armani and had a penchant for raw meat? I don't think so. I really don't think so."

Vlad pressed out the door next, head bent, with Harley's book open and balanced on his palms. I felt my eyes widen and a fist of fire scorching my insides.

"You have got to be fucking kidding me. You, Vlad? You don't exist. According to this, *you don't exist!*"

Vlad used his index finger to hold his place and flopped through a fourth of the book, holding it out for me to inspect. "And according to this, neither do you two."

I stared at the text, my mouth falling open.

Angels—Fallen and in Grace— And the Vessel of Souls

One of the most popular religious myths is that of angels not only as Guardians of the living but as Guardians of a mystical, mythical Vessel that is said to contain all human souls while in the stage commonly referred to as "limbo." Texts abound documenting the whereabouts of this Vessel, and references have gone so far as to say that the graced angels, as a way of keeping the Vessel safe from the clutches of the fallen, will hide the Vessel as they say "in plain sight." Each iteration of the so-called Vessel of Souls is protected by a Guardian—a human graced and chosen by "higher" mythical authorities, charged with the protection and care of the Vessel. According to legend, the Vessel's shape can shift and the Vessel itself can take any form. I have done exhaustive research on the Vessel of Souls and have documented

here the many iterations of the Vessel and its le-
gions of human Guardians.

From a scroll found embedded in the wall of an
Irish monastery, circa 1216, we find that the Vessel
of Souls has taken the shape of an emerald that has
been embedded in a necklace worn by a noble
woman. In 1481, the Vessel turns up in Italy, where
it has taken on the guise of a painting (La Prima-
vera*) by "Vessel Guardian" Sandro Botticelli.*

I blinked up at Will. "Did you know Sandro Botticelli?"

Will nodded, his eyes wide as saucers; the gold
flecks were dancing and alive. "Sandro was my great-,
great-, great-grandfather. Times fifty." He managed to
get the majority of his statement out before collapsing
into ridiculous guffaws.

"This is serious!"

"No, love," Will said, shaking his head and using the
heel of his hand to wipe at his moist eyes. "This is bol-
locks. Harley doesn't have the foggiest what he's talking about, so he just spews. It's not like anyone's going
to call him on it."

I shrugged, considering, while Will took the open
book from Vlad's hands. He read to himself, then snorted.
"According to old Harley, you were an organ in a Roman
Catholic church, a crumbling penny fountain in a small
town in Greece, and a paper crane in Japan."

"Why is that so funny?"

"Because everyone knows the 'crumbling penny
fountain' was at a Golfland and the paper crane thing?
Way off. It was an actual crane in Detroit, back in '71."

"Did you learn all of this in Guardian school?"

Will raised an annoyed eyebrow and went back to reading the book; Vlad scanned the text while looking over his shoulder.

"This book is great," Vlad said, sharp edges of his fangs showing through his goofy, happy-vamp grin.

"Really?" I asked.

Vlad nodded. "Think about it. We're not exactly the kind of people who want our existences documented. So the way I see it, Harley is doing us a favor."

Will shrugged and snapped the book shut. "Sounds about right to me. Now who's up for a pint?"

I looked at Vlad and then at Will; for the first time since I'd known them, they seemed to be in relative agreement. Leave it to them to agree on the one thing that pissed me off.

"But it's all lies!" I hated how whiny I sounded, and I knew, intellectually, that Vlad was right. Another person debunking ghost myths, or laughing at those of us who considered the idea of "others" among us, actually did help the Underworld inhabitants far more than a book confirming their existence ever would.

Right?

Nina came outside then, carrying a stack to her nose of Harley's books.

"Did you buy all those?" I asked.

Nina grinned. "Yep. I'm supporting my man. I think they'll make excellent Christmas gifts."

"Leave me off your list," I said. "Can we just get out of here?"

"Yeah," Nina said, "we need to get home and straighten up the place. Harley and Roland should be there in about a half hour."

"You invited Harley and Roland to our *house*? Where we *live*? Actually, where I live and you cease to live?"

Nina rolled her eyes. "Really, Sophie, you can be so close-minded sometimes. Harley is really a great guy. He just happens to have a different way of viewing things. Cut him some slack, okay?"

I felt my lips kick up into a ridiculous, incredulous smile. "A different way of viewing things?"

Nina blinked at me, arms crossed, and I did the same. Finally I sucked in a large breath of what I hoped was calming air. All it did was highlight the fact that my ears were blowing steam.

"You know what? I'll meet you at home. I'm going to walk."

"You can't walk alone," Will said.

"Is that spoken in your official guardianship capacity?"

"Nope." He tossed Harley's book to Vlad and slung an arm across my shoulders. "I can't be official when I'm nonexistent, now can I?" He eyed me, a mischievous grin playing on the edges of his lips. "Now, how about that pint?"

Chapter Thirteen

Will and I strolled through the hordes of tourists as we walked away from the bookstore, stopping at an Irish pub on the edge of Geary Street. Will raised his eyebrows and I pushed past him, muttering, "After Harley's speech, I need a drink. Or maybe a tranquilizer."

It took a moment for my eyes to adjust; but when they did, I felt instantly at home. Not that our home featured posters of half-naked girls hawking beers in the mountains or anything. It's just that the pub was cozy, with a long, smooth, dark wood bar, mirrors etched with curlycued Guinness slogans, and a worn leather couch set in front of a crackling fire.

"I like this place."

Will nodded to the bartender; and before I had a chance to shrug out of my jacket, he had a pint glass in each hand, walking steadily so as not to spill any of the to-the-rim pour. We sat down on the leather couch, and my kneecaps immediately felt toasty from the heat of the fire.

"Are you drinking both of those?" I asked.

"Not tonight," Will said, sliding one pint glass toward me. "I'm a gentleman."

I stared at the glass he handed me, the thick black liquid a foamy brown on top. "So you got me motor oil?"

"It's a Guinness. Try it."

I wrinkled my nose, but I took a small sip, anyway. I felt a smile spread across my lips. "Mmm. It tastes chocolaty. I like it."

"So what do you think about this Harley bloke?"

"I think he's a quack and an idiot, and I'm wondering what's going to happen when he finds out his beloved is a vampire."

Will took a slug from his glass. "You really think he'll find out before he takes off?"

I shrugged. "Probably. I don't have many more purses."

Will raised his eyebrows and I waved my hand. "Roommate thing, nothing to worry about."

"Hm."

"Hm."

Will and I sat and drank in companionable silence for a few minutes, both of us staring at the fire.

"So," Will said finally, "any word on what happened at the dragon's place?"

"You mean Mrs. Henderson?" I shook my head, taking another sip of my drink. "I told Dixon and he said they had an investigative team look into it, but I think he just said that to shut me up. I don't know, Will, I just have this feeling. I think Dixon might have something to do with this—with everything."

Will seemed to consider that for a moment. Then he replied, "I'm not doubting you, love, but what would

Dixon want with a dead dragon? Or beating up a . . . What was she exactly?"

"Bettina? Banshee."

Will sat back, looking impressed; I shook my head, worrying my bottom lip. "I don't know. He's replacing all the UDA higher-ups with vampires. If he were to take out some of the less desirable clientele, then . . ."

Will sipped. "Then?"

The word hung in the air and I turned it over and over, trying desperately to figure out why Dixon, his toothy brethren, or even VERM would start taking out other demons. Coming up blank, I shrugged, took a heavy slug of my beer. "I have no idea, but that doesn't mean it's not possible. Vampires can be zealots. And someone did try to stake me through the heart." I rubbed the fat bruise that marred my skin.

"Why would a vampire try to kill you, Sophie Lawson, human, with a wooden stake?"

"It could have been a sign."

"Or coincidental. Or the theory of three."

I cocked a scrutinizing brow. "All bad things happen in groups of three?"

Will opened his arms and looked around the half-empty pub. "And yet, nothing bad has happened since we've been here, right?"

"So we're out of the woods?"

"It's possible."

I set down my drink and used my index finger to trace the exposed wood grain on the coffee table. "I'm afraid everything that has happened has had a common link."

"That link being you."

I nodded woefully. "Of course. Closing in on me.

Killing people around me to let me know they have the power. Its practically textbook. I mean, you're my Guardian. You should know. Doesn't the Vessel always draw"—I dropped my voice, my eyes darting around the room—"unrest? And what about it being a fallen angel? Alex said that once Ophelia was . . ."

I still had a hard time saying "once Ophelia was dead"—both because I was the reason she was dead and technically (however technical demon blood lines went at least), she was my half sister. For a while there, she was the only family I had.

Unfortunately, she spent our entire sisterly relationship trying to kill me.

I swallowed hard. "He said even after Ophelia, it wouldn't be over. Another fallen angel would just come and take her place."

Will held up a silencing hand. "True. And generally, that's how it is. Once Ophelia was stopped, all it meant is that someone else will take her place and come after you, trying to get the Vessel for himself. But, Sophie, no one knows about you. Ophelia had a connection to you."

I sat back, both startled and impressed. It must have shown on my face because Will stiffened. "What? You don't think I know anything about this whole fallen angel business? You're my charge, love, and I'm well-versed in all the things that go bump in your nights."

An inappropriate hot blush washed over me. I clamped my knees together, mentally claiming that the fire was the reason for the sudden sweat at the back of my neck—it had nothing to do with Will and what went bump in my nights.

I took a refreshing sip of my beer. "What about

Adam? He was working for Ophelia and he knew what I was. He said he did."

"Just before the building he was in went up in flames." Will smiled. "Remember? I was there. I was the bloke with the rubbers"—he pointed to his shoes—"and the enormous hose."

The hopelessness of the situation must have gotten to me, because I found myself giggling uncontrollably when Will said "enormous hose." He watched me, his hazel eyes catching the gold glow of the cracking fire. The warmth raged inside me again and I sucked down half my beer in a single gulp. I winced, burping softly.

"'Scuse me. And I don't mean to be naïve, but aren't fallen angels like"—I struggled for the words—"immune to fire? Adam didn't even flinch, and the flames were right on us."

"Adam isn't here, love."

I finished my beer. "So you're just going to dismiss this whole thing? Just like that?"

"I didn't say that. As per our otherworldly agreement, I'm keeping an eye on you, and you're keeping an eye on the Underworld." Will smiled and clinked his glass with mine; then he finished his beer. "Another?"

"I guess," I groaned.

By the time Will came back with our second round, I had kicked off my shoes and had tucked my legs under myself, enjoying the calming warmth of the fire, the comfort of the little pub with its beer-and-shepherd's-pie scent.

"I guess I could be wrong," I said, taking a hearty sip.

Will turned to stare at me, full in the face. His eyes were wide with incredulity. "You don't say!"

I took another gulp. "Shut up. I do have another theory."

Will raised an interested eyebrow. "Do tell."

"Well, Mrs. Henderson burned Nina up." I held up two fingers. "Twice." Then I hiccupped and took another sip to wet my mouth. "And Kale . . ." Here I looked over each shoulder, scanned the bar for intruders, and crooked my finger, beckoning Will closer. "Kale," I started in a hoarse whisper, "and Vlad were almost *doing it* on my living-room couch. I walked in on them." I didn't know if it was the beer or the recalled image of Vlad's deathly white chest, but a shudder washed over me. I clamped a hand over my mouth because suddenly the idea of Kale and Vlad—*Vlad!*—writhing on my living-room couch was far more hilarious than disgusting. "Get it?"

A mask of confusion—or maybe disgust—set across Will's handsome features. "Get what?"

I gestured wildly, slopping some beer on my wrist and licking it up. "Mrs. Henderson burned up Nina."

Will grabbed my near-empty glass as I tried to negotiate it to my other hand to make the requisite two-finger gesture.

"I know, twice," he said. "But you told me yourself there is no way Nina is involved, and I have to agree with you."

I scooched closer toward Will, until he and I nearly were nose to nose. I began enunciating exaggeratedly, certain that that is what it would take to get my point across. "And then Kale seduces Vlad, and she gets hit by a car." I took my drink from Will and finished it, wiping my foam mustache with the back of my hand. "Get it? It could be VERM, out for revenge. They're protecting their kind."

Will blinked at me and I fanned myself. I leaned over and deposited my empty beer glass on the table and took a healthy slug from his. "It's hot in here."

A waitress stopped by and poked at my glass with the nub of her pencil. "'Nother?"

"No," Will said, eyes firm on me.

"Yes," I said, eyes just as firm. "He's trying to be my party pooper."

The waitress returned with another round of beers and a selection of appetizers, which Will had suggested. He read off the menu and I nodded to each one. Now we had an army of deep-fried deliciousness picking up the comforting flames of the fire.

I smashed a hunk of deep-fried mozzarella in between two slabs of boneless buffalo wings and tossed the whole thing in my mouth, reveling in the hot, deep-fried goodness as I licked the gooey residue from my fingers. I finished off my bar menu canapé with a slug of cold beer. "So what do you think?"

"I think maybe you've had enough."

I slapped down my glass. "You know, I'm really tired of you patronizing me. You would be out of work, if not for me."

"You do realize I work for the San Francisco Fire Department, right?"

I nodded my head hard and rolled my eyes. "I mean out of guardianship work. And what's with that, anyway? Do I need to remind you who drove a stake through the last fallen angel? Shouldn't that have been"—I poked Will in the center of his rock-hard chest—"your job?"

Will looked unfazed. "Do I need to remind you who climbed out her flat's bathroom window to fall into dubious battle with the fallen undead?"

"And whose fault was that?" Somewhere in my sober subconscious I was fairly aware that it was me, but I could see the alarm growing in Will's four eyes, so I left it alone.

"You might want to calm down, love."

"I'm calm." I pointed at him with a half-eaten chicken wing. "I'm just trying, once again, to give you a little heads-up to the things that go bump in the night." I smiled, gritting my teeth against a hiccup.

Will stopped trying to fight his grin and it pushed up to his earlobes. "All right, then. I'm listening."

The setting sun was glistening off the line of empty pint glasses on the sticky little coffee table as I polished off the last potato skin, licking sour cream off my fingers.

"I might be wrong," I started, then hiccuped, "and I hope I am, but I am not being overdramatic. It just kind of adds up a little bit. I mean, their whole organization . . . Hey, isn't it weird that in England they spell 'organization' with an *s,* not a *z*?" I grinned, and Will's eyes were intent on mine. I knew I was in the zone. I knew I was onto something. I knew if I didn't stop sucking down Guinness and chicken wings, I would be seeing both again later tonight. "Their whole organization is dedicated to the restoration and empowerment of *vampires.* They're all, 'Vampires good—arghh, arghh, arghh!'" I feigned bashing with my chicken wing. "It's right there on their website."

"VERM has a website?"

"Everyone has a website."

Will nodded, picking bits of chicken from the front of his shirt. I finished off my chicken leg, gave myself a makeshift bath with a Wet Nap, then blinked.

"Do you think everything is going to be okay, Will?"

Will's grin was easy and slow as he tangled his fingers in my hair. His fingertips brushed my naked neck, making me shiver. I closed my eyes and let the warmth from the fire—and from the beers—wash over me.

Will nodded. "Nothing is going to happen, love—not if I have anything to say about it."

"You have pretty, pretty teeth. Do Guardians get good dental?" I hiccupped again.

"I think you've had enough."

"Now I think I've had enough."

Will slung his arm around me and carried—er, led—me out the door. A slow drizzle had started in the ink black night and I pulled my jacket up over my head, feeling the flaming red curls that I had so carefully relaxed frizz and bounce around my head. I could smell the yeasty scent of beer on my own breath; but when Will turned to me, his breath was minty fresh. Before I knew it, my arms were around his neck, and my chest was pressed up against his. I leaned forward, focusing on the stern set of his chin. I brushed my fingertips over the sprinkle of stubble there, and Will grabbed my hand and kissed it.

"Thought we were workmates," he said in a throaty voice. His index finger gently tapped my chest. "Guardian and guard-ee."

"We are friends, too," I murmured. My eyelids felt heavy. "And friends can do all sort of things."

Will whirled me around so we were standing under an awning, slightly shielded from the rain.

"No!" I said. "I like the rain!"

My hand trailed down his arm; my fingers interlacing with his. I pulled him into the cool rain and rolled up onto my tiptoes, mashing a rough kiss against his lips. My knees went weak and my whole body exploded in titillating warmth. I pressed my tongue through Will's slightly parted teeth and found his tongue. Will's arms tightened around my waist and he pulled me closer. I let out a little groan and slumped against him, enjoying his firm chest and the secure way his hands fit at the small of my back.

"You're drunk," he whispered down to me.

"You're pretty," I said to his chest.

"Come on, Sophie."

"Don't you want to kiss me some more?" I was trying to smile in the sexy way I had seen Nina do so many times, but my cheeks felt like bubble gum and fishing weights. I shrugged. "Hey, where does it say in my supernatural job description that I can't occasionally imbibe? Besides, I was just going to get a Coke." I poked his firm chest. "You were the one who bought me the beer. What kind of angel is that?"

I may have been a little out of sorts, but not enough to miss the look of disappointment that flitted across Will's face.

"I am your Guardian. Alex is the angel."

I shrugged and continued down the sidewalk, feeling light and silly. "You say potato . . ."

Will stepped around me so he was walking closest to the curb. I stopped and snickered. "Alex does that so I don't get mud on my petticoat."

He looked at me skeptically. "Come again?"

"Boys from his time walk on the outside so that girls"—I thumped my chest in a most ladylike gorilla fashion—"don't get splashed with mud from wagon wheels on their dresses." I attempted an imaginary dress-fluttering twirl, but instead I stumbled over my own feet and landed against the cold bricks of a boarded-up Zain's Liquors. I hiccupped and giggled, pointing at the wall. "When did that get there?"

Will wagged his head. "Let's get you home." In one quick move I was hanging over his shoulder, my hair flopping in my eyes, arms hanging Raggedy Ann style over my head. I was watching the sidewalk roll by . . . until I realized that if I straightened up, I had a perfect view of Will's rump, and it was quite, well, perfect.

"You know, for a Guardian you've got a hell of an—"

But my words were drowned out by the *pop-pop-pop* as it echoed through the empty city streets. I tried to straighten up, to see the car as it backfired, but Will broke into a run and my stomach thunked against his shoulder. I could feel the beer slosh around in my gut and my cheeks started to burn. I was able to crane my neck and catch the shiny wheel covers of an SUV before Will dove behind a Dumpster, both of us flopping onto the wet concrete.

"Are you okay?"

"Were those—"

There was one more echoing *pop!* and I saw the sweat beading above Will's upper lip. My teeth started to chatter. "Gunshots?"

The last shot melted into squealing tires and Will

pushed me back as he peered around the Dumpster. I could feel the cold wetness of the concrete seeping into the seat of my jeans, and my palms were rough and stung from hitting the ground, raking through the gravel.

"Is he gone?" I was surprised I was able to get the words out as my teeth hammered together.

"Stay back," Will commanded.

I did as I was told, holding both my breath and my stomach. I felt my beer and potato skins climbing up my throat. "I don't feel so good."

Will turned back to me and did a precursory examination as he knelt beside me. "Are you okay? You weren't hit at all?"

I shook my head, unable to talk. "Wha-wha-wha," I mumbled dumbly.

"Don't move. I'm going to make sure they're gone."

Will reached behind him and fished a gun from his waistband. I could feel myself blanch. "Since when do you carry a gun? Fire people don't carry guns! Is it Guardian-issu—"

Will shushed me, and I clamped a hand over my mouth, parting my fingers to whisper, "I can't believe you had that the whole time."

He answered me with a hissed "shhh!" and crept around the Dumpster after cocking the gun once. I heard the safety slide and felt like I needed to pee. My heart thundered in my temples, replaying the rhythmic *pop* of every gunshot.

"Oh God," I grumbled. *It is happening again.*

I could still see Will's shoes as he crept along the side of the Dumpster, but I felt so incredibly alone. A tongue of icy cold air dipped down the back of my coat. The tears started to fall, and I darted after Will, pushing myself in front of him.

"Sophie!"

"They want me, Will. They're after me!" I turned to him; tears and snot were mingling at my chin, and my eyes blurred. "I can't let you get hurt, too!"

Will yanked hard on my arm and I flopped to the concrete, letting out an inelegant "oof!" as I hit the ground.

"What are you doing? What the hell are you doing?" I screamed as Will worked to still me.

"Sophie, stop!"

I finally stopped flailing and looked up at Will; he was straddling me, sitting gently on my hip bones. I sobbed miserably.

"All my friends are going to die, and it's all because of me. I'm going to give myself up. You can't stop me. Don't try to talk me out of it. I'm going to do it!"

I was midway through my suicidal soliloquy when I realized that Will had climbed off me, tucked his gun back in his waistband, and was crouched down a few feet from me, studying the concrete.

I pushed myself up. "What are you looking at?"

"Shell casings," he said without turning around. "Do you know what shell casings are made of?"

I shrugged, thinking back to the single shooting lesson I had with Alex a year ago. "I don't know. Brass, right? Aren't they usually made of brass?"

Will nodded and I crouched down next to him, following his gaze to the litter of shell casings gleaming on the wet concrete.

"They're usually brass or aluminum." Will picked up

one of the casings and held it up between thumb and forefinger so we could both examine it. "But look. These are made of silver."

"Silver?"

"Silver bullets."

I felt my eyebrows go up. "Silver bullets? That's either—"

Will licked his lips and forced a small smile. "Skunky American beer."

"Or the only thing that could kill a werewolf."

We both looked out to the deserted street and noticed the lone silver bullet at the same time. It was lolling against the black concrete, winking in the night.

Suddenly I was stone-cold sober. I sucked in a sharp breath.

"My God, Will. Someone is hunting werewolves."

Chapter Fourteen

In my imagination I am *Sophie Lawson, Badass Investigator, Paranormal Specialist.* I wear black leather, like a second skin; I wield a sexy, jeweled sword; I have the kind of hair that flies in gorgeous wisps over my naked, carved shoulders.

In real life I was crouching behind a Dumpster, sputtering and making snot bubbles; my skin was pasty white and "I'll hit the gym tomorrow" jiggly.

"Someone's hunting werewolves?" I finally bellowed; my voice was choked with tears and terror. "Does someone think I'm a werewolf?" I pointed to my own chest and then focused on my index finger. "Have I always had hair on my fingers? Oh, holy lord, I'm becoming a werewolf, and someone is trying to kill me!"

Will grabbed my halfway-to-a-paw hand and pushed it to my side. "I don't think anyone thinks you're a werewolf, love."

I shook my head. "What's going on, Will?"

He gathered up the last of the silver bullet casings and slipped them in his pocket.

"Are you okay?"

I gave myself a mental pat down and a short scan for bullet holes. Other than a bladder that was suddenly, shamefully empty, I was unharmed. "I think I'm okay," I said, my voice a cracked whisper. "Are you?"

Will nodded coolly as though a shower of bullets was a common occurrence in his English life; then he helped me to stand.

He brushed little bits of gravel from my shirt and frowned. "I think Bettina was right. Someone is definitely out to eradicate their kind."

My stomach quivered, gooseflesh breaking out all over my arms. "Oh my God."

"This guy might be after anyone mythical."

I licked my lips in a vain attempt to stop them from trembling. "So not VERM? Not just vampire defense."

Will shot me a noncommittal glance. "I'm not sure any of this is a coincidence anymore."

I slowly began to process what Will was suggesting— a serial killer of mythical creatures?—when I heard a gruff wince coming from the street. My whole body went hot again; the hair on the back of my neck pricked up. My legs trembled like Jell-O and I thanked God that my bladder was empty.

"What was that?"

Will pushed me behind him again and my inner Gloria Steinem was stomped out by my overwhelming girlie desire to climb up on his shoulders and bury my head in his neck.

Will picked his way across the wet sidewalk to where the wincing was coming from; the collapsible iron gate that locked the storefront next door was gaping open, and there was a dark shape hulking inside.

"Hello?" Will asked. "Sir, do you need help?"

Though I trusted Will implicitly, a large part of me considered taking off, running—if only to get help for the downed stranger. To get help and possibly to crawl under a bed somewhere and scream bloody murder until everything was calm again.

Instead, I stayed glued to Will, certain that my thundering heart would bash through my rib cage and kill us both.

I could make out the shape of a large man lying on his side against the brick wall. He made a sound, somewhere between a grunt and a growl, and I stiffened.

"Is he hurt?"

Will shrugged me off. "Sir, I'm an EMT and a fireman. I'm not going to hurt you, but I'm going to come in and check on you. Again, are you hurt?"

"No," came the gasping reply. "Don't come in here. Just leave me alone." A painful breath punctuated every word, and I narrowed my eyes, peering deeper into the shadows. I could make out the man's rumpled coat; the hem dipped into a shard of streetlight and I noticed that the stitching was even and hand done, the luxurious gray silk lining exposed.

"I think he's a businessman," I whispered to Will. "Ask him if he's a businessman."

Will glared over his shoulder at me and took another step toward the man, who shifted and lurched. The man jumped out of the darkness and his face was thrust into the light, teeth bared, upper lip snarled. Though he remained crouched, I could see the guy was huge, with biceps the size of melons and a chest at least three feet across, smeared with blood. A vein bulged in the man's neck, and his dark skin was stretched tight. His brown eyes were wild, and sweat stood out above his eyebrows and lips.

"I don't need any help," the man snarled.

"You need a doctor," Will said. His full body was tensed and seemingly ready to pummel the man.

"I don't." The man doubled over and crumbled before he could finish. I whipped around Will and knelt down, just a few inches from the man's face.

"Sophie!" Will yelled.

I felt Will's fingers brush past my shoulder as I put my hands on the man's chest. His head railed against my palm and his breathing came in sharp, fast breaths.

"I'm calling an ambulance."

"He doesn't need an ambulance," I told Will. "He needs to come home with us."

"What?"

I looked into the man's dark eyes, which were now hooded and weary. "He's a werewolf."

The man started to shake his head and I steadied him. "It's okay. I recognize you from the UDA, but I don't remember your name."

"Sergio," his dry lips whispered. "My name is Sergio."

Will's eyes went wide. "Werewolf?"

I had a hot, sinking feeling in my belly. On a daily basis I surround myself with immortals, angels, and the occasional fire-breathing dragon. From time to time, having that kind of posse tends to make me feel rather invincible, but coming face-to-face with the kind of firepower that could take down a werewolf—let alone turn me into a runny hunk of Swiss cheese—had the uncanny ability to turn me into jelly.

I blinked at the velvety bubble of black-red blood as it made its way out of Sergio's wound. I felt hot bile rise in my throat. "I don't feel so good."

I felt Sergio's baseball mitt–sized paws holding my shoulder, guiding me softly to the concrete. Will pressed his palm to my forehead.

"Is she going to be okay?" Sergio asked.

I blinked and gulped down a lungful of stale, urine-scented air; then I gagged and coughed.

"Yeah, she's fine."

I tried to glare at Will, but I was feeling a little barfy. I swung my head out of the vestibule and sucked in some semiclean air.

Will crouched down next to me. "So, do . . . these guys . . . bleed out like normal humans?"

I looked back to where Sergio was holding his wound and nodded. "Yeah."

"Then we need to stop the bleeding or we're going to lose him." Will gently pushed Sergio's arm aside and Sergio let him. "Looks like he was shot in the chest."

Sergio shook his head again. "Shoulder. It's the upper shoulder. Not a big deal."

"Let's get him home."

We helped Sergio up and I was astonished to see that he was almost a full head taller than Will; but Will wielded Sergio as if he weighed nothing.

I stared into the street, frowning. "Should we get a cab?"

Sergio shook his head with concentrated effort. "My

car is right over there." He dug in his pocket and dropped a shiny set of keys in Will's hand. "Do you mind?"

Will shook his head silently, continued to guide Sergio and me toward the car. We helped Sergio lay down in the back of his SUV, then drove home in near silence. The only sounds were Sergio's occasional groans and ragged whooshes of air. I glanced over at Will, noticing his own arm lying limp in his lap, covered with blood. He was slowly flexing and unflexing his fist.

"You okay?" I wanted to know.

I watched the muscle twitch in Will's jaw. I saw the pink tip of his tongue slide across his lower lip. He leaned over to me.

"What does it take to make a person . . ." His eyes flicked from the windshield to his blood-covered forearm.

"Into a werewolf?" I finished for him.

Another whoosh of air from the backseat and Sergio pushed himself up. "Don't worry, man. You're fine. I didn't nick you, did I?"

My eyes went wide. "He didn't nick you, did he?"

Will wagged his head and I let out a tiny, relieved breath. "You're fine," I said. "It's only a bite, a really significant scratch, or drinking from his footprint."

Will knitted his brows. "Drinking from a footprint?"

I shrugged. "I'm just the messenger."

We rounded a corner and Sergio winced again; I angled myself over the back of my seat. "You're going to be okay, Sergio. We're almost back to my apartment." I eyed the man and his well-tailored suit—that gorgeous coat now glistening with a growing sheen of wet blood. "Do you know what happened? Do you know who did this?"

Sergio shook his big head. "I don't really know. I was walking home from the office and I heard tires squeal. I didn't really pay attention because, you know, downtown San Francisco."

We all nodded knowingly, used to the constant honks, tire squeals, and inarticulate shouting from the downtown residents and tourists.

"Then I heard the first pop. Naturally, I ducked, but I didn't think it had anything to do with me."

"Gangbangers?" I asked.

"Something like that. I really try and keep to myself mostly. There are a lot of thugs out there, a lot of bad elements. I like to keep my business clean."

I socked Will on the shoulder. "See? I told you."

"Good guess," he said without looking back at me.

"I felt the first shot whiz by me, so I dove into that doorway. I wasn't too worried because"—Sergio's dark eyes glanced from Will to me—"well . . ."

"Werewolf," I finished. "Yeah, we get it."

For the first time Sergio seemed to brighten. "You too?"

"No"—I pointed to Will—"Vessel Guardian." Then I jabbed a thumb at my chest. "Supernatural Tupperware."

Sergio grinned, his teeth practically glowing white in the dim car. "Vessel Guardian. You don't say! I thought that was all just a bunch of religious mumbo jumbo."

Will stepped on the gas and easily maneuvered us through an intersection, finding a space just in front of my building. "You don't say," Will mumbled.

"And Tupperware? What's that like—"

"Vessel of Souls," I confirmed, shrugging nonchalantly.

Sergio's eyes went wide, and Will cut his eyes to me. "Way to keep that one under wraps."

Will put the car in park and we helped Sergio up to my apartment. He was groaning less and starting to stand up a little straighter by the time we reached the third floor. You gotta love that supernatural healing power.

I sank the key into my lock and kicked the front door open. Vlad, seated on the couch, snapped his head toward us; his nostrils flared, and his brow furrowed.

"Vlad, this is Sergio," I said. "Sergio, take off your coat. Let me have a look at the wound." I nodded to Will. "Go grab the emergency kit underneath the bathroom sink. And there's extra Bactine in the medicine cabinet."

I would like to say that I kept a fully stocked emergency kit and a Costco-sized bottle of antiseptic just for Florence Nightingale situations like these, but, the truth was, I had a tendency to walk into things. Or fall off them. But I was still feeling very much like a lifesaving battlefront nurse, until Will returned with a heap of bandages and Bactine. I turned back to Sergio, who was now down to his white shirt, the blood soaking through to his collar and all the way down his breast pocket.

There was a lot of blood.

But I was used to blood in copious amounts—when it came from a blood bag and wasn't attached to an actual bleeding person.

That was the last thing I thought before the room started to spin. . . .

I felt ice-cold fingers pressed to my cheeks. When I blinked, Nina was hovering over me. "She's awake. She's going to be okay."

"Are you sure she doesn't have a concussion?" It was a gruff, unfamiliar voice and I struggled to sit up, but Nina held me down, fingertips pressed against my shoulders, surprisingly strong.

"What's your name?" Nina asked.

"Let me up, Nina."

"Answer the question," she commanded.

"Sophie Annemarie Lawson. And you're Nina LaShay." I pointed. "That's Will Sherman and . . . I have no idea who you are."

"Sergio, remember?" Sergio grinned at me and I cocked my head, remembering. "Nice shirt," I said finally.

He had traded in his bloodstained button-up for a borrowed shirt from Vlad. It was three sizes too small, emphasized Sergio's bubbly muscles, and the VERM logo was stretched unmercifully across his huge chest. Sergio smoothed it, grinned, and patted the two inches of exposed belly under the hem of the shirt. "It's the best we could do."

"Whatever," Vlad mumbled.

I sat up and smiled at Sergio. "You're okay." I pointed to my own shoulder. "The gunshot?"

Sergio blushed, his dark skin tinged a deep red. "Your Will is quite the nurse."

Will's eyebrows disappeared in his bangs. "Hey! No, it must be the werewolf-healing thing." He snapped his fingers. "Quick. I had nothing to do with it."

I stood up and brushed off my pants. "I'm glad. But I thought the silver bullet would, you know . . ."

Sergio wagged his head. "No, only through the heart."

"Oh," I said, "like vampires. But with the stake."

"*Not* like vampires," Vlad said, taking his seat behind his laptop.

Will leaned in to me. "They're not going to start the whole werewolf-vampire arm wrestling thing, are they?"

I looked from Sergio to Vlad, narrowing my eyes on the scowling century-old sixteen-year-old. "No, they're not. Besides, the whole vampire versus werewolf thing has mainly been fabricated by the media."

"That sounds very VERM."

"We *DON'T* shorten it!" Vlad groaned.

Sergio clapped his hands together. "So, now that this is all sorted out, I should probably be on my way."

I grabbed him by his ham-hock bicep. "You can't go. You've just been shot. You need to relax and we need to figure out what's going on. Your shoulder might be healed, but you're probably still a little weak, right?"

Sergio frowned and rubbed his flat belly. "A little, I guess."

"Can I get you something? Crackers or something?"

"No, thanks." Sergio wagged his head. "Do you have anything with protein?"

"Oh," I said, "because you're a werewolf."

"Actually, it's because I'm gluten intolerant."

Will followed me into the kitchen while I pulled open the fridge, willing a turkey breast and a hunk of Brie to magically appear. My powers of astroprojection being nil, I was greeted with the usual selection of blood bags, condiments, and a carton of vanilla soy milk.

I shook the carton, then upended it in a glass.

Will winced. "Is it supposed to be chunky?"

I tossed the carton in the trash. "Do you think I could pass it off as chocolate chip?" I blew out a sigh. "Hey, Sergio, what do you like on your pizza?"

We were all sitting around the dining-room table—Vlad, glowering at Sergio; Sergio, oblivious, enjoying his fourth piece of Veggie Madness on a gluten-free crust; Nina, working a bag of AB negative and typing away on my Mac; and Will and I trading uneasy glances between a half-decimated all-meat, extra-cheese pizza.

I wiped my grease-soaked fingers on my napkin and pushed away from the table. "Okay! So, are we going to talk about the elephant in the room?"

Nina raised her eyebrows. "Sophie, you may have put on a few pounds, but I wouldn't call you an elephant."

"I think she is talking about him." Vlad's dark eyes went to Sergio, who popped his last bit of pizza in his mouth and wiped his hands on a napkin. Sergio's back stiffened, and his eyes held Vlad's.

"What about me?"

"I thought you said there wasn't an issue between vampires and werewolves?" Will asked.

"Hey, before you guys start comparing incisors, and before I completely kick Nina's ass for calling me an elephant—"

Nina held up a single finger without looking up from my laptop. "I called you *not* an elephant."

"I'm talking about the fact that Sergio was shot with silver bullets. Kale was plowed over in an intersection. Bettina was hammered in the streets. Someone tried to drive a stake through my heart. What else needs to happen for you to believe that someone is out there? We're seriously being Van Helsinged, and no one is paying attention."

"Who has it in for demons?" Will asked.

I huffed. "Who doesn't?"

Will's eyebrows went up and Nina sighed. "There is always someone hunting vampires. Buffy wasn't exactly an original idea."

"There's always been people after us," Sergio said.

"Yeah. They're called dogcatchers!" Vlad snorted.

"Guys!" I shouted.

Nina finally looked up from the laptop, clicking it closed. "Okay, if someone is out for demon blood, what are we supposed to do about it?"

"Um, maybe find out who wants you dead and why. If this guy knew that Sergio was a werewolf , and that silver bullets would *actually* kill him—"

"Then he's probably got a pretty decent foothold in the Underworld," Will finished.

"Right. Because most people just pretty much assume the whole werewolf-silver-bullet thing is legend," I said.

Vlad blew out an exhausted sigh. "Still more trouble in Gotham."

"We were shot at." I thought yelling and stamping my foot with each word would get the weight of the issue across, but Vlad just straightened his ascot to Thurston Howell-perfect—quite a feat since the man had no reflection to check—and looked at me.

"I'm really sorry about your incident, Sophie, but I fail to recognize how this affects me. Or"—his eyes cut to Nina—"us."

Nina frowned. "Are you sure it wasn't gangbangers?

Maybe they picked up the bullets by mistake." She crossed her arms in front of her chest and narrowed her coal black eyes. "Bastard gangbangers. We could do the city a real service if the UDA would just lift their ban and let us eat them."

Vlad wrinkled his nose. "Ew. I don't like gang-bangers. They're usually so thin and stringy."

"It wasn't gangbangers." I dug in my pocket and picked out the one shell casing I had nicked from Will's stash. "This bullet isn't something you inadvertently pick up at Walmart."

Vlad examined the shell casing and gave it a small sniff.

"Anything?" I asked.

He narrowed his eyes. "I'm not a dog." Then, "Do you keep Skittles in that pocket, too?"

Nina leapt off the couch and snatched the casing from Vlad's fingers. "A silver bullet. How odd. Maybe one of my characters gets shot with a silver bullet!"

Sergio leaned over, flashed a big grin. "You're a writer?"

"Novelist, actually," Nina said, oozing pride. "I'll read you something later."

"Hello!" I sprang up from the couch. "My clients go missing, a banshee is bashed up with the message about eradicating 'her kind,' and now someone shoots at me and Will with *silver* bullets. Don't you get it? Someone is trying to clean up. Someone knows about the Under-world and is trying to clean up."

No one seemed to register the amount of shock and awe that my proclamation required, and I huffed. "Hello? Guys? There is a serial killer out there and you're what he's looking for."

Nina bit her lip. "I don't know, Sophie. Demon hunters can't exist. Have you read Harley's book?"

I was sputtering. "Wh-what? Harley's book? Nina, Harley's stupid book says *you* don't exist! You're in love with a man who has mathematically proven that you"—I jumped forward and batted her on the shoulder, to show how corporeal she was—"don't exist. Yet, here you are, standing in our living room, looking at me like that."

"Like what?"

"Like you think I'm completely Looney Tunes for suggesting that we might be in danger."

Sergio leaned over to Will. "What book is this?"

Vlad patted my shoulder in an effort to placate me. "It's not that we think you're Looney Tunes, but look at the facts. Someone shot at you and Will with silver bullets—silver bullets that only kill werewolves."

I held up a single finger. "And can make a hell of a dent in your everyday average human."

"You're not everyday," Will put in.

"Or average," Nina chimed in.

"But I'm still human, and I was still shot at. And, Nina, I swear to God, if you say that being mistaken for a werewolf is proof positive I need to wax in the winter, I will drive a stake through your heart myself."

Nina crossed her arms in front of her chest and jutted out a hip. "You said it, not me."

"You guys, this is serious. Can't you see?"

I looked into the unconcerned faces surrounding me: Nina, surreptitiously eyeing my winter-hairy legs; Vlad, dark eyes cutting from the clock to the front door;

Sergio, intently flipping through the promotional copy of Harley's book, which Will handed him.

This was going to be harder than I thought.

I looked around, feeling my eyes widen while my stomach dropped. "What if this is another fallen angel?"

Nina blinked at me. "If it were, don't you think they'd toss out the middle man and kill you directly? I mean, no offense."

"I don't know." I looked at Will. "Maybe they're playing—trying to get me nervous or something?"

Will rubbed his chin. "There has been no information on any fallen angels coming into town. As for them playing with you? Nina is kind of right. Fallen angels don't play. If they're after you, it's pretty direct."

"And frankly," Vlad stated, eyes glued to his screen, "everything that has happened so far has been pretty coincidental. Kale got hit by a car—a hundred cars run through that intersection every day. It was bound to happen."

I put my hands on my hips. "And Bettina and Mrs. Henderson and the centaur and me getting staked?"

"Muggings, break-ins—they happen. The economy is tanking, breathers get desperate. Unfortunately, both of those can end in murder."

I tried to shoot a questioning glance at Will, but he was fully immersed in the last piece of pizza. I cleared my throat; and when he looked up, he opened his mouth, looking as though he was about to agree with Vlad. I pinned him with a glare and he snapped his mouth shut.

"The guy said he was going to eradicate her kind, Vlad. Do you really think that was just your average thug?"

Vlad shrugged. "I got mugged in New Orleans by a

guy who told me he was mugging for Christ. It takes all kinds."

Sergio stood up, dropping his napkin onto his plate. "Look, everyone, I appreciate your concern, and even more so appreciate the hospitality, but I really should get running."

I felt hysteria rising in my chest. "But someone just tried to *kill* you!"

Sergio patted me on the shoulder and smiled at me kindly. "Again, I appreciate everything, but I'll be fine."

I watched Sergio walk out the door; then Will gave me a quick hug and turned to go, too, but not before telling me, "I'll keep an eye out—poke around and see if there is anything that seems a little"—his eyes cut left and right—"angelically abnormal. But you never know, Sophie. Vlad could be right and this could all be a chain of coincidences."

Will stiffened, and I sensed he could feel the ice-cold waves of disbelief wafting from me.

He tried an unconvincing smile. "Besides, why would someone want to attack the Underworld?"

I dug my teeth into my lower lip. *If anyone is going to save the Underworld,* I thought, *it's going to have to be me.*

Chapter Fifteen

I set the pink donut box next to the coffee and tea service on the credenza; then I set a tray of artfully arranged blood bags next to that, trying to make the UDA conference room look welcoming. I was buns to the sky, rooting around in my shoulder bag, when Will's lilting voice broke the silence.

"I love this country."

I turned around and shot him an icy glare. "This is serious, Will."

"Obviously." Will stared skeptically at the fuzzy purple earmuffs I offered him.

"Go on. Put them on."

He reached out, tentatively taking the earmuffs, his fingertips brushing mine. Though we were in the throes of a potentially life-and-death situation, my body reacted with all the hormonal decorum of a twelve-year-old girl at a Justin Bieber concert.

I waggled the earmuffs. "On."

To his credit, Will snapped them on. To my credit, I didn't wet myself laughing.

"Would you like a donut?"

Will's brows went up. He plucked one fuzzy earmuff away from his ear. "Can't hear you, love. I'm wearing the muff."

I rolled my eyes, dropped a donut onto a plate, and handed it to him.

"Cheers," he said before settling into a chair.

Vlad and Nina filed in next, each selecting a blood bag and a pair of earmuffs, then settling around the conference table. Dixon came in and I shut the door behind him, offering him a pair of earmuffs.

His razor-sharp eyebrows formed a tight V; his dark eyes slitted as he looked at the earmuffs. "Are those really necessary?"

I shrugged. "It's your afterlife."

Dixon pressed his lips in a pale, thin line and took the earmuffs, snapping them on.

"He's so vain," Nina said with a matter-of-fact head shake. "It's part of the reason we didn't work out."

"I can hear you," Dixon returned.

Nina's stunned face broke into an easy grin. "Kidding," she sang, quickly looking away.

"Okay, since everyone's here now . . ."

Each of the vampires looked at me, vague interest on their timeless faces. Will, on the other hand, kept chewing happily while humming a jazzy version of "Swing Low, Sweet Chariot."

"Will?"

Nothing.

In my brilliant calculations I failed to note that while vampire hearing is ultrasensitive—even when encased by a set of fuzzy earmuffs—human hearing was not. I gestured for him to slide off the earmuffs and I started again.

"I know that you are skeptical about Mrs. Henderson's disappearance. You think the guy who tried to turn Kale into a speed bump was a coincidence, and the guy who shot silver bullets at Sergio was—what?—a gangbanger. I know none of these are coincidences, so I wanted to prove to you, firsthand, that even if these events are remotely coincidental, we need to pay attention. Bettina? Could you come in here now, please?"

Will's eyes widened, earmuffs locked securely in place, as I led Bettina into the room. In the day that had passed, her bruises had become more pronounced. Her gray skin had puckered and dropped into a deep purple; cuts and scratches, which I hadn't noticed yesterday, looked blue-red and menacing today.

Bettina's lower lip started to tremble, her lips parting a millimeter, hands curled into fists. I dove across the table, coming face-to-face with a startled Will. I clamped my palms over his fuzzy purple earmuffs just as Bettina started to shriek.

Will's eyes were wide; terror and surprise sank in the deep hazel. Sweat beaded on his upper lip, and his body started to quake gently underneath my palms.

"Bettina, please!" I was shocked that I was able to scream over the choking knot of tears locked in my throat.

Will's face was turning a mottled purple. His eyes bulged; a drop of sweat rolled from his hairline.

"Shut up! Shut up, shut up, shut up! You're killing him!"

Bettina clamped a hand over her mouth and the silence

seemed just as loud. Will crumpled forward. His shoulders slumped, his head deadweight in my hands.

"I'm so sorry, Sophie," Bettina whispered as she backed out of the conference room.

"Will?" I said, the word barely crossing my lips before a torturous sob wracked my body. My cheeks itched as the tears flooded over them.

"Will . . ."

"I can't hear you, love!" Will yelled in my face, pointing to his head. "Got the muffs on, remember?"

"Oh God, Will." Relief washed over me and left a cold sweat. I slid the earmuffs from his head, but Will continued yelling.

"And I think that gray bird tried to kill me!"

I wiped the heel of my hand across my cheeks. "Momentary lack of judgment on my part," I croaked.

Will plucked a piece of donut out of my cleavage and popped it in his mouth. "We're all allowed one."

"Ms. Lawson? Perhaps your guest should take a breath of fresh air. Vlad, Nina?"

Nina and Vlad led Will out of the room. I worried my bottom lip as I watched them leave and Dixon approached me.

"Your demonstration was eye-opening."

My stomach was in my shoes. "I didn't mean for that to happen."

Dixon held up a dismissing palm. "Regardless if the previous events are connected, Bettina's experience has demonstrated that as an organization we are not doing enough to keep our clients safe. The Underworld Detection Agency will work to rectify that, and I will allocate all the resources necessary for you to conduct a thorough investigation."

"For me to conduct an investigation?"

Dixon nodded curtly.

It should have been a victory, but it didn't feel like one. But whether it was Will's near-death experience, Dixon's blood-tinged, conciliatory smile, or being charged with finding the Underworld killer and saving my friends, I wasn't sure.

Dixon turned to leave; in a moment of confident solidarity, I stopped him.

"May I ask you something?"

Dixon nodded and took a seat at the conference table. I fished the silver bullets from my shoulder bag and laid them in front of him.

"Do you know anything about these?"

For a beat Dixon didn't make any motion that he had heard me; did nothing to acknowledge the bullets glinting on the table.

"Silver bullets," he said, sucking air in through his teeth. "Where did you get these?"

"From the wrong end of a gun."

"Was anyone hurt?"

I shook my head and Dixon picked up one of the bullets, fingering it gingerly. Something in his eyes registered.

"You know something about these bullets?"

"Well, silver bullets are routinely used to kill—"

"No," I said, feeling the frustration roil through me, "these bullets. These particular bullets. You know where they came from."

Dixon tapped the bullet on the table, then cut his eyes to me. His smile was icy smooth, the entire visage glacial. "I'm sure I don't know what you're talking about, Ms. Lawson." He stood up and sauntered out of the room; the door slammed behind him with an ominous thud.

I gathered up my things and plodded to my office, where I dumped my papers and a donut box onto my now-naked bookshelf. Finally I lowered myself into my desk chair on a desperate, whooshing sigh.

"Exaggerating a bit?"

Vlad appeared behind my door and pushed it shut with a gentle kick. I clawed at my chest and willed myself not to pee. "My God, Vlad, can't you announce your presence like a normal person? Or is that against the Vampire Empowerment bylaws?"

He grinned, showing a toothy mouth of fangs and imperfect teenaged teeth, and sat down across from me in my visitor's chair. "It's not against the bylaws, but it's a lot of fun to surprise you. Should I get you a glass of water or something?"

I got my heartbeat—and bladder—under control and glared at him. "And to what do I owe this terrifying intrusion?"

Vlad paused. His tongue darted across his lips, just touching the fanged edge of one tooth. He drummed the fingers of his left hand against his knee. "I was listening to what you said today."

My ears perked, but I remained wary. "And?"

"And I think you're right to worry. I think we're all right to worry."

I sat up a little straighter. "But nothing has happened to any vampires yet. So far it seems your"—I cleared my throat—"kind is pretty safe."

"If any demons of the Underworld aren't safe, then none of us are."

"So? Do you want to help me investigate?"

Vlad looked over his shoulder at my closed door; a millisecond later I heard the clatter of footsteps down the hall. Once they had passed, he leaned into me. "I can't do that." He reached across his chest, one hand sliding under his jacket. My breath hitched.

Is he pulling out a gun? No! This is Vlad! He could kill me in my sleep if he wanted to!

"Are you going to be sick?"

I shook my head. "No, no, sorry."

Vlad retrieved his hand, and a thin file folder. He slid it across my desk. From the official Underworld Detection Agency crest, I knew it belonged to upper management. From the scrolled writing across the top, I knew that "upper management" was Dixon.

"The UDA keeps tabs on breathers and demons who produce weapons that could be used against our communities."

"Where did you . . . ?" But when I looked up, Vlad was gone, door shutting softly behind him. The trailing scent of his earthy cologne was dissipating slowly.

I slid the file onto my lap and opened it slowly, feeling my pulse speed up. Several pages were clipped together under the heading "werewolf." The top page was a photograph of a newspaper clipping covered in thick Chinese characters. I didn't need to read the language to know that the article oozed with rage and invectives; the hashes in the characters were deep and sharp. There was a name and address scrawled in red ink on the bottom of the paper. I was surprised to see that it was local, and was more surprised to see a tiny plastic bag with a silver bullet locked inside, taped to the back of the page.

Once I got home, I was pacing a bald spot in my carpet, rolling the bullet between my fingers when Will let himself in.

"Do you ever knock?" I asked, jitters going all the way up to my scalp.

"How's that for a Guardian's welcome?" Will smiled, unfazed, and shook his tea mug. He set the kettle on the stove and motioned to me with his empty mug. "So what's that about, then?"

"What?"

"The pacing, the brooding"—he straightened—"the bullet."

"I know where the bullet came from."

Will took the bullet from me and led me to a kitchen chair. "Well, then, let's go there. Where is it?"

I swallowed hard. "Chinatown."

Will stood up. "So what are we waiting for?"

I bit down hard. "I'm not sure. I . . . It was Vlad."

Will's eyebrows rose and he sat down again. "Vlad is responsible?"

"No!" I shook my head. "Vlad gave me the information. He took it from Dixon."

"Nicked it?"

I nodded. "I think so. And something about it just doesn't feel right."

"Okay, okay, okay," Nina said as she tore out of her room. Her red silk kimono was flailing behind her.

"Listen to this." Her eyes went wide when she saw Will. "Oh! Hey, Will. I thought I smelled you."

Will smiled uneasily and looked relieved when the teakettle started to whistle. He disappeared into the kitchen and I went to assist, but Nina commanded me to "sit," pointing at the chair I had just come from. I sank down and swallowed hard. "Go ahead."

"Lady and gentleman," Nina stated, her pale face positively beaming, "today I am proud to present to you the first reading of my new novel/memoir, *Pale Is the New Black*."

I raised my eyebrows when Nina flopped a three-inch-thick manuscript onto the tabletop and fixed a pair of glasses at the end of her ski jump nose.

Have I mentioned that vampires have impeccable vision in their afterlife?

I must have furrowed my brow because Nina pushed the cheaters up her nose and said, "They make me look more literary."

I couldn't tell whether it was Nina's fake glasses or the great tower of manuscript pages, but I wasn't feeling Nina's literariness, and I wasn't all that thrilled about it.

"Now"—Nina began again as her small, pale hands clutched her book—"this first portion might be a little emotional for me, so I'm going to read the scene the whole way through."

I looked over my shoulders, half expecting to see the literary masses Nina seemed to be speaking to.

"If you need any bathroom breaks," she continued, "I suggest you go now and hold all questions and applause until after I've finished."

In retrospect I should have run for the relative safety of our little 1920s-style bathroom, with the chipped black-and-white tile floor.

"Ahem." Nina cleared her throat and began to read in earnest.

"'Darkness touched the Paris night sky like a gentle kiss, and I—young, beautiful, supple . . .'"

I shifted in my chair, and Nina pinned me with a death squad glare.

"'. . . was bored. I waited for something to happen, for something to whet the appetite for blood that was stirring within. I could taste my want. My need rose until it was almost too much to bear, and then I saw him. Tall, warm, soft, in the darkest night.'"

I raised a tentative hand. "What kind of book is this again?"

Nina snarled, a single nostril flaring. "I asked you kindly to please hold all commentary until the end."

"I was just—"

"Please hold all commentary until the author has finished, thank you. Now where was I?"

"Supple," I reminded her.

Nina fixed her glasses and started again.

"'He turned and I could see the vein throbbing in his neck. I longed to sink my teeth into the flesh, to taste of meaty life juice.'"

I clamped my jaws shut. Every muscle in my body winced and I bore down against the torrent of laughter.

"'Suddenly my fangs were in him and he was underneath me, writhing.'"

My stomach dropped into my fuzzy slippers when

the heroine was introduced as she plunged her fangs into her beau Horatio's "tender virgin neck."

When Nina was through, she looked up, beaming, expectant. "Well?" she asked breathlessly.

Somewhere around Cecilia falling into Horatio's arms and her going back for a second taste of "that meaty life juice," Will must have returned from the kitchen. He stood in our doorway; his face pale, his lips drawn. The little Arsenal Football logo on his chest was jumping as his heart thudded underneath. He held his tea to his lips, a statue with darting eyes.

Will eyed the stack of papers Nina held. "Is that her diary?" he asked, voice low.

Nina's eyes went wide and her chest swelled. "Do you really think it's that good? That believable?" She shook the papers. "Because I wrote it."

Will eyed her. "You wrote it down or made it up?"

"Made it up."

He cocked an eyebrow. "Inspired by true events?"

"A little."

Will's smile showed a small amount of relief. "Then you're either a hell of a writer or a very, very scary woman."

Nina preened. "Thanks. On both counts." She flopped into a dining-room chair, forearm thrown over her forehead, fainting Victorian style. "I can't read anymore. It's very emotional." Nina's gaze was steady on me, waiting, and I took the hint. I jumped to my feet and started clapping. Will joined in.

I know you should never lie to a friend, but when that friend has two-inch fangs, I consider it warranted.

"Thank you!" Nina's grin was so wide that it went

to her earlobes. "So what are you two still doing up?"
She bobbed her small shoulders and waggled her eyebrows. "A little nightcap?"

Will and I exchanged a glance. "Actually, we were
just talking about the case a little bit."

Nina's eyes lit up. "Wait, wait, wait one second." She
jumped up, bounded over to our junk drawer and pulled
out a pen and notepad. "I'm thinking my next novel
might be romantic suspense or, you know, espionage.
So . . . go ahead. I want to take notes."

I licked my bottom lip. "There isn't that much to tell.
I think I know where the silver bullet came from. I have
an address in Chinatown."

"Sophie, that's huge! How did you figure that out?"

I pinched my bottom lip, quiet.

"Vlad nicked a little something from Dixon."

Nina blinked. "Oh. Well, why aren't you checking
it out?"

"I—I'm not sure. There just seems—maybe . . . I
don't know . . ."

Nina put her notepad down and dropped her pen.
"You think Vlad has something to do with all of this?"

My eyes went wide. "No. No, I don't think—"

"Do you think my nephew is trying to lure you into
some kind of trap or something? Because if that's what
you think—"

"No," I said definitively. "I don't think that at all. I
just got the information, so I haven't really had a chance
to look into it. I know Vlad wouldn't do anything like—
like this."

The lie tasted sour on my tongue.

* * *

I was reading the same line of an Elle Adair romance novel over and over again when I heard the lock tumble and Vlad walked in. He was wearing an ankle-length duster over his pressed black pants and clean white shirt. I expected a top hat or another stupid ascot, but he looked almost twenty-first century.

"Where have you been?" I asked.

"Out" was his quiet reply.

He went directly to the fridge and yanked it open. "Where's Nina?"

"Poe's. She's still working on her novel."

Vlad snorted and snatched up a blood bag, piercing it with his fangs. For the first time that motion, which I had seen every day of my life with Nina, made me wince, made me consider those sharp fangs digging into soft flesh.

Vlad grinned; and with his teeth stained a hearty bloodred, he looked momentarily sinister. "What's with you?"

"What do you know about the murders?"

"Murders?" Vlad continued working on his blood bag, then flopped down on the couch, clicking on the TV. I perched myself in the chair-and-a-half (that cost me a paycheck-and-a-half) next to him.

"The Underworld. Mrs. Henderson. Bettina," I elaborated.

"I thought Bettina was fine." Vlad didn't look at me; he kept his eyes transfixed on the glowing TV screen as he clicked past the guy from CHiPs selling Lake Shastina real estate and an ad for Mister Steamy.

"The file you gave me."

I watched his nostrils flare; his top lip curled into a bloodstained snarl. "I thought I was helping you out."

I straightened, feeling a spike of nerves rushing through my body. "I know, I was just curious."

Vlad looked at me now; the snarl moving up into a gruesome smile. "You don't have to be upset, Sophie. I was just saying."

I fought to slow my heartbeat to a normal rate. "I'm not nervous."

Vlad went back to watching his stream of infomercials "What do you want to know about the file?"

"How did you get ahold of them?"

Vlad's eyes cut from the TV, cut across mine, and flashed back again. "I'm holding them for a friend."

"Come on, Vlad. These aren't condoms or cigarettes. They're official Underworld Detection Agency files. They're Dixon's files."

"Like I said, I thought I was doing you a favor."

I held up my hands placatingly. "I'm just trying to get to the bottom of this. I don't suspect you, personally, of anything. I'm just trying to explore all of the options. Maybe look into some factions that might have had a grudge against other demons."

"Factions?" Vlad cocked an eyebrow. "You mean the Empowerment Movement, don't you?" Vlad stood up so quickly that I lost my breath.

"It's just that Dixon is also a part of the movement—"

"I don't believe you, Sophie. You say that you're on

our side—the Underworld side—but when it comes down to it, the first thing you do is start pointing fingers at demons. Whatever happened to 'never judge a demon by his horns,' huh?"

I gripped the chair arms, burrowing my fingernails into the soft fabric. "I'm just following the facts."

"There are no facts that lead you to the Empowerment Movement."

"Vlad, the goal of the movement is to advance the vampire race."

I could see Vlad's jaw clench.

I could see his fingers roll into tight, pale fists.

"And you think the only way a vampire can advance is by taking out the competition?"

I steadied my voice. "You have to admit, it's a little odd. A banshee, a dragon, a centaur, a werewolf—but no vampire hits? Vamps are the majority in the Underworld. Statistically speaking, they should have been hit, too."

"Statistically speaking, vampires are much more intelligent than any of those other demons," Vlad snarled. "We don't have to take them out. Given enough time, they'll do it themselves."

"Vlad, I . . ." I stood up and tried to put a calming hand on Vlad's shoulder.

Truth was, I believed what he was saying; and deep down—and maybe even more on the surface—I didn't believe that VERM could be responsible for the Underworld murders. VERM had been around a long time— and the Underworld murders were just beginning. Vlad let my hand rest on his shoulder for a chilling millisecond before he flicked it away; he spun on his heel, and snapped his black leather duster from the hook by the door. He shot a look over his shoulder—anger? disgust?—and said nothing before he stomped into the foyer and slammed the door hard behind him. I let out a breath, which I didn't know I was holding, and it was like every bone in my body turned to jelly. I collapsed on the couch and stretched out, pulling my grandmother's afghan over myself and falling asleep.

Chapter Sixteen

The next morning when I rapped on Will's door, I convinced myself that I was out to cover all my bases. My gut told me that Vlad and his VERM brethren had nothing to do with the Underworld killing, but over the long night, something niggled at me. Something whispered that maybe I was missing something, that maybe it was possible— however unlikely I wished it to be—that Vlad and VERM *might* have had a hand in the Underworld violence.

He answered in his usual guise—shirtless, low-slung jeans showing off his taut belly, the light sprinkle of hair across his pectoral muscles. He grinned when he saw me; then plunged a spoonful of cereal into his mouth.

"Good to see you here. Thought maybe you hated me after all the vampire mumbo."

"It's not me you have to worry about on that front."

Will paled and looked over my head at our closed door. I waved my hand.

"You're fine right now. How would you like to go for a little adventure? Might help us find out for sure."

Will's eyebrows rose. His smile went from cute and lopsided to sly and interested. "Go on."

"I think I might have some information to follow up on." I pinched the bag of bullets between my thumb and forefinger. "About these."

The smile dropped from Will's eyes, but he shrugged. "If we're going into the mouth of Hell, best to have your Guardian with you."

"I wouldn't call it 'Hell,'" I said.

We were seated side by side, rolling across Sutter, when Will poked the paper I was balancing on my lap.

"Now *that* is an impressive power," he said.

I told him how I had dropped by Lorraine's office and she had done a mental scan for the Du family, coming up with the address on the paper. Having a witch on staff: way better than Google Earth.

The bus lurched around a corner and Will sat up straighter, his knuckles going white as he gripped the seat in front of us.

"Wait a second," he said, swallowing heavily. "Are we headed toward Chinatown?"

"Yeah. This is right." I waved the paper. "I have an address."

A light sheen of sweat broke out above Will's upper lip. "Isn't this business something the angel boy should be doing? I mean, I wouldn't want to step on any toes or . . . wings or whatever."

"What's going on, Will?"

He clapped a hand to the back of his neck and blew out a sigh. "I hate Chinatown," he said under his breath.

I knitted my brows. "Nobody hates Chinatown."

Will and I stepped off the 30 Stockton, squinting into the rare shard of city sunlight. I started to walk—hands fisted, zigzagging with dire purpose through the throngs of tourists—when I realized that Will hadn't moved at all. It was as if his Diesel sneakers had melted to the ground.

Which, given the city, wasn't entirely impossible.

I beelined back to him, grabbing his arm. "Hey, come on. We don't have much time."

Will's eyes were focused over my head; his lips pressed together. I watched his Adam's apple bob as he swallowed slowly.

"What?" I looked over my shoulder at the two carved cement lion/dragon statues that guarded the mouth of Chinatown. "Those? They're not real. Promise. They don't come to life during a full moon or a *Keeping Up with the Kardashians* marathon or anything."

"It's not that," Will said, starting to shuffle with the tourist crowd. "It's"—and here he wagged his head from side to side, hazel eyes scanning, scrutinizing— "Mogwai."

I stopped dead and crossed my arms, feeling one eyebrow creep up. "Mogwai?"

We had crossed through the Chinatown gates and were flanked by a couple with thick Midwestern accents, who were pausing to photograph everything, and a guy power walking while listening to his iPod loud enough to hear every one of Steven Tyler's wailing screams.

"Yeah," Will said, voice lowered, "Mogwai."

"Look, Will, I know every single demon in the Underworld. And the majority in the upper world, too—wait. A Mogwai?"

Will nodded nervously, as if saying the word would bring one about.

"That's a Gremlin, Will."

"If you feed it after midnight, it is. And whose midnight, you know? They're Chinese, right? Is it when it's midnight in China or here? And, well, I'm British. Does my Mogwai become British—"

"It's a freaking Spielberg movie, Will!"

Will stopped, putting his hands on his hips. "And you don't think it was based on something real?"

I could feel my left eye begin to twitch. "Fine." I put out my hand, wiggling the tips of my fingers. "Give me your wallet."

"No. Why?"

"Give it to me."

Will reluctantly fished his wallet from his back pocket and handed it to me. I pulled out his credit cards and all of the cash—seventeen dollars, all in ones—from it; then I handed it back.

"Hey!"

I shoved his money in my pocket, clapped a hand on his shoulder. "See? Now I've got *all* of your money. There is absolutely no chance of you buying a Mogwai, unless you've got some magic beans in your pants. Now let's get going."

Three uphill blocks and six wrong turns later, I had lost my spunky, go-get-'em spirit and was bemoaning the city as a whole. I spotted the Chin Wa bakery and its glistening selection of glazed confections in the front window and began fishing Will's dollars out of my pocket.

"Pineapple bun?"

I pushed in the heavy glass doors of the bakery and was immediately hit with a blast of hot, pastry-scented air. I huffed it until my head felt light, and then traded some of my pilfered dollars for a bag of toasty pineapple buns and a Diet Coke. I offered the white bag—as it quickly became spotted with grease stains—to Will.

"Want one?" I asked, my mouth watering.

"Don't like pineapple."

"Don't worry," I said, fishing one out and taking a huge, satisfying bite. "There's no pineapple in them."

Will took a bun and shook his head. "I'll never understand you."

"So what does the map say?"

Will pulled the map from his back pocket, unfolded it, and smoothed it across his thigh. I leaned over, smattering the crudely drawn map with pineapple bun crumbs.

"Okay, from the looks of it"—I looked over both shoulders, feeling my ponytail bob against my cheek—"we should be here. It should be right there." I pointed to a squat building across the street that housed a Chinese/American/Japanese delicatessen, a handwritten sign in the window proudly touting, *Free Wi-Fi/bathroom for paying customers ONLY.*

"Wow," Will said, "they really cover all their bases."

I popped the last of my pineapple bun into my mouth, taking a half second to revel in the sugary, buttery, custardy bliss. I washed that all down with a Diet Coke so my thighs would remember that I was serious about slimming them and grabbed Will by the wrist. "Let's go."

Will stood up with me, and his palm slid up to meet

mine. Our fingers instinctually laced together. I sucked in a sharp, guilty breath and tried to convince myself that the speed up of my heart was due to our impending meeting, rather than the comfortable way our hands fit together; the ease of our conversation, even when we were walking in circles; the way the golden flecks in his hazel eyes exploded when he looked at me.

"Ready?"

Will stayed rooted, his thick lips pressing up into a slow smile. "You're blushing, love."

I clapped a palm to my cheek. "I'm flushed. It's warm out here. We should go."

We ran diagonally across the street, making our way through four lanes of tightly packed cars, some inching forward at glacial speeds; some parked and littered with tickets.

We stopped in front of the door and checked our address. "'Du,'" Will read from the fading painted sign. "This should be it. You ready?"

I stepped back and examined the plate glass windows, trying to find a shred of clarity among the years-old Chinese calendars, ads for cheesy videos, and poster-sized displays of Sanrio imports. I knew that behind the cheery posters, something awful could very easily lie inside.

I squeezed Will's hand. "Do it."

A series of bells tinkled as we pushed open the door. My heart clunked painfully and I felt the horror, felt my jaw hanging open, felt my lips go slack. This wasn't what I expected.

It was much, much worse.

"Will—"

"I don't know what to do, either, love. Is this . . . Are you sure this is the right place?"

I unfurled the paper, having swiped it after covering it in crumbs. "Number 32." I looked around. "This has to be it."

Du—the Chinese/American/Japanese restaurant—was, apparently, where wide-eyed Japanese anime went to mate. Life-sized schoolgirls, with melon-sized boobs pressed up to their chins, were painted in all manner of fighting poses wielding swords, along with their pigtails and knee socks. The blue Formica tabletops were covered in figurines of the same, and seated around those tables were wide-eyed, big-boobed anime knockoff people and their sailor boy counterparts.

"Are they dead?" Will whispered out of the side of his mouth.

"Hello! May I help you?"

The woman behind the counter had waist-length black hair pinched into a glossy ponytail. Her straight-angle bangs met thin eyebrows over eyes that were a dazzling, unnatural lavender; bits of brown swirled behind the colored lenses.

Her smile was wide and welcoming, and she was dressed like a 1950s diner waitress—if '50s diner waitresses doubled as schoolgirl-style sex kittens. Will was staring and I gave him a shove.

"Um, right, then. We're looking for . . ." Will's eyes cut to me, and I gave him a small nod—the universal sign for "don't just gape at the manga cover girl, talk!"

"It was suggested that we, uh . . ."

"We are looking for Xian Lee."

The girl behind the counter stiffened, causing her ponytail to sway with the sharp movement. "Why?"

"Do you know him?"

"Why do you want to know?"

I leaned forward so that I was a hairsbreadth from the anime girl. "I'm from the Underworld."

Anime girl blinked at me, and it was hard to discern which one of us was crazier.

"Do you know Dixon Andrade? Vlad LaShay?"

Her eyes widened and she stiffened almost imperceptibly, but just enough to make her long, thick ponytail bob again.

"What do you want?"

I licked my lips. "I work at the Underworld Detection Agency. Right now, my friends are dying, and it's only going to get worse for them—and maybe for you—if you don't help us."

The girl stepped back. Her shoulders slumped a bit with the movement. She held my eye and studied me for a full minute before calling out something in Chinese that I vaguely feared was "Anime friends, eviscerate the nonbelievers." But, to my relief, an older man came from the hallway. His slippered feet shuffled against the industrial tile. He waved us in and we followed through the kitchen, toward a ratty screen door. The wood was tarry with decades of cooking fat; the rusty hinges barely keeping the door on.

The old man pushed through and so did I; Will hung back in the dank kitchen, letting the screen door work its slow snap shut.

"Come on," I hissed to Will.

Will shook his head slowly, silently mouthing the word "Mogwai."

I opened the door again and yanked him by his shirtsleeve. We caught up to the old man, who gestured toward a door, then turned around and walked away.

"What are we supposed to do here?" I asked.

"There's a door, I'm guessing we open it."

Will looked at me, rubbing his jaw with his palm. "Vlad just handed you this information, didn't he?"

I looked around the dim alley, heard the *plink!* of water dripping off one of the fire escapes into a greasy pool on the ground. "Yes."

"How do you know he's not leading us into a trap?"

I stopped, cement filling my body. "I don't."

Will's eyes were wide, focused. "So what should we do?"

I swallowed hard. "We trust him."

I sucked in a slightly nervous breath—not due to Mogwai fear, by the way—and pushed open the door. The room was large and empty, with hardwood floors. When I blinked, a woman was standing in front of me. She looked nearly identical to the anime girl, save the sexy-waitress costume and the surrounding of big-eyed followers. Even though the room was dim, I could see that her hair was black, waist length and stick straight. Her eyes narrowed and menacing.

I was about to offer a hand—a shiny, friendly "I'm Sophie Lawson, here to save the Underworld" hand—when I felt hands around my throat. Suddenly I was vaulting backward, crushed against Will, who was crushed against the wall. I kicked out and landed a blow to the woman's gut; she doubled over and let me go. I gasped, drinking in as much air as I could while Will rushed her. He struck and she blocked; he rushed and she ducked. There was a spinning, dizzying sequence of Will-then-her and her-then-Will; and suddenly Will was pinned to the floor. The only sound in the room was the ominous cock of a gun—its barrel lined up with Will's nose.

"What do you want?" the woman asked. She had one knee on Will's chest, a half inch from his windpipe. Her other foot was planted firmly on the ground. In her hand she held a heavy black gun, which she wielded as though it were a tube of lipstick.

I pressed myself against the wall, feeling my shoulder blades against the cold, hard steel of the door. I wanted to do something, to rush her, to take her down in a move that would make Angelina Jolie or Jackie Chan proud. Instead, all I could do was think how badly I needed to pee, and that if I were to make a sound, that lady would squeeze the trigger and Will would be dead.

"What do you want?"

"We come in peace!" I blurted it out before I thought about it. Both Will and the woman about to blow his brains out turned and stared at me.

"She's got a gun, love, not an alien life-form," Will said, sounding way too calm for imminent doom.

I dug in my pocket and the woman swung the gun on me. "Hands up!"

I threw my hands straight up—and to be honest, a little bit of my lunch—while Will knocked the stunned gun girl off him, did some sort of barrel roll, and pinned her. He yanked the gun out of her hand and shoved it in his back waistband.

"Let's none of us try to kill each other for about thirty seconds, okay?"

The woman writhed underneath Will, but she slowly stilled.

"What do you want?" she spat.

I pulled the ziplock bag of bullets out of my pocket and rushed over, shaking it in front of her. "We're looking for the person who made these."

Her eyes sliced down to the bag and then held mine. "You'll have to let me up. I can't get a look at them."

Will looked at me and then at her. "How do I know you're not going to try to kill us again?"

"You have the gun. How do I know you're not going to try to kill me?"

Will handed me the gun. "Go put this up." And then, to her, "I'm going to let you up now. We just want some answers. No trouble."

"Are you Xian?" I asked.

"No." The woman rose up on her elbows. "You already met Xian, out there. I'm her sister, Feng. Why do you want to know about these bullets?"

"Do you recognize them?" I pushed the bag into Feng's hand.

"Maybe."

I sighed. "Look, we're not cops. We're not after you or looking to cause any trouble. Someone shot at me with these bullets. They shot at me and my friends."

"So?"

I took the bag back and pushed one of the bullets out. "So these are silver bullets. Silver bullets are only used to kill very specific things."

Feng said nothing, but everything was held in her stare.

"They kill werewolves," I said.

Feng's eyebrows rose. "Who did you say you were, again?"

Will helped Feng up.

"I'm Sophie, and this is Will. We've . . . we've been

having some problems, and we need to know where someone would get bullets like these."

Feng cocked her head, seemingly not understanding. "Why did you come here? To me?"

I glanced around the dismal cave of a workshop and determined that the likelihood of Feng placing an ad in the *Guardian* or on public-access television was probably a long shot.

"Dixon Andrade." It wasn't a complete lie.

Feng shook her head. "Dixon, huh?" But she seemed pacified and almost smiled. "Okay. So what do you want?"

"Do you know where to get the bullets?"

Feng sat down, kicked her booted feet up, and popped a handful of nuts into her mouth. "I know who makes them."

I felt my eyebrows rise. "You do?"

Feng smiled. "Yeah. Me." She opened the toolbox on the table and plucked out a silver bullet and set it on the table next to the one I brought in. She examined mine from all sides; then sat back, satisfied. "I made this one in the spring."

"How do you know?"

"Is it some sort of Underworldy voodoo thing?" Will wanted to know.

Feng looked confused, then spun the bullet. A tiny Chinese symbol was carved on the blunt end. "All of our bullets are marked with a seasonal sign."

"That's a lovely sentiment for an instrument of death," Will said, smiling nervously.

"*Our* bullets?" I asked.

"It's kind of a family business."

I felt like someone had let all the air out of the room.

Feng's cheery smile swirled in front of my eyes. Will slid a chair underneath me, just as my legs went wobbly.

"You're werewolf hunters?" I asked breathlessly.

Feng beamed with something that looked shockingly like pride.

"There's barely a dog left in the city, thanks to my family." Feng gestured to the large, painted family crest behind her. The surname *Du* was intertwined with the American spelling, a stylized painting of a wounded werewolf dying behind the heavy black print.

On a daily basis the Underworld Detection Agency processed at least a dozen vampires coming or going, a good handful of zombies (more, lately), plus a smattering of all other matter of demon. But werewolves were rare.

Now I knew why.

"My family has been here for over a hundred years. We were sent to America—San Francisco, particularly—to deal with hordes of dogs out here."

"Werewolves," I said, meaning to correct her; but Feng just nodded, as if I was asking just to make sure.

"We've been tracking and hunting for thousands of years."

"And the bullets?"

"They're specific to what we do." Feng tapped the bullet. "The silver cuts through the fur and pierces the flesh—the only thing that will. Our bullets explode inside and launch an elephant-sized amount of tranquilizing poison. The dog just lies there until they bleed out."

I was horrified, completely forgetting to hide it, until Will came up behind me and began massaging my clenched shoulders. He nuzzled my hair; his lips brushing my ear.

"Stay calm," he whispered. And then, to Feng, "She's just a bit jumpy, this one. Doesn't like anything with fur. Had to toss her UGG boots in the rubbish bin. That was a terrible Christmas, wasn't it, love?"

"So, do you have a werewolf problem?" Feng wanted to know.

"No, actually it was just a curiosity."

I swallowed down the bile that lodged in the back of my throat. "Do you sell the bullets?"

"Yeah. Not too often, though. Occasionally people get worked up and start buying if there are dog sightings. Or we get an onslaught of buyers anytime a werewolf movie or *Twilight* comes out. Man"—Feng shook her head—"those Team Edward girls are ruthless."

"Can you tell us who bought this bullet?"

Feng's lips turned down. "Look, I'm really not in the business of advertising my client list."

"There's a whole list?" My voice was a hoarse whisper, betraying my discomfort.

"So, do you want to buy or what?"

"Yes. Yes, of course we do." Will's voice sounded a million miles away as my head felt like it was stuffed with cotton.

I squinted in the sunlight when we left Feng's lair. Will clutched a paper bag full of werewolf-killing bullets; I stumbled with a numbness which started in my feet and went up to every follicle on my head.

"They're werewolf hunters, Will."

He took my hand and pulled me across the street. "I know that, love."

"Do you think they had something to do with Sampson?" I asked.

"One crisis at a time." Will hailed a cab and stuffed me in it, sliding in behind me.

I let out something halfway between a chuckle and a gasp. "One crisis at a time."

"And we aren't even a step closer to solving this one."

"Well, actually . . ." I unbuttoned my sweater and slid out the rubber-banded, handwritten wad of receipts that I filched from Feng's countertop while she showed Will her selection of bullets.

Will stiffened; surprise registering all over his body. "You stole them?"

"I don't suppose I could get away with saying I'm borrowing them, huh? Besides, the woman choked me. She owed us something."

Will sat back, clearly looking pleased. "Looks like you've got a little bit of street cred, after all, love."

I felt myself grin. *Sophie Lawson, True-Life Badass*.

"I just can't believe you stole something from a woman who decorates with deadly weapons and tracks demons for a living.

My knees shook a little bit. *Sophie Lawson: Badass, as Long as She Doesn't Think About It.*

Chapter Seventeen

I let myself into my apartment and was pleasantly surprised to find the only inhabitant was ChaCha, who did berserk circles around my ankles. She finally settled into a bowl of Alpo and I shrugged out of my clothes, took a hot shower, and oozed into some comfortable clothes. I popped a Lean Cuisine into the microwave and watched it spin, trying to keep my mind off Bettina, Kale, who had just been let out of the hospital, and what was going on in the Underworld.

I must have fallen asleep somewhere between my knockoff spicy chicken enchiladas and an *Extreme Couponing* marathon, because suddenly I was being shaken awake. I scrunched my eyes shut, and from far away I heard Nina's assertive voice.

"Fine. If you're going to play sleep, things are going to get rough."

I felt fingers on the collar of my sweatshirt inching slowly toward the naked skin of my neck.

"Wake up, Sophie. . . ."

I thought that if I could just keep my eyes closed a

little longer, then it would be a new day and this would all have been some terrible dream.

"I warned you. . . ."

Nina plunged both hands down the neck of my sweatshirt, pressing her palms and icy fingers against my once-warm skin. I jumped and howled and landed with a thud between the couch and the coffee table.

I glared at Nina, and she grinned at me, her fingers raised like six-shooters. She blew each pointed index finger and tucked them into imaginary holsters. "I warned you."

I rolled my eyes and kicked the plastic enchilada tray onto the floor; ChaCha pounced on it with gusto. Nina beelined for her bedroom, a tiny tornado of slick black hair and flying couture. "We don't have much time."

"For what?" I helped myself to a marshmallow pinwheel. I had eaten a Lean Cuisine, so I deserved it. I took two.

Nina had done a marathon makeover in eight seconds. She had slipped into a body-hugging black dress and slid a lacy black skirt on over it. Glovelets, fishnet tights, and an Art Deco brooch weaved into her hair finished her look.

"You look amazing!" I complimented, slightly jealous that the same outfit would make me look like a ballerina hooker.

Nina blew out her "I can't eat you, but I could smack you" sigh, and I jumped back a quarter inch. She rubbed her forehead. "Did you forget about tonight already?"

I fished in the marshmallow pinwheel bag. "Forget what?"

"Our date!"

I chewed, relishing the feel of oozing chocolate as it melted over my teeth. "We have a date?"

"We have dates. Plural. Didn't you get my message?"

I crossed my arms and jutted out one hip. "Were you sending me telepathic messages again? I told you that doesn't work."

"I wrote it down here." Nina picked up the notepad we kept by the phone and waved it at me. "And I left a message on your cell phone and I Facebooked you. I would have sent a carrier pigeon, but I ran out of time."

"And you're scared of birds."

"I'm not scared. I just find them winged and disgusting. Apparently"—Nina snatched the last pinwheel out of my hand—"I should have written it in chocolate and marshmallow. Get ready. Harley will be here in twenty minutes."

I took the notepad and read: *S, We're going out tonight. Yes, you are. Look cute, six o'clock, Neens.*

"I can't go out tonight. I'm grieving."

"Over your roots or the death of elastic?" Nina snapped my pajama bottoms for effect.

I crossed my arms, fighting off a growl, and I shook my head. "This whole Underworld violence thing. Aren't you worried?"

Nina bared her fangs. "Not really. Besides, nothing more you can do but clear your head. Start with a tabula rasa tomorrow."

I frowned. "It's never good when you speak Latin."

"Come out tonight. If you stay here, you're just going to obsess and cry and mope, and your pity quota is totally up. Clear your head and get a free dinner. Wear that black dress from Wasteland."

I groaned. "Why do I have to look cute for your date? I'm going to be like a third wheel. I don't want to be a third wheel."

Nina brushed past me, stomping into my bedroom. "You're not going to be a third wheel."

She was standing in front of my open closet, hands on hips, her fangs working her lower lip as she scrutinized my wardrobe. "Don't you have anything that's not from the Talbots 'Administrative Assistant Collection'?"

I angled myself between Nina and my offensive wardrobe. "Why?"

"Because."

I fought to hold Nina's gaze, but her eyes flitted all around me.

"Do I have a date tonight, too?"

Nina nodded. "And you don't even have to thank me."

I smiled sweetly. "Don't worry, I won't."

Nina tossed me a silky green dress that lived at the back of my closet. "Put this on and wear your hair up."

I paused. "Am I going out with one of Harley's writer friends?"

Again Nina avoided my eyes. "Not exactly. But he's seriously in the business. I'm borrowing your chandelier earrings, okay?"

"In the business?"

Nina dangled the earrings. "Okay?"

I nodded.

"Now get dressed. We've got"—she checked her watch—"fifteen minutes."

I slid into my green dress. Well, slid with a back-and-forth combination of groaning and yanking—and used a bath towel to dab the new round of sweat under my arms. I'm neither a big fan of double dates or Spanx, so I wasn't about to spend extra time on glossy lips or smoky eyes (which made me look like a prizefighter who lost, anyway). Instead, I did an understated wash of pressed powder, mascara, and ChapStick. When the doorbell rang, I met Nina in the living room, where she gave me an appraising once-over.

"You'll love Roland, I promise," she whispered.

"Roland?" I hissed back. "As in Harley's agent, Roland?"

"I know he's not much to look at, but give him a chance. Harley says he's really a great guy and super-loyal to Harley."

"Great," I groaned, crossing my arms. "You get the hot writer and I get Old Yeller."

Nina pasted on a gorgeous grin and I tried to turn my scowl into something remotely welcoming when Nina opened the door.

"You look amazing." Harley's voice, slow and rich, floated through the open door.

I craned my neck to see over Nina's shoulder and caught Roland's eye, an unremarkable brown. He smiled at me; then dug into his pocket and pulled out his trusty, yellowed handkerchief. wiping up the beads of sweat that popped up on his balding forehead.

Nina was going to owe me big-time for this one.

"Roland Townsend," he said to me, offering his surprisingly delicate hand. I took it, and he pumped my arm. "Good to meet you."

I was about to remind the moist little man that we had met before; but when I opened my mouth, Nina shot me the kind of narrow-eyed, eyebrows-down look that reminded me that behind her MAC Pure Pink pucker was a set of fangs.

"Nice to meet you, too," I said.

Harley slapped his hands together. "Shall we go? We've got an early reservation at Ruth's Chris."

"The steak house?" I said, eyebrows up.

Roland rubbed his bulbous belly proudly. "I pulled some strings to get us a last-minute reservation."

"Lovely," I said, shooting Nina a glance that, I hope, said there would be no filet mignon shoved in my purse tonight.

"That sounds wonderful," Nina purred, completely avoiding my gaze.

Harley reached out for Nina's hand, and hers delicately slipped into his. His eyes darkened. "Oh, sweetie. Your hands are as cold as ice."

Nina flashed me a frantic look and I dipped back into the apartment, yanking out two coats. "Our heat has been on the fritz lately," I said, handing Nina a coat. "The place is an ice box."

Harley and Nina shared nauseating sweetheart looks as he helped her slip into her coat.

"Let me help you with that," Roland said, taking his cue from Harley.

"I really think I can—"

But Roland's girlish hands were on the neck of my coat, yanking it up to my earlobes.

I gritted my teeth. "Thanks so much."

"Oh, what's this?"

Will was in the doorway of his apartment, door flung wide open displaying his impressive lawn furniture couture. He was shirtless, shoeless, and balancing a bowl of what looked like Cocoa Pebbles in one hand and a spoon in the other.

Ruth's Chris be damned—I would kill for those Cocoa Pebbles right now.

Nina wound her arm into Harley's and batted her big eyes as she said, "Will, you remember Harley Cavanaugh, the writer, and Roland Townsend . . ."

"Agent," Roland said. Then he offered his hand to Will, a business card tucked expertly into his palm. Will shook tentatively, retrieving the business card with his spoon hand. He glanced at it. "And there it is right there. 'Roland Townsend, Agent.'" Will looked up at me with a Cocoa Pebbled grin while I implored him—silently— to tell me that Roland was a fallen angel who needed immediate pummeling.

"Well, you kids have a nice time tonight," he said, shoving a heaping spoonful of cereal into his mouth.

"Thanks," I said, trying to avoid gaping at Will's chiseled chest while dodging the beads of sweat Roland mopped up with his yellowing handkerchief. "We were just leaving."

I stomped down the hall, pausing only when I heard Roland's raspy breath as his stumpy little legs worked to keep up.

The drive to Ruth's Chris was mercifully silent, or it would have been, if the gods of dating hadn't forsaken me. As we inched through the Friday-night traffic, I had to hear about Roland's meteoric rise to literary agent superstardom—from his humble beginnings floundering and ultimately failing out of junior college in Hollis, Queens, to the brilliant business opportunity that brought him and Harley together. Namely, the fifteen-year high-school reunion of the Hudson High Cougars.

As the maître d' led us to our table, I tried to get Nina's attention, but she was too lovestruck to pay any attention to me. She floated gracefully into the chair that Harley pulled out for her, and Roland landed with a wheezing thud in the chair the maître d' had pulled out for me. I sat down and inched as close to Nina as I could.

"This is a disaster," I hissed to Nina as Roland handed the tuxedoed maître d' a folded-up bill.

"So, Sophie," Roland started, his tongue darting over his bottom lip in a way that made me think of salting slugs. "What makes Sophie Lawson tick?"

I grabbed Nina's hand under the table and dug my nails into her palm; then I cursed myself when I remembered that vampires can't feel pain. She took a second away from batting her eyelashes at Harley to bat her eyelashes at me.

"Oh, Sophie likes lots of things," Nina piped in. "Sometimes she just gets shy." Nina dug a finger into my ribs and commanded me to "be polite."

I scanned the menu for any item that might come on a wooden stake.

"I hope you're hungry, honey bear," Harley said with a lovesick drawl that brought bile to my throat.

"I haven't eaten a thing all day," Nina said truthfully. "I called to see if you wanted to have lunch, but you didn't answer."

Harley and Roland exchanged a fleeting look, which anyone not counting the minutes would have missed.

"We were doing a round of interviews," Roland said. He snaked his clammy hand around my arm, thumping his chair hard on the floor as he bounced it closer. "It would have been nice to meet you a little earlier."

"We're ready to order," I said to a passing waiter.

Roland waggled his bushy brows while I untangled my arm from his. "This one seems to want to get out of here as soon as possible," he said with an obnoxious grin.

Oh, if you only knew.

We had just ordered our dinner—another raw-meat extravaganza for Nina, a petite filet for me (watching my weight, remember?)—when I dragged Nina to the bathroom.

"Are you having fun?" Nina asked, obviously oblivious to the three shades of purple I turned after a half hour of gritting my teeth.

"So much. Like Pap smear fun."

Nina rolled her eyes and glanced in the mirror—her eyes steady on her lack of reflection while she glossed up her pout. "Give him a chance."

"I have given him a chance."

"Harley says that Roland just gets nervous, but once he's over that, he's really a great guy."

"I've given him a chance and now I'm climbing out the bathroom window."

I spun on my heel and Nina grabbed my wrist, her cold fingers nearly cuting off my circulation. Her eyes were wide and pleading, and her newly glossed frown was real.

"Please, Sophie. I really, really like Harley, and I think things could go somewhere for us. I've never met a man who I've got so much in common with."

I cocked an eyebrow.

"I mean, we're both Tauruses. We both like to dance. We're both writers."

"And one of you is alive, and the other one is—"

I clamped my mouth shut as the bathroom door swung open and a centerfold blonde walked in, teetering on enormous heels and balancing an enormous chest. She glanced down at Nina's hand on my wrist, then quickly up at the mirror. I saw the confusion register in her eyes, and Nina and I both stiffened until the blonde teetered past us and locked herself in a stall.

"Just be nice until dinner is over, and then I'll never ask you to do anything for me again. I swear."

Nina looked earnest, but the last "something" I did for her was still lurking on our living-room couch.

"Come on. For me? For true love? I'll even eat anyone you want."

"Fine."

Dinner passed uneventfully; and although I prayed for everyone to pass up dessert, Roland ordered a conglomeration of everything on the menu, plus a cup of tea for the "little lady."

It's times like these that I wished I had taken up with Steve, the blue cheese–smelling troll.

"That was torturous," I said to Nina as I trudged through the apartment vestibule after our date finally ended.

Nina didn't answer; she just continued her love-swept twirl and her tonally challenged rendition of "Up Where We Belong."

Chapter Eighteen

My blaring cell phone woke me from a deep sleep, but I managed to catch it on the second ring, mashing it to my ear and upsetting ChaCha.

"Sophie Lawson," I answered.

"Lawson, I need you." Alex's voice was tense on the other end of the line.

Sophie Lawson: Hot Commodity Once Again.

A delicious chill zapped down my spine and I sat up straight, glancing at the red glowing numbers on my alarm clock. It was three o'clock and Alex needed me. My whole body went on high alert; everything jumping to attention. Maybe this night was looking up, after all.

"Are you here? Where are you?"

"Do you have a pen?"

I fumbled in my desk drawer—my pen poised over the back of a plea to save the whales, or to avoid circuses or something.

"Take down this address."

The little chill in my spine dropped below my belly button and worked itself into a full-on heat.

An address? Alex didn't have a home address, so was this . . .

"It's a crime scene."

Everything dropped inside me. "Of course it is."

"Romero called me. He said you and he had a little meeting on the dock a few days ago."

"How come you haven't answered any of my calls? Things are exploding—"

"Look, Lawson, I don't have much time, and I can't be on the phone. Romero called this in and I need you to look into it."

I felt a lump forming in my throat, felt my eyes start to mist. "I need you."

"I know you can handle it. I won't be away forever. I need you to get down to the Paradise Hotel, 101 Folsom Street."

I bit my lip. "I don't have a car."

I could almost see Alex's eyebrow cocking. "What happened to your car now?"

I thought of my beat-up car, and the scrawling across the front windshield. "Nothing. I'll just grab a cab."

There was a quick knock on my door. When I opened it, Will was standing there, a big goofy grin on his face. His car keys were pinched between forefinger and thumb.

"Ready?"

"I can't talk now, Will. I've got to get to—"

"One-oh-one Folsom."

I blinked. "Were you listening in on my phone call?"

Will snorted. "Like I don't have better things to do. Your angel boy told me I'd better help you out with this one."

I gaped at Will. "I can handle a lot of things, Will, but you and Alex working together?"

Will just shrugged and ushered me toward the stairs.

The Paradise Hotel was a little slice of 1970s Key West, smack-dab in the left ventricle of the Fillmore District. Its thumbprint-sized pool was lagoon blue and surrounded by brightly colored homages to tropical birds and potted banana trees, whose enormous leaves were fraying in the cold ocean air. In its heyday the whole building was painted a cheery yellow and each door to Paradise a pale, tranquil turquoise. Now the yellow paint had hardened into something sallow and showed its age as it warped and peeled around what remained of the turquoise door frames. Some of the numbers were missing on the doors; the once-shiny doorknobs were grubby with black fingerprints and scratches from years of abuse, neglect, and drunken lock picking.

I saw a trio of uniformed officers staring blankly at a broken pot—its banana tree was severed on the concrete, soil scattered all around. Officer Romero turned finally and beckoned me over.

"Officer Romero," I said.

"Hey, thanks for coming, Sophie. I called Alex, but—"

I nodded. "He's on a stakeout."

"Right." Romero looked past me. "And you must be the private investigator?"

Will absolutely beamed. "That I am."

"So what's this all about?" I wanted to know.

"That's what I'm hoping you can tell me."

Officer Romero led Will and me to room 34, where a naked bulb flickered and buzzed outside.

"We got a call about forty minutes ago." He jutted his chin toward the lady with the dog. She was listening to the officer in front of her; her wrinkled lips set in a hard, thin line. "She called in. Said there was a ruckus with her new tenant. Said it sounded like someone was being murdered out here."

I shivered, though the early-morning air was unusually warm. "And?"

"And that's it. She looked out her window and saw two people struggling. Said she couldn't be sure it was her new tenant, but from the size of her"—Officer Romero's eyes flashed—"it looked about right. The lady called the cops, and the first car was on the scene in less than three minutes."

I nodded, impressed.

"And there was nothing here."

"Nothing?"

Romero nodded his head. "Not a thing."

"So what made you call Alex?"

Romero dug into his pocket and produced a business card wrapped in a plastic Baggie. I examined it under the flickering light.

"It's yours."

I nodded and Officer Romero went on. "It didn't have a phone number, so I called Alex. He said that your firm was covering this case. I didn't know that the FBI had an underworld division out here."

I opened my mouth and then closed it again, dumbly, as Officer Romero prattled on. "So mobsters, huh? I thought that was, you know, purely a Jersey, *Sopranos* thing."

"Oh. Underworld. Like the mob. Yes"—I straightened—"yes, we'd appreciate it if you kept it quiet."

Romero nodded, impressed. "Absolutely. We'll clear out. You do what you need to do."

Once Officer Romero stepped away, Will crossed his arms and grinned at me. "We're detectives now. Underworld detectives."

I rolled my eyes and speed dialed Alex, willing him to answer the phone.

"Good, Lawson, I've been waiting for you to call."

"What is this all about, Alex? And why can you miraculously talk all of a sudden?"

I heard him suck in a deep, slow breath. "I'm on a dinner break. Do you want my help with this or not?"

I looked at Will, then looked at the broken plant and the flickering light. "Sure. Why did you think this was about us?"

"Because the woman staying in that room was Bettina Jacova."

I paused. "Oh. But she didn't check out?"

"No. The only thing the guys could find was that overturned pot."

I balanced the phone on my shoulder. "So everything is gone, there's no evidence. Why did you need me here?"

"The officers said they couldn't *see* anything."

I nodded, finally understanding. "And you want me to make sure you're not missing something."

"Bingo."

I looked over Will's shoulder, surveying the "blue

lagoon," the aged patio furniture, and banana trees. "I don't see anything right off."

"Will's there with you?"

"Yeah."

"Take a walk around the property. Just take a look around. If there's nothing there, there's nothing there. If there is, maybe it'll help you get down to the bottom of all this."

I felt a warmth at the base of my spine. "Thanks, Alex."

"I've got to get back to work. 'Night, Lawson."

I hung up the phone, and Will and I strolled the property for a minute. We paused at the blue lagoon–colored pool.

Will put his hands on his hips. "What do you think?" he asked.

I shrugged. "I don't see . . ."

I stopped, my eyes catching a trail of scattered soil leading to matted grass. There were footprints pressed into the dirt, and I felt my throat tighten as I bent down to examine the two distinct sets of prints there. "Footprints."

Will crouched down with me and shrugged. "Doesn't look like anything more than a scuffle, though."

I wish I didn't see anything else.

"There's blood," I said, feeling a lump form in my throat. "Lots of blood."

Will cocked his head; his eyebrows mashed together. "I don't—"

"It's not human. It's demon."

Will seemed unfazed, until I straightened up, crossed my arms in front of my chest and held my elbows tightly, trying to ward off the shudder which I knew was coming.

"It's Bettina's. There are some drops here," I said, not willing to point.

I knew the official word was blood "spatter," and that was easy to say when the blood was anonymous, left at the crime scene from a victim I felt sorry for but never knew. This was the blood of someone I knew, talked to, cared for. The realization made me queasy.

"Can we just get out of here?"

Will touched me gently at the small of my back. "We still have no idea what happened, love. If it's just a bit of spatter—"

I sucked a gulp of air and blinked away tears. "See where the grass is all matted there?"

Will nodded.

"There's more blood."

Will looked toward where I was pointing and then shook his head. "Well, if the blood is covered by some magical shield, then that must mean our guy is a demon or something, right?" His voice was almost hopeful.

I took his hand and we both sank down to a squat. "Look." I pointed again, and the world went deathly still. The light from the naked bulb stopped flickering; the banana trees stopped their gentle flap in the breeze; the city seemed to hold its breath.

"Can you see that?"

Will cocked his head the way I showed him; and as his eyes started to register, to see what I was seeing, his mouth went slack.

"Is that—is that it?"

Demon's blood isn't wildly colored or Hollywood glittery. It's as angrily red as our blood, and thick and viscous, but there is an almost blue-black sheen to it, which seems not to register to human eyes.

Unless, of course, you're looking for it.

Will paled and I watched his Adam's apple bob as he swallowed hard.

Bettina's blood was spattered in the plant soil, then smeared where there had been a definite struggle along the walk. It looked as though she had struggled for about four feet before the grass was matted when she was pressed into it. Her blood seeped through the broken blades of grass, pooling at the edge of the walk.

"Tell me demons have an inordinate amount of blood and we're looking at a skinned knee here."

I shook my head, unable to form the words. Will twisted toward me, his hazel eyes miles deep. "You know with this much blood loss, there isn't a lot of hope that this bird—"

"Bettina. Her name is Bettina."

"That Bettina could have survived."

My fingertips went cold. My lips went numb. I should have been crying, but my eyes were tired. I felt like I had already done that. I looked somberly at the crushed grass, the pooled blood.

"We have to find out who did this. We have to find him and kill him."

Will stepped back, his eyes wide. I could tell he was considering whether to placate me ("We will, love") or to correct me ("An eye for an eye is not justice, love"). But all he did was take my ice-cold hands in his, straighten us both to our feet, and gather me to his chest. I swallowed against the knot in my throat.

"Is that all?" Will asked, raking his fingers through my hair.

I wanted to melt into his palm.

Chapter Nineteen

I heard her before I saw her. The unmistakable pounding of Jimmy Choo stilettos backed by 102 pounds of pissed-off vampire was thundering up the three flights of stairs toward the apartment. The front door flew open; and although I knew it was coming, I jumped, my skin immediately feeling too tight for my body.

"Nina?" I asked.

If the flames of Hell were to live in a woman, Nina would be that woman. Her coal black eyes had a glossy, smoky sheen to them; her lips were pursed tightly, the corners pulling down, and her hands were clutching what remained of a photocopy of a typed business letter.

"Can you believe this?" She shook the letter over her head. "I'm incensed. I'm going to file a UDA-V injunction, then suck the crap out of Lilia Hagen Literary Management."

"Something wrong, hon?" I asked, trying on sweetness and light.

Nina's nostrils flared. "Is something wrong? Yes,

Sophie, something is *very* wrong. Listen to this." Nina whipped the letter back in front of her; electricity shot through the room. "'Dear Author.'" She slapped the paper against her thigh. "Can you believe that? 'Dear Author'? Don't they know who I am?"

I knew better than to answer one of Nina's rhetorical questions (and yes, I found out the hard, pointy-toothed way), so I knitted my brows and worked up the best indignant/disgusted look I could muster. "I can't believe that!"

"Oh," Nina spat, "it gets better. 'Thank you for your manuscript submission. However, I didn't feel compelled enough to keep turning the pages.'"

Nina gaped at me, eyes glittering, saliva at the corners of her mouth. "I am going to compel that woman to kiss my cold, dead ass!"

I pried the letter from Nina's hand before she threw herself on the couch in a diva move that would make Streisand envious. "Well, look, Neens. She says that another agent might feel different and she wishes you the best of luck. That's nice, right?"

"Nice? *Nice?* I practically opened a vein for that woman and she *thinks* another agent *might* feel different?"

"With all due respect you don't"—I pointed to my wrist, then thought better of it—"You know what? You're right. Who is this Lilia Hagen, anyway? What does she know?" I went to tear the offending missive down the middle, but Nina sprang up, eyes wide, cold fingers snatching the letter from mine.

"Lilia Hagen is a legend! She's a genius. If she doesn't think I have talent, then maybe it's over for me." Nina sank to her knees on the high-pile carpet. "Maybe I'm just no good!" I watched my best friend slump over and draw her knees to her chest, cradling her legs and whimpering. ChaCha trotted over and gave her a precursory sniff, then went on to her dog bowl.

"Wanna get a bite?"

Nina rolled over and blinked up at me, her lips spliting into a smile. "Oh, Soph. You always know the right thing to say. I'll drive."

It didn't take us too long to find a restaurant in North Beach that served homemade gnocchi and had a cache of blood donor waiters—mainly because there is only one restaurant in North Beach with homemade gnocchi and blood donor waiters. I noshed my way through the bread basket while Nina scanned the waiters passing by, deciding whom to order. She frowned, pulling on her bottom lip.

"I can't decide what I want," she groaned as a particularly anemic-looking blond strode by. "Why didn't you tell me this was going to be so hard?"

"Ordering lunch? You usually go for that meaty guy, Toby."

"Not eating lunch! And yes, Toby sounds good. I mean with my career!"

"At UDA?"

Nina's eyes rolled back like slot machines. "No! My writing career!"

"Oh?" I popped another piece of bread in my mouth. "That."

I learned early on to keep my nose out of Nina's extracurricular activities—except for the one time she decided she had a real future in toddler beauty pageant coaching. Then I had to bail her out of jail and explain why a grown woman trolling elementary schools for "Auntie Nina's Perfect Princesses" was a very bad idea.

I was pushing around the remaining bites of spaghetti and meatballs, and Nina was polishing off what remained of a bag of Toby, when I put down my fork and took a deep breath. Nina cocked an eyebrow, knitted her hands, and rested her chin.

"I heard you coming in awfully early this morning." She grinned, her fangs tinted a healthy pink. "Anything you want to tell me?"

It had been close to dawn when Will and I had returned from Bettina's hotel. Though I know Nina doesn't sleep, her door was closed and all the lights were out, so I decided against disturbing her—especially since what I needed to tell her was so disturbing to me.

"Alex called."

Nina's ears perked. "Ooh, I bet he heard about all this time you're spending with Will. I bet he's jealous."

"He wanted Will and me to go to a hotel."

"Jealous and kinky!"

"Nina, I went to a hotel where Bettina checked in. She wasn't there. It was a crime scene."

Nina stopped. "What do you mean?"

"Bettina . . ." I gulped. "Her body wasn't there. Oh, Nina, it was horrible. There was blood everywhere."

"What happened?"

I swung my head, pushing my plate away. "It looked like she had been attacked. It looked like someone pushed her into the ground, and there was blood everywhere. She couldn't have survived it, Neens. There was no way. The person who attacked her must have come back. He must have come back, and now she's dead."

Nina looked away; her bottom lashes glistened. "This is real, isn't it?"

I swallowed hard. "It's real, and it's not going away."

Nina pressed her keys across the table toward me. "Will you take the car home?"

I reached out and squeezed her marble-cold hand. "I can drive you home, Neens."

She gathered her purse and started to scooch out of the booth. "I need to go see Harley right now."

I flopped on the couch, blowing out a miserable sigh.

ChaCha, my ever-faithful companion, was snuggled up in her dog bed. She cracked one dark eye open to witness my misery; then flopped around and went back to snoring. I tried to soothe my jangled nerves with a tall glass of ice water and something on KQED—okay, it was a bottle of Yoo-hoo recovered from the back of the fridge and a *Real World* marathon—but I was still filled with the overwhelming sense of dread. I had sat and watched, frozen, as Nina's black hair swished across her back when she walked out of the restaurant to go find Harley—a man who wrote off demons for a living.

In print.

And it made him millions.

My breath caught in my throat and I hiccupped chocolate Yoo-hoo. I fumbled through the highbrow reading material we kept stacked on the coffee table—*InStyle, US Weekly,* a three-month-old *Cosmo*—until I found what I was looking for.

Nina's copy of Harley Cavanaugh's book *Vampires,*

Werewolves, and Other Things That Don't Exist was on the bottom of the stack. I ran my fingers over the raised letters and groaned when I read the message Harley had inscribed to Nina in his quick, slanted scrawl: *To the beautiful woman standing before me—maybe I should reconsider whether angels exist? Truly, Harley.*

I gagged so loudly that ChaCha jumped from her bed, yipping.

"Sorry, Cha," I mumbled, turning the page and settling in for the read.

I paged through Harley's introduction, where he established himself as one of the foremost debunkers of so-called spooks, haunts, and legends. I yawned when he opened chapter one with a meant-to-be-humorous anecdote about dressing up for Halloween. I was halfway through his description of a drugstore-purchased Dracula costume when I jumped to the index, looking for trigger words.

Is Harley more than just a bigoted blowhard?

I flipped until I found *Underworld, The pg 67.*

I found the page and scanned. *The Underworld is just that—a world under our own.*

I snorted. "Way to use a dictionary, Professor Cavanaugh."

I continued reading.

There are many differing beliefs about this Underworld. Some will argue that it is a parallel universe that encompasses all manner of human evils. Here on Earth (the "upper" world) exists God (or central protector/creator), light, growth, life, and humanity. The Underworld is looked over by Satan and em-

*braces demons, fire, chaos, and death. It is signified
by its absence of light.*

I thought of the brightly lit UDA hallways, the
orderly lines, and the neat stacks of paperwork that
were handed over by my smiling (well, for the ones
that had lips) UDA regulars. Then I thought of the
fires that I'd experienced—my father's house, my old
job—and the chaos that ensued. Both were in Harley's
"upper world."

The description continued:

*The inhabitants of the Underworld are demons with
horrible features, faces, and traits, and those not demonic have been banished to this alternate world for
being obstinate in their evil. Some well-intentioned
humans have slipped into the Underworld via portals,
curses, or mistakes, and those poor souls are tortured
and fed upon by the demonic population.*

I scanned Harley's reasoning about the fallacy of the
Underworld (Earth-core drilling has not encountered
Satan's underworld bachelor pad, for starters) and started
to feel a little better, betting that Harley's book was nothing more than a scientist on a soapbox, until I got to the
chapter titled "Demon Races." I sucked in a breath and
read over Harley's vampire mathematics (wildly flawed,
as vampires do not "turn" or kill every person on whom
they feed) and grimaced at his detailed description of
loony bin–ready "vampire slayers." I tossed the book
back on the coffee table, but it thunked on the ground, instead. It fell open to a handful of colored pages right in
the center. The book fell open on a page entitled simply
"Weaponry." And under that, "A cataloging of actual
tools used in the hunt and eradication of demon races."

There was an ornately carved wooden stake (vampires), a clefted silver knife (Kishi demons), silver bullets (werewolves).

A long, thick club.

Banshees.

My heard thudded in my chest.

Bettina.

I kicked aside Harley's book and beelined for the kitchen, tearing through our newspaper recycling stack. I found last week's *Chronicle,* with a big, torn hole in the "Books" section, and groaned.

"She's going to go see him." I sucked in a terrified breath. "She's going to see him and he's going to figure out what she is." I crumpled the paper and yanked the door to Nina's bedroom open, then sighed.

To call Nina's bedroom a "*bed*room" is a radical misnomer, but I could never get used to saying I share a one-bedroom, one-showroom apartment. Having no use for a bed (being a nonsleeping vampire) and needing a ridiculous amount of closet space (being a fashion-whoring vampire), she had expertly turned the entire room into the kind of walk-in closet that would make any fashionista worth her Jimmy Choos weak in the knees. Every item of clothing—from Old Navy today to 1800 antique—was cataloged, grouped by decade, and kept in pristine condition.

And then there were the shoes.

Nina was obsessed with the evolution of shoes and maintained that her affair—and nauseating procurement of shoes—was nothing less than an anthropological, sociological study. She kept a scant collection of greased Victorian boots and bootlets with their delicate buttons from ankle to toe; there was a selection of saddle shoes and Sandra Dee cotton candy-colored pumps, which bled to an earthy collection of shaggy boots and love-beaded sandals (two pairs complete with Woodstock mud). Then came the chunky platforms, the 1980s color blocked pointy numbers, the 1990s fashion flats, and finally a selection of sky-high stilettos, peep-toe booties, and sexy strappy numbers emblazoned with names like Manolo and Louboutin. Her shoe collection alone was worth more than my car and made my current selection— a pair of shaggy Payless Shoe Source slippers in a leopard print—seem that much less exotic or cute.

It didn't take me long to find what I was looking for. The torn-out article emblazoned with Harley's smug, smiling face was pinned to Nina's wall. I groaned, and my stomach churned as I thought about poor, battered Bettina, Sergio, and Mrs. Henderson—somewhere. Mrs. Henderson was one of the most annoying clients I'd ever met, but I certainly didn't want her—I gulped—dead.

I grabbed my cell phone and speed dialed Nina, shifting my weight from foot to foot and muttering, "Come on, Neens, come on. . . ." When the last ring bled into Nina's voice mail—her gleeful, recorded voice telling me to leave a message—I felt the lump form in my throat. I choked out, "Neens, it's me. Call me right away." I paused, then added, "Love you" before hanging up.

I traded in my slippers for boots, shrugged into my coat, snatched up my shoulder bag, and charged into the hallway, where I stopped dead, frowning.

It was the middle of the night and that meant that Nina was at Poe's.

The vampire coffeehouse.

Though I spent forty hours a week surrounded by all manner of the undead, being the only breather in a vampire haven wasn't exactly tops on my bucket list. I bit my lip and then dialed Alex, squeezing my eyes shut when his voice mail clicked on, sternly telling me to leave a message or dial 911 if this was an actual emergency.

I considered it.

Then I rushed across the hall and sucked in a deep breath before hammering on Will's door. He was a breather, but still . . . two breathers in a vampire bar were better than one, right?

When he didn't answer, I felt the sting of tears burning my eyes. My best friend could be in serious danger, and everyone I knew—and everyone I knew who owned weapons—was out.

They'd better be planning a surprise party for me.

It was a quick drive to Poe's, which was tucked between an empty storefront and a Chinese herb shop at the beach end of Clement Street. I had never actually been there before. When I stood out front, I realized the dreary, hand-painted Poe's sign—complete with a beady-eyed raven—did little to quell my angst.

Ditto with the blacked-out windows.

I paced for a few minutes and left pleading voice mails on everyone's phones for a second time— something between "I really need your help" and "If I die at the fangs of a rogue vampire tonight, it'll be on your shoulders." (Rogue being UDA speak for a nonadherent client.)

Then I called the only other person I could think of. . . .

"Sophie was right to call Steve," Steve said with an authoritative pat of my hand while I desperately tried to breathe through my mouth.

Trolls in general—and Steve, in particular—have a very distinctive smell. It's distinctly horrible. Like an unholy combination of sewer rot and ripe blue cheese. And although Steve was the last person on my call list—and generally the first on my "stay far, far away from" list, I did have a soft spot for the little moldy man ever since he had been instrumental in saving my life. Besides, being a troll, he would give me some badly needed Underworld cred and we should fit right in.

But that didn't mean I enjoyed hanging out with him.

"Now," Steve started, "Steve thinks Sophie should pretend to be Steve's love monkey."

I gave Steve an unamused once-over, which he ignored, threading his graying arm through mine, his lichen-covered knuckles closing over my fingers. I caught our reflection in the blacked-out glass: me, stylishly disheveled in skinny jeans, UGG boots, and a herringbone hooded jacket; Steve, dressed in his trademark velour track suit, dripping with enough gold chains to give Mr. T a run for his money. His stubby troll arms wrapped around my right thigh; his flat, stone gray eyes looked up at me lovingly while his pointed tongue slid over his snaggled yellow teeth lasciviously.

Oh boy, we wouldn't stand out at all.

Chapter Twenty

The inside of Poe's was uniformly dim and beatnik chic. The dark wood tables were crowded with fabulous-looking intellectuals reading newspapers and having conversations in low murmurs. Everywhere pale hands were wrapped around bowl-sized mugs that wafted little bits of steam. The only indication that Poe's was anything more than your average Starbucks-refuting coffeehouse was that those mugs—the ones that were empty and stacked on the counter—were stained a deep, rich red.

I pushed my fire engine red hair over my shoulder and pasted on my most confident-feeling smile, while covertly trying to shake Steve off my thigh. Though, even without three feet of gray skin and swamp lichen attached to my leg, I don't think I would have been able to blend in. I barely had one foot through the front door when all heads turned and swung toward us, nostrils twitching.

I gulped, willing my heart to continue along at its natural clip, praying that what I heard was not my blood roaring through my veins because if I heard it, everyone else did, too. A very tall woman, with blue-black hair pulled back into a slick ponytail, bangs cut high on her forehead, cocked her head toward me, clearly listening. My heart continued to do its siren-sounding thump, and the woman licked her lips. A glistening hint of saliva colored her lower lip. I stiffened and grabbed Steve's hand, holding tight.

"Steve knew Sophie would come around."

Sophie knew that with the vampires' supernatural sense of smell, Steve's personal odor could work as a kind of shield.

Despite being the only breather in a coffeehouse filled to the gill with people who dined on people like me between meals, I wasn't a complete idiot.

I glanced around. "I don't see her. Maybe she left?"

I watched the woman with the ponytail stiffen in her chair; her body was erect and she leaned slightly forward, as though she were about to pounce. I didn't recognize her from the UDA, which meant it was possible that she was newly created or new to town—two things that meant she didn't know or possibly didn't care to adhere to the UDA's strict no-eating-me policy.

With one eye on salivation girl, I limped over to the front counter, where an adorable-looking Leighton Meester knockoff was pushing a white towel in small circles on the sparkling granite.

"Hi," I said, brightening. "Hi, excuse me. I'm Sophie Lawson . . ."

The *Gossip Girl* doppelganger grinned at me, her small fangs glowing a bright white in the overhead light. "I know you. You work at the UDA with Nina LaShay, right?"

I nodded spastically; relief washing over me. Maybe little Leighton would protect me from ponytail girl.

"I'm Avey."

"Oh, hi, Avey." I held out my hand and Avey took it in hers for a microsecond; then she let it go as though my skin had burned her.

"Oh! I'm sorry," she said, her bluish violet eyes going wide. "I didn't realize you would be so warm."

"Ahem!" Steve cleared six inches of phlegm from his throat, and I wanted to gag.

Avey leaned up on her tiptoes and peered over the counter to where Steve stood, little tree stump legs askew, fists on hips.

"Steve is here to protect Sophie. May Sophie lift Steve up, please?"

I watched the terror shoot across Avey's face—mainly her nose—and wagged my head.

"It's okay, Steve. I'm fine." I turned back to Avey. "Is Nina here?"

"No. Actually, she was here a bit ago, but—"

Steve yanked hard on my hand and kicked one snakeskin-booted foot against the wood base of the counter.

"Steve is here to protect Sophie. Sophie cannot trust these bloodsuckers!"

Suddenly the murmuring din of conversation stopped, and the whole room plunged into stunned silence.

"Steve," I started to whisper.

Avey's eyebrows shot up, alarmed. "You should go."

A cold chill slid over my bare neck and I shivered

despite my coat. The girl with the ponytail was a hairsbreadth away from me now, the tip of her nose brushing against my hair. I watched her fingertip curl around my wrist, then draw a fine line toward my elbow.

"Go!" Avey yelled, but in the same instance that delicate finger turned into a circulation-cutting grip on my arm. I winced, paralyzed, stunned, and appalled by her strength. I felt the blood throb in my veins; I felt the tip of ponytail girl's hair as she angled her head and bared her fangs.

A high-pitched, girlish scream pierced the drop-dead silence. I was stunned to find that the howl wasn't coming from me. It was coming from Steve, and fading quickly as his fat little legs propelled him toward the door.

I tried to wriggle, but I was held tight. The cold from ponytail girl's marble-hard, lifeless chest seeped through my coat to my skin.

"Let her go, Devora," I heard Avey cry. "It's illegal. And Sophie's practically one of us!"

"You mean she's practically killing us," Devora hissed back.

I whimpered and then squeezed my eyes shut, when I felt the warm prick of fangs against the thin skin on my neck. I felt the pierce—two thick, hot pinpricks as Devora began to sink her fangs into me as her fingers tightened around my arms, making my hands go numb. I squeezed my eyes shut as my stomach rolled over and my knees weakened. I thought I would crumple to the floor, but was instead pushed against the counter with such force that I lost my breath. Groaning, I felt my ribs protest against the pressure. My forehead smacked against the granite countertop—and Avey's damp polishing cloth—and black spots flooded my eyes. I sank down to the cold tiled floor, stunned as Devora flew backward, the ridged soles of her black-stacked motorcycle boots in the air. The vamps who were sitting and sipping at the crowded tables around Poe's barely gave a hint of recognition as Devora landed between two chairs with a thud, howling and clawing at the figure who was wriggling on top of her. I huddled against the counter and watched as Devora flailed uselessly against her attacker, who, with hands securely around Devora's throat, turned to me and called over her shoulder, "Are you okay, Sophie?"

I blinked at Nina, shocked as my fashion-forward best friend sat astride Devora, holding her taut without so much as upsetting a hair on her head.

I opened my mouth to speak, to thank Nina, but nothing came out—save for a strangled, whimpering gurgle. Nina pinned her knees firmly on Devora's chest and asked, "What the hell were you doing to my best friend?"

I coughed and found my voice. "It's okay, Nina. I'm fine. When did you—when did you get here?"

Nina ignored me, leaned forward so she was nose to nose with the terrified girl, and told her, "If I ever see you around Sophie again, I will personally break your neck, set you on fire, grind your bones with a sledge-hammer, and sprinkle them over a scone. Do you understand me?"

Devora made no attempt to move. Her eyes remained big and fixed on Nina. "Yes," she said finally, "I get it."

Nina straightened up. "Now I'm going to stand up, and Sophie and I are going to walk out of here, and all three of us are going to pretend none of this ever happened. Except, of course, for my non-idle threat against your afterlife."

Nina hopped up and sauntered over to me, hunching down and examining my neck. "Doesn't look too bad," she said, offering me a stack of napkins. "But no reason to go sending up food smells in here."

I pressed the wad of napkins to my neck and followed Nina out of Poe's. Even in the cold night air, my fingers started to warm up and regain their circulation, but my arms still throbbed from being gripped and pinned to my side.

Once on the sidewalk Nina stopped and turned to me. "Do you have a death wish, Sophie? What the hell were you doing alone in Poe's?"

"I wasn't alone," I said, feeling the bite of anger. "Steve was with me."

Nina wrinkled her ski jump nose. "*Steve* Steve?"

"I called everyone. And besides, I thought his smell would distract them."

Nina rolled her eyes and fished in her suitcase-sized Marc Jacobs bag. "Well, you didn't call"—she checked the readout on her phone—"oh, look at that. You did."

I pulled the napkins from my neck and glanced at the bright red spots dotting them. "Does it look okay?"

Nina glanced at my neck. "It's barely a scratch, but two seconds later and you would have been dinner. What were you thinking?"

Nina and I fell into step. "I was worried about you."

Nina cocked an eyebrow. "You—Sophie Lawson, breather—were worried about me hanging out in a vampire coffeehouse?"

I tossed the soiled napkins in a trash can. "I wasn't worried about you there." I stopped and cornered Nina. "Neens, I need to talk to you. It's about Harley."

Nina eyed me with a wry smile. "If you're going to give me the sex talk, you're about one hundred years too late."

I clapped my palms over my ears. "Ew, Nina, boundaries."

"Fine. Talk to me about Harley."

"Not here. We should go home."

Nina cracked her neck and brushed her waist-length hair over one shoulder. "I guess there's nothing exciting going on tonight, anyway. Let's go."

I watched the stoplight change in front of us, and watched the largest, gaudiest Cadillac I have ever seen coast to a stop a few feet from me.

"One sec."

I beelined for the car and rapped on the driver's-side window. Steve stared out the windshield, trying his hardest to ignore me.

"Steve!" I yelled, pounding.

He finally relented and rolled down the car window. I saw that he had a stack of phone books wedged securely on the leather bucket seat where he sat. I crossed my arms. "Some protector you are."

A blush washed over Steve's face, tinting his cheeks a sort of pocked mauve. "There you are, sugar bun! Steve ran out to grab some coffee."

I raised an eyebrow. "You ran out on me and I almost got fanged, you asshat! You left me alone in a vampire den!"

"Steve ran out for comforting hot beverages."

"I didn't need a hot beverage! I needed a wooden stake!"

Steve clicked his tongue and wagged his head solemnly. "Steve can't please everyone."

When Nina and I got back to the apartment, I sat her down at the dining-room table and paced, wringing my hands, wondering how I was going to tell my very best friend that her new beau was hunting demons.

"My God, Sophie, sit down. You're making me nervous."

"Okay." I sat, taking a seat and sighing heavily. "Here it goes—Harley is dangerous."

Nina rolled her eyes, stood up, and rummaged through the refrigerator. "Do we have an AB pos?"

"Didn't you just hear me? Harley is dangerous, Nina. He is behind all the demon issues. He got rid of Mrs. Henderson and attacked Bettina. Have you even read his book?"

Nina popped a straw in her blood bag and her cheeks went hollow as she sucked. "Of course I've read his book. Most of it."

"Most of it? Most of it! Nina, it's practically a blue-print to kill demons!"

"Sophie, Harley doesn't believe in demons. His books specifically tells people that they don't exist."

I crossed my arms in front of my chest. "No, his book specifically tells people that demons *can't* exist."

"So?"

"So don't you find it a little suspicious that suddenly demons start disappearing right when Harley and his demons-can't-exist book comes around?"

Nina sucked out the remainder of blood and then crushed the bag, pitching it into the trash. "Yep, it's a coincidence."

"Or it's Harley making sure that the world agrees with the findings of his book."

Nina's newly red lips cracked into a bemused half smile. "You actually think that Harley is going around playing Whac-A-Mole in the Underworld so no one proves him wrong? Sophie, that's completely ridiculous. He's an author, not a killer. I've talked with him. He's spent his entire career debunking things. He doesn't believe in the Underworld. He can't see through the veil. He had dinner with me, for God's sake, and trust me—as far as Harley is concerned"—Nina's fingers slid over her hips and thighs—"I'm all woman."

"That's fabulous—and disturbing. But all the evidence points to Harley."

"Is that so, Columbo?"

I stomped into the living room and snatched Harley's book from the floor, where I left it, opening to the page with the weaponry photos. "Notice anything?"

Nina glanced nonchalantly at the pages. "That doesn't prove anything."

"Think about it, Nina. Harley makes millions based on this debunking thing. What would happen if his loyal public found out that we—*you*—really do exist and that their beloved guru was the actual sham?"

Nina's eyes went up as if the answer were written on the ceiling. "Um, I'd say that if Harley actually did uncover the Underworld, and its fabulous inhabitants"—Nina stretched out her slim, long legs and kicked them onto the table—"he would be an instant celeb."

"Like that Scottish guy who proved that Nessie really does exist?"

Nina frowned. "Who was he?"

"Exactly! No one knows who he was, because he's in a loony bin!"

Nina tugged on her lower lip. "I'm still not seeing the connection here, Sophs."

I blew out a tortured sigh and held up my index finger. "One—Harley Cavanaugh inks a one-point-seven-million-dollar deal—"

"One-point-seven million dollars? Where did you hear that? Did he tell you that?" Nina's eyes went big. She turned to me and grabbed both my hands. "Did he tell you that because he's planning on buying me a ring?"

"I read it on his website," I huffed. "Now listen. Harley Cavanaugh inks a huge deal."

"One-point-seven million," Nina sang.

"To write a book proving that vampires and whatnot don't exist."

"Whatnot?"

"Stay with me here. Two—the book isn't even in print and Harley makes millions in presales." I pointed at Nina before she could start. "Also from the website, no jewelry involved."

Nina shrugged and I kept going, ticking my fingers.

"Three—Harley discovers that demons really exist, making his entire book a work of fiction."

"Four—Harley finds out that I exist and writes another book, which sells millions," Nina challenged.

"A book that he writes on spit-soaked napkins while holding a pen in his mouth and wearing a straightjacket because everyone—his publisher, his fans—believe that ole Harley, the debunker, has gone off the deep end. See my point?"

Nina cocked her head, raking her fingers through her long hair and examining it for split ends. "Kind of. But I still don't buy it. Harley really has no need to pick off demons."

"He does if he wants to save his contract!" I sputtered.

Nina put both elbows on the table and leaned in toward me. "You know what I think, Sophie? I think you're scared."

"I'm scared?"

Nina nodded, dark hair bobbing. "Yeah." She reached out and grabbed my hand, squeezing it. The chill from her skin went all the way up my arm and I shivered. "But you don't have any reason to be scared, Sophie. I'm not going anywhere. Harley won't take me away from you. We're a package deal, you and me."

I felt my jaw slack open and I jumped up, yanking my hand out of Nina's. "Seriously? That's what you think this is about?"

"I know how you feel, Sophie. You're like a kite without a tail. Just bobbing along in the atmosphere of love. You're not connected to anyone, romantically—not Alex, not Will. . . ."

"You're kidding me, right? A tailless kite?"

"Hell, you could be a tailless monkey without any bananas if that works better for you. The point is *not* what you are *metaphorically.* The point is what you are *physically,* which is afraid of being alone."

I jabbed my index finger toward Nina. "No more Dr. Phil!"

Nina ignored me and stood up, mashing me against her marble-solid chest. "It's okay, Sophie. You don't have to be afraid. Harley is not going to take me away from you."

I pushed Nina away. "I'm not worried about you leaving me. I'm worried about Harley killing you!"

Nina's eyes were sympathetic as she pushed a lock of my hair behind my ear. "You can use whatever metaphor you like, honey, but you and I—we're in for life. And, you know, afterlife."

It was hard not to trust Nina. She had never let me down before; and when it came to strong women, Nina was the strongest.

"Promise me you'll think about it, okay? And maybe stay away from Harley?"

Nina cocked a warning eyebrow.

"Okay," I backpedaled, "just think about it, and maybe only see Harley in well-lit public places?"

Nina grinned and gave me an icy peck on the forehead. "I'll think about what you said, but I'm seriously avoiding the well-lit places. Okay?"

"Okay."

"Now go to bed. You look awful!"

Chapter Twenty-One

I wrestled myself into an oversized San Francisco Giants sweatshirt and whistled for ChaCha; then both of us flopped into my bed. ChaCha started snoring immediately—small, puppy pants of kibble-scented air. I clicked off the overhead light and stared at the pattern the streetlights flashed on my ceiling. Finally I clamped my eyes shut and willed myself to fall asleep.

All I could see was Bettina's face, tormented, bruised; then Kale, lying lifeless on the wet cement, her head flopping like a rag doll.

I wasn't going to let that happen to my best friend.

I wouldn't.

I kicked off my covers and tiptoed to my bedroom door, inching it open a crack. Nina was stretched out on the couch, the silvery light from the television glowing ominously on her marble skin.

I slid into a pair of yoga pants, socks, and tucked my Reebok EasyTone sneakers under one arm. Hey, crime fighters need good glutes, too, right?

I peeled open the door again and dropped down to

my knees, crawling from my bedroom doorway to dive behind our side table. If I could just get out the door, I could do in Harley myself, and Nina would never have to know. My heart was pounding in my throat, and sweat started to prick at my upper lip. I crawled from behind the side table to behind the couch; my hands and knees moving silently on the carpet.

Sophie Lawson, Savior, I thought with satisfaction as I crawled toward the front door.

"Can I help you?"

I stopped—rather, Nina stopped me—when my forehead banged against her shins. She was blocking the front door, hands on hips; her charcoal eyes glaring down at me.

"Um," I said, sitting back on my bum, "I was looking for one of ChaCha's chew toys." I felt a smile of relief pushing up to my earlobes. *Yes! A chew toy! That's right!*

Sophie Lawson, Incognito.

Nina cocked a single eyebrow; her smile was wry. "A chew toy?"

I nodded spastically. "Yep."

Nina crossed her arms in front of her chest. "Oh, I know what this is about."

I gulped. "You do?"

"Uh-huh. You're sneaking out to meet a boy, you little minx. Now, who is it? Alex . . . or Will?"

"You caught me, Nina. Nothing gets past you." I forced a tittering laugh. "Yeah, I'm going to meet Alex. He just got back from Buffalo. Tonight. I would have told you, but—"

"But you knew that I would never let you leave the house looking like that?"

"What's wrong with the way I look?"

Nina rolled her eyes. "Are you kidding me? You look like—like . . . Well, I can't even come up with a funny retort. But you look awful. Yoga pants, no makeup? I know Alex is all good angel and stuff, but trust me, Sophie, looks matter." A wide grin spread across her face. "Wait here. Just give me two minutes and Alex will not be able to resist you."

Nina hopped cleanly over me. Once I could see that she was in her room, knee deep in lace and see-through camis, I continued on my hands and knees out into the hallway.

"Did I mention how much I love this country?" Will said, grinning down at me from his doorway. He was shirtless and barefoot, wearing a pair of faded jeans, which hung in all the right places. His naked chest was slim, but every single muscle was brilliantly well defined, a la David Beckham or one of those anatomy posters.

I felt myself start to salivate—the last hint of male chest I had been privy to had been gray, lichen covered, and dripping with gold chains.

Screaming hormones or not, I was a woman with a mission.

"You're pretty," I heard myself say.

Sophie Lawson, Quivering Puddle of Undersexed Jelly.

"I mean, pretty . . . jerky," I corrected in an uncertain cadence. I stood up, brushing off my already achy knees. "I'm sneaking out of my apartment."

"Nice strategy. Where you headed?"

I pushed Will's chest until we were both in his apartment; then I slammed the door. "To the Mark Hopkins hotel. I need to go find Harley. He's the one who's responsible for all this. He's the one who tried to kill me." My eyes drifted from Will's brilliantly hazel eyes to his broad shoulders . . . those ropey muscles . . . the two-inch tuft of hair that led from his navel to the top button of his Lucky Brand jeans.

Will seemed amused, his eyes following mine.

"Harley. Yes. Bad," I said, pulling out all the stops in my impressive vocabulary.

"Harley's responsible. Are you sure about that, love?"

"Of course I'm sure! I read his book! And besides, who else would want to pick off demons?"

Will bit his lip. "How about Alex? You said yourself it could be a fallen angel picking people off to make you crazy. What happened to that theory?"

I blew out a sigh. "It's not Alex. Alex wouldn't hurt a fly. He won't even go to the circus because of the way they treat the animals."

"Are you sure he's not just afraid of clowns?"

I was about to fire back my own witty retort, when there was a quick rap at the door.

"Is that—"

"No!" I pantomimed silently. "She can hear you!"

Will yanked the door open and I dove behind the selection of lawn chairs and Wii games, which passed as Will's living-room set.

"Nina! What an unexpected surprise! Come round for a spot of plasma, did you?" I could hear the absolute glee in Will's voice and it made me growl.

"That's very sweet of you, Will, but I'm looking for Sophie. By the way, nice outfit."

I peered out from behind two slats of tan lawn chair and caught a glimpse of Nina, eyes doing that incredibly sexy-smoldering thing, the tip of her tongue feeling her fang. A surprising surge of anger started to simmer low in my belly. *She wouldn't . . .*

"Can you just tell Sophie, when you see her"—Nina peered around Harley and looked directly at Fort Lawn Chair—"that these are for her?"

I gaped as Nina piled a selection of black lacy things—topped with a pair of stiletto heels that would have been better suited for a *Playboy* pictorial than for anything I would ever do—into Will's outstretched arms.

"Sure."

Nina leaned up on her tiptoes, caught my eye, and gave Will a slightly sensual peck on the cheek. "Thank you, Will," she said coyly.

Will slammed the door and I stood up, raging. "You know, Will, we're going to have to get you some big-boy furniture!"

Will shrugged and shook the heap of garments out of his arms—save for some shimmery black dental floss or possibly a thong. (My lingerie IQ was woefully low.)

"Aren't you supposed to put these on?" he asked, grinning. The dental floss/thong was hooked around one finger.

I snatched it. "No. She was just doing this for— for . . ."

Will's eyebrows went up expectantly. I made up my mind to stop Harley and then kill Nina myself. "I've got to go stop Harley."

Will pointed to the heap of satin and lace. "What am I supposed to do with this?"

I shrugged. "Donate it. This city is full of needy people."

"Needy sexy people?"

"I've got to get out of here."

Will held up a finger. "Wait one second." He disappeared into his bedroom—what I assumed was his bedroom, as I had never been in and would not be going in, I told myself sternly. He came back out, sliding a red football jersey over his head.

"Don't you have anything that can't be worn on a soccer field?"

"It's called football, love, and you should talk."

I looked down at my Giants ensemble. "Baseball is America's pastime."

"Ditto football in the UK. Hold this, please?"

I put my hands out. "Ew!" I shouted, dropping Will's socks onto the floor.

"What'd you do that for?"

"They're socks!"

Will rolled his eyes, beelining for the kitchen. "They're clean." I watched as he selected a pair of long barbecue tongs, then pulled open the oven door.

"What are you cooking?" I asked, rolling up on tiptoes to look over his shoulder.

Will extracted a single sneaker, held between the tongs. He touched the sneaker delicately and grinned. "Perfect."

"You're baking your shoes?" I gaped.

Will extracted the other sneaker and set both on the counter. "I'm drying my shoes. We had a game in Golden Gate Park today."

I cocked an eyebrow. "I didn't know there was a Guardian Intramural League."

He flashed a grin. "Lucky for you, there is."

"There is?"

"No. Now, would you hand me my socks, please?"

I picked up his socks between forefinger and thumb. Not that I'm that delicate a flower, I just didn't have a lot of experience holding men's underclothes. Even their . . . lowest . . . underclothes.

"What are you suiting up for?" I asked as Will yanked on a sock and tried to tie his shoelaces with a pair of oven mitts.

"I'm coming with you."

I put my hands on my hips. "Why?"

"I'm your Guardian, remember?" He slipped on his second shoe and shook out of the oven mitts. "Ready?"

"Yeah, but when did you suddenly get all Guardian-y?"

Will grabbed his keys off the rack and spun them around one finger. "I thought I was pretty Guardian-y not getting you shot in the alley." He flashed me a grin that was part admonishment, part "I told you so."

"Yeah," I harrumphed, "barely."

"You know, I only work in fallen angels. That's all I'm contracted to guard you from," Will murmured, holding the door open for me. He locked the door behind us and we continued down the stairs and out into the frigid night.

I crossed my arms and stopped dead on the sidewalk. "What does that mean?"

"That means, love"—Will sank his keys into his car lock—"that if you wish to take your life into your own hands hunting writers, I don't necessarily *have* to help you." He opened the car door with a flourish. "Get in."

I narrowed my eyes. "So what are you coming along for?"

"I'm not the kind of guy who lets a girl go to her doom all by herself."

I offered Will a sarcastic smile. "What a gentleman."

"And I got nothing better to do."

I shrugged. "Suit yourself." I dug a crushed bag of popchips out of my shoulder bag. I saw Will eye the bag with unrestrained horror.

"You want?" I asked tentatively.

Will grabbed the bag, wound the window down, and tossed out my chips.

"Hey!"

"You do not snack in a 1958 vintage Porsche 365."

"When did the Boring Police make you their huffy English master?" I grumbled.

Will rolled his eyes and gunned it up California Street, his little car huffing as we rounded Nob Hill. "This it?"

I looked up at the hotel, stately in a uniquely San Francisco way. "Yup."

Will yanked the car toward the curb, and a white-gloved bellman, who kindly opened my door, offered me a hand.

I made a mental note to hire myself a bellman, once I became filthy rich.

The valet came around and opened Will's door. Will gave him a quick once-over before handing him the keys, holding his eye.

"She's precious, you know."

"I assure you we'll take the best care of"—the valet eyed Will's rust-colored clunker—"her."

"What was that about?" I hissed as Will threaded his arm through mine, guiding me into the lobby.

"Have you not been paying attention, love? I'm your Guardian, and people—things, whatever—are after you."

"And you think the valet was going to get to me through what? The giant rust stains on the side of your car?"

Will whirled to face me. "Nigella is a vintage 19—"

"I know!" I groaned.

"She just needs a little TLC to be restored back to her former grandeur."

I rolled my eyes. "So how are we going to find Harley?"

Chapter Twenty-Two

Will sized up the broad-shouldered woman behind the front desk. She was looming in a navy blue blazer and smart haircut, head bent, chin jutted out as she held a phone receiver between her shoulder and ear. She was barking short, little retorts every few seconds.

A slow, suggestive grin spread across Will's face. He licked his puckered pink lips, and I ignored the urge to slide a feather of kisses over him. He was my Guardian; and good-looking or not, he was annoying as hell.

Also, he had a car named Nigella.

He raked a hand through his hair, making the spiky, sand-colored strands stand up in a charmingly disheveled way. He jutted his chin toward the cluster of neatly upholstered chairs that were set up to look like a cozy living-room set. "Wait over there."

I wandered over to the faux living room and scanned the magazines fanned out attractively on the coffee table, while keeping one eye on Will as he sauntered up to the phone lady. His back was toward me, but that sly grin practically shot out like a force field or an English mating call.

Phone lady didn't seem to be swayed.

Will leaned seductively against the front desk, and the woman hung up her phone. Her pinched face and naked eyes fixed on him. She offered him what looked like a stock, courteous smile and Will leaned a bit more over the front counter, saying something that I supposed was sexy and suggestive. From the look on the lady's face, Will was either about to get a master suite or slapped with a restraining order.

He slowly turned and grinned over his shoulder at me, giving me a double thumbs-up, while the lady got back on the phone. From the looks of the dark-suited man quickly barreling toward Will, she had summoned security.

I fished around in my purse for an envelope—this was one time it really paid to pack the world in my shoulder bag—and mashed several magazine pages inside. Then I popped up and wedged my way between the hulking guard and Will.

"Hi, um, excuse me. I'm supposed to deliver this to Harley Cavanaugh. The writer?" I wagged the thick envelope just under the security guard's nose. Close enough for him to think it was chock-full of very important information; fast enough for him not to realize the envelope said YOU MAY HAVE ALREADY WON $1,000,000!

By the time the security guard pushed me aside, Will had slipped away, and the phone lady turned her static smile on me.

"Did you say you have something for Mr. Cavanaugh?"

"Yes." I waggled the envelope. "Very important documents. Mr. Cavanaugh needs them right away."

Now that I was close enough, I could see that the phone lady wore a little engraved nametag on her lapel. "Sharona," I added, eyeing her name tag.

Sharona pursed her lips and gave me a suspicious once-over. "And who did you say you were?"

"I didn't. What I did say was that Harley Cavanaugh needs these documents right away."

Sharona held her palm open. "I'll see that he gets them."

"I would really prefer to deliver them myself."

"I'm sorry, but that's not possible."

"I understand. But will you please ring him right now to let him know that they're coming?"

Sharona let out an exasperated sigh and waved the security guard away. He retook his post by the front door, apparently content that Will, the English threat, was gone.

Sharona's ultralong nails clicked away at her keyboard and she was back on the phone. I could hear the shrill ringing as she cradled the receiver. I stood up on my tiptoes and whispered the word "bathroom."

Sharona rolled her eyes and jabbed one clawed fingernail a little too close to my left ear, but I got the gist. I slid the envelope in my pocket and beelined across the foyer toward the restrooms.

I was pacing outside the ladies' room when Will came up to me, smiling broadly. "That was brilliant, love, really."

"Did you see the computer screen?"

"Three thirty-seven. Thanks for getting security off my back, too."

"Next time, let me do the talking."

We took the stairs and I was huffing by the time we reached the third floor. I assumed it was the altitude and helped myself to a chocolate off the maid's cart as we counted off the rooms.

"Here we are, room 337," Will said.

"Okay."

We stood and stared at each other. "Okay, what?" Will asked.

"Knock."

Will rapped on the door and we stood, waiting, silent. Nothing happened. I pressed my ear to the door.

"Do you hear anything?" Will asked.

I shook my head. "Well, that was a big waste."

"Not at all." Will threw on that charming, sheepish grin, which he did so well, and strolled down to the maid who was locking up room 341.

"Hi there. My wife and I are here on our second honeymoon"—he looked over his shoulder at me and I gaped, wondering how he could muster a bashful blush on command—"and we seemed to have locked ourselves out of our room. It's our first time here, and we're just so excited to see the city."

The woman looked around Will at me and I nodded quickly, feeling my ponytail bobbing.

"We're from the UK," Will continued.

"Yes, yes," I said, coming closer to Will and pouring on my Madonna/Gwyneth faux English accent. "I thought I had the key in the boot, but the hubby here thinks we left it in the room when we went out for a pint."

Will looked at me. "Cut it out," he whispered.

"Blimey," I continued, slapping a palm to my forehead. "I'd forget me head if it weren't attached to me shoulders, that I would."

The maid said nothing, but slipped her keycard into the lock. The little green light flashed and Will pushed open the door, smiling gratefully. "Thank you."

"Pip-pip," I called, waving.

Will pushed me into Harley's room and slammed the door behind us. "'Pip-pip'?" he mocked. "'Blimey'? Where the hell did you get your English?"

I put my hands on my hips. "I was playing along, asshat. And now I'm wondering why."

"What do you mean?" .

I flicked on the light and Harley's hotel room looked like every other hotel room in the Mark Hopkins hotel—elegant, lushly appointed, without a blood-written message alerting us to the room owner's murderous desires.

"We're here in Harley's room. You know who's not here? Harley. He's probably out killing Nina as we speak."

"This was your idea, love."

I slumped on the bed. "I guess I didn't really consider what would happen if we didn't find Harley."

"What were you planning if we would have found him?"

I shrugged. "I don't know. Citizen's arrest. Mythical ass kicking. Maybe get him vanquished by those sisters on *Charmed*?"

Will sat down next to me and slung an arm over my shoulders; then handed me his cell phone. "There's only one way to find out if Nina is safe tonight."

I took the phone and dialed Nina's, counting the rings.

"Wait a second," Will said, ears pricking. "Listen."

I pulled the phone from my ear and cocked my head. "Nina's phone is ringing in stereo."

"Wait a second," I heard, "it's my roommate."

Will and I looked at each other. Nina's voice was muffled, slightly. "Let me just turn this off," Nina said.

The dial tone droned in my ear. "She just turned me off!"

Before I could continue my tirade, Will grabbed me by the wrist and hurled me to the floor.

"What—"

He clamped a hand over my mouth—hard—and slid with me under the bed. It was then I heard the lock jiggle and Nina's voice came closer.

"They're here!" I hissed in Will's ear.

"Way to get in the game," Will whispered back.

I watched Nina's elegant heels walk across the surprisingly plush carpet; then I watched Harley's polished wingtips follow. There was some murmured conversation; by the cadence and tone Harley and Nina were exchanging some grossly sexual banter. I looked at Will; my lip curled into a disgusted snarl. He waggled his eyebrows at me. If the intent was to be suggestive, it missed the mark and lodged securely in "ew."

My ear pricked when I heard Nina's voice drop into her singsong, sexy, sweet sound—the one usually reserved for big fangs and large favors. I pressed my forefinger in front of my lips, should Will decide to talk.

"Listen," I mouthed.

"Harley, sweetie," Nina said while I watched her press up onto her tiptoes. "I'm so thirsty."

Will looked at me. Even under the faint, dusty light

of the bed skirt, I could see that he was clearly alarmed. Frankly, so was I.

"Well, maybe we should see what we've got in the minibar," Harley said, his voice deep and sexy.

"Oh, sweetie. You know what I'm really thirsty for?"

I felt a hot wire split down my spine. I couldn't believe what I was hearing. My own roommate gone rogue? My heart thumped painfully, and my fingers curled into the carpet. I gripped down to the studs.

"I just have this absolute craving"—Nina's voice was a slow, seductive drawl—"for a French 75."

Even from under the bed, the dumb-dog smile was evident on Harley's face.

"Oh, yeah? What happens in a French 75?"

"It's a cocktail, silly."

Harley's "oh" sounded crushed.

I watched Nina's pointy-toed shoes move closer to Harley's shiny ones, and I guessed she was pressing her body up against him in that way she had, snaking her arms around his neck, lips brushing his ear.

"I would do anything for a French 75. Be a dear and get me one."

Harley broke toward the phone. "Let me call room service."

"No"—there was an audible pout—"that will take too long. Run downstairs for me, sweetie? I would be so happy." Harley didn't answer and Nina drawled on. "And it would give me some time to freshen up."

Will and I exchanged relieved looks when we heard the quick smack of Harley's lips on Nina's; we watched his wingtips hightail it for the door.

"What the hell is wrong with you two?"

"Aghhh!" Will and I both shrieked at the two coal

black eyes that glared at us from under the dust ruffle. Will must have tried to make a break for it, because the next thing I heard was the unmistakable thunk of skull on box spring and Will grumbling while his hand massaged his forehead. "Son of a bitch."

"Both of you perverts, out of there. Now."

Nina pointed to the ground and Will and I shimmied out from underneath the bed like panicked puppies. If we'd had tails, they would have been firmly planted between our legs.

"What are you guys doing here?" Nina hissed over her shoulder as she crossed the room and threw the lock on the door.

Will leaned into me and barely moved his lips. "Oh God. Does that mean she's going to kill us now?"

"Maybe," Nina said, nostrils flaring. She was suddenly—noiselessly—a half inch from Will's nose.

"Nina," I said, sighing, "we need to talk to you."

Nina lodged her hands firmly on her narrow hips. "And you couldn't use the phone?"

I put a gentle hand on Nina's cold forearm, then led her to the end of the bed. "Sit down, Neens. This isn't going to be easy to say." I licked my lips and looked from Nina to Will, who lowered his eyes solemnly. "Nina, Harley's going to kill you."

The edge of Nina's lip twitched, and then the other one. She blinked, probably a half-dozen times. I watched her form fists, then stretch out her fingers. She wouldn't look at me, and I put my hand on her knee.

"Are you okay?"

I felt the tremor roil through her before I heard the

sound—a wild, high-pitched gurgle. I looked at Will; his eyes were wide, alarmed.

"Nina?"

She was shaking now; her tiny shoulders spasming; tears streaming down her face.

And then came the laughter.

"This is funny to you?" I gaped.

"No," she barely managed to gasp out.

"We're here to save your life!"

"That's what's so funny," Nina gushed, pressing her palms against her mouth.

I stood up and stomped ineffectually. "Shut up! I've saved your life before! Why should this be any different?"

Nina doubled over, still engulfed in silent, hilarious spasms. When I looked at Will, he simply shrugged his shoulders; then cracked his own toothpaste-commercial smile.

I shook Nina's shoulders, forcing her to look up at me. "Look, Nina. I've read Harley's book, and all signs point to him as the Underworld killer. If he knows you're onto him—or that you're a vampire—then you're probably next."

Nina waggled her fingers at me. "Oooh, ominous! Sophie, Harley is no killer." She patted my head affectionately. "But I love your paranormal paranoia. It's sweet. And besides, don't you think I could handle myself against Harley if"—she held up a single finger—"it was necessary?"

Will sat down next to Nina on the bed and I wriggled between them.

"Normally, you aren't the one I worry about in hand-to-fang combat. But Harley knows things, Nina. He

knows about silver bullets and banshees and stuff. He'd
know how to take down a vampire. He'd know how to
take you down," I implored. All of the angst of the occasion finally came out and walloped me. Suddenly I
was hunched in Nina's lap, crying, her cold fingers tenderly sliding through my hair.

"There, there, Sophie. It's okay. I'm not dead. No
one's going to kill me."

"I couldn't stand it if anyone hurt you!"

"Oh, sweetie . . ." Nina pushed me up so I was looking directly at her. She thumbed away the tears that kept
spilling down my cheeks. "Will's going to drive you
home. Right Will?"

I could see Nina look over my head, her eyes focused
on Will. He must have nodded or done something else
in the affirmative because Nina zoned in on me again,
cocking her head at a sympathetic angle.

"Nothing is going to happen to me, I promise. I'll
just have one drink with Harley and then I'll come
home directly, okay? We'll watch some TV, make fun of
Vlad's horrible fashion sense, and maybe post a few
fake online profiles on eHarmony. Sound okay?"

I sniffed and nodded, and Will handed me a Kleenex.
Nina chucked me softly under the chin, then said, "Now
get out of here. I'd rather have Harley think I'm a vampire
than the three of us are swingers."

Nina led us to the door. Before we left, Will turned
to her.

"How did you know we were under the bed?" he
asked.

Nina pointed to her nose, cocked one annoyed eyebrow. "Now get out."

"Well, that was pointless," Will said as we waited for the elevator.

I blew my nose. "Nina might trust Harley, but I still don't. There is something about him that gives me the heebie-jeebies."

"Is that the paranormally technical term for Spidey sense?"

The *ding* from the elevator interrupted my plan to slug Will and we quickly spun to examine the opulent arrangement of orchids on a side table, our backs to the open elevator.

"Was that Harley?" Will murmured.

I chanced a glance over my shoulder and watched Harley sauntering down the hall toward the room we had just exited, balancing a bottle of champagne and a couple of flutes.

We caught Harley's elevator and I crossed my arms while Will mashed the CLOSE button.

"You still think Harley's the one, huh?"

"Who else could it be?"

"Nina's a big girl, love. With, you know, fangs. She can take care of herself." He slung an arm over my shoulders and pulled me close to him. I breathed in his clean, refreshing scent of bath soap and detergent. I allowed myself to rest my head against his shoulder, to consider the idea that the fate of the Underworld might not be on my shoulders for the next fifteen minutes.

"Fancy a pint?" Will asked when the elevator doors opened on the lobby.

I bit my lip, then smiled. "I fancy something with frosting."

Will reflected my bright grin back. "I'm not really into all of that kinky stuff, but for you, love, I'm willing to risk the sticky."

Chapter Twenty-Three

I slept restlessly. ChaCha was walking over me and covering me with hot doggie slobber. My mind alternately raced through every Underworld murderer scenario and images of beautiful red roses bursting into flames. I woke up with a start, and went nose to nose with Nina.

"Augh!" I screamed, and clutched at my chest. "My God, Nina, I told you not to do that."

"I'm sorry," she said, smiling sweetly. "I'll send trumpeters ahead of me next time."

My heart thundered in my ears. "That would be nice," I yelled over the beat. "What are you doing in here?"

"I heard you tossing and turning." She pulled her knees up to her chest, and dug her bare feet underneath my covers. "Want to talk?"

"I thought you were mad at me."

She shook her head, pushing a lock of silky black hair over her shoulder. "I know you just worry about me."

I nodded. "Not just you, Neens. This is *big*. I know I said that before, but I'm scared. This is big and it seems so close." I looked at her; then I looked back at my bed-spread. "And you and Harley are getting so close. . . ."

Nina slung a frozen arm over my shoulder and pulled me to her. "I told you, Soph, you and I are a package deal. I'm not going to go hightailing it off into the sunset with Harley."

"Because that would make you burst into flames."

Nina rolled her eyes. "Even when my novel gets picked up—"

"I'm not worried about you running off on a book tour with Harley, Nina. I'm worried about him being dangerous. His book—"

Nina held up a hand. "Soph, two days ago Dixon and VERM were responsible for all of this. A day before that, it was a fallen angel. Before that, it was random acts of demonic violence."

"I wasn't sure then."

"And you're still not. You're looking for someone to fit your theory, and you're making Harley fit. What about VERM? Their one goal in this afterlife is to re-store vampires back to their former glory. Well, that and bring back the ascot." She grinned. "Two major goals."

"Nina, you know if you're accusing VERM, you're accusing Vlad."

I could see Nina's jaw stiffen as she gritted her teeth. "Not exactly. Dixon has his hands in VERM, too. He could be using them—using Vlad even—to do his dirty work. It would make sense, you know—the whole pull to bring the vampire population up by bringing the demon population down."

"You really think VERM would have people out at-tacking demons—attacking me?"

Nina crossed her arms in front of her chest. The act wasn't defiant, so much as challenging. "Do you really think my boyfriend would be out attacking demons—or you?"

I wanted to nod. I wanted to tell her, yes, that was exactly what I thought, but I couldn't push that tiny, three-letter word past my teeth.

Instead, I looked over Nina's head, looked at the clock, and said, "We're going to be late for work."

I spent the majority of my workday hiding in my office reading an ancient Nancy Drew mystery that I found under my bookcase and drawing a crude flow chart of Harley-as-the-Underworld-killer versus Vlad/VERM-as-the-Underworld-killer. Neither of them got me anywhere, but no one bothered me, and no one came into my office—especially now that I was not only a breathing pariah, but also a pariah with nothing but a broken file drawer stuffed with fast-food menus and a very well-organized line of Post-it notes.

I waited for most of the other employees to leave the office before I gathered my shoulder bag and the remains of my lunch and headed down the hallway. Eldridge was shrugging into his jacket and talking on his cell phone—an animated conversation about meeting someone for a *Sound of Music* sing-along. He missed me in his enthusiasm, and he also missed locking his office door behind him. I took the opportunity—and my renewed girl-power crime-fighter zeal—to sneak into his office. I clicked the door shut behind me, and dropped to my knees in the darkness. I knew better than to turn on a light, so I dug out my cell phone, crawling toward Eldridge's desk by the pale, silvery cell phone glow. I slipped open his file drawer and pushed aside a stack of glamour magazines, only to find another stack. His calendar was filled with hair appointments and lunch dates—nothing incriminating. My heartbeat sped up when I looked over my shoulder toward Dixon's office. The lights were out, and the door was cracked open a half inch. I pressed the cell phone out in front of me once more. Proud of my cat burglar prowess, I took a timid step forward—then another. My cell phone and extended arm were past the threshold into Dixon's office. My heart was thundering in my ears; the blood coursing through my veins in tidal wave–sized torrents.

I crossed the threshold. I was breaking into a vampire's private office.

I held my breath, willed my heart to slow to a nonfrenetic pace. And when my cell phone rang, I peed my pants. I also dropped my phone. Grabbing it, I shoved it into my pocket as I sped for the door, taking the corner of Eldridge's desk to my midthigh. It threw me off balance, as did my shoulder bag loaded with a mushy banana, a bottle of water, and the aforementioned Nancy Drew book. We all went down in an inelegant heap on the industrial carpet. My head hit hard. The Nancy Drew book came around to wallop me in the temple, and I clamped my eyes and my teeth, biting down hard on my tongue. Pain seared through my jaw, and light flashed before my eyes.

It took all of a millisecond to realize the flashing light was coming from the fluorescent light above me and that

Dixon was staring down at me, brown eyes sharp, lips pressed into something that resembled annoyance.

"Ms. Lawson?"

He leaned down gallantly and offered me a hand; I took it tentatively, pushing myself up with my other hand.

"Dixon, hi. I'm really sorry." I looked over both shoulders, worried my bottom lip, trying to stall and buy time to come up with a good explanation. "I thought I heard something in here, and I thought everyone had left, so I just thought . . . well, you know, with everything going on and all. . . . I wanted to make sure that everything in here—everything in here, and with you, was secure. And maybe to see if you needed me to do anything."

I grinned widely, stupidly, praying that Dixon would see past my terror, sweat, and pee smell—and would send me home or fire me on the spot.

But he didn't seem to have listened to a word I said.

His eyes were fixed, narrowed, and laser sharp on my lower leg, on the enormous tear in my panty hose. On the velvety red bead of blood that bubbled there.

"Oh." I looked from the tear to him, at the sharp focus of his eyes, the faint flick of his nostrils. I saw a muscle in his cheek flick, saw the slight bob of his Adam's apple as he swallowed.

He was salivating.

"Dixon?"

Dixon avoided my gaze, his whole body bristling. It looked as though it took effort—*physical effort*—for him to tear his eyes from my cut, from the blood that had now started to dribble in an anemic, itchy trail.

"You need to go home now, Sophie."

I picked up my shoulder bag and pointed toward Dixon's office door. "I need to get my cell phone. I dropped it when I"—I paused, licking my lips—"when I tripped."

"Get it. And then you need to leave right now, Ms. Lawson. You shouldn't be in here. My office is private, and I need for you to leave right now."

"But I just need to—"

Dixon's mouth was open, his sharp fangs glistening with saliva. "Go!"

His palms were on my chest and he gave me a shove. His push knocked me out into the main hall, making me slide across the linoleum on my butt and lose my breath when I finally hit the wall. My heart was pounding in my throat, and my whole body felt hot, covered in a fine, sticky sweat.

Dixon stood in his office, fists and teeth clenched. I scrambled onto hands and knees, pushed myself onto my feet, and took off at a dead run to the elevators.

I didn't stop hiccupping, crying, or sucking in great gusts of fresh night air until I was at the base floor of my apartment building. I was able to breathe normally, was able to go a full minute without a snot-filled hiccup, by the time I got to Will's door.

"Whoa, whoa, whoa, love," he said, opening the door and letting me fall into him. "What happened here?"

I dumped all of my things on the ground and thumped down, too. "Dixon tried to eat me."

Will's fawn-colored brows rose. "Isn't that quite frowned upon at UDA? The boss eating his employees?"

I breathed deeply. "Well, I guess he didn't try to eat me, so much as he wanted to eat me. And didn't."

"Well, that was nice of him. Right?"

I dropped my head in my hands. "What's happening, Will? My life is coming apart at the seams."

Will sank down next to me and gathered me in his arms. I sucked in his sweet, toasty scent of hops and sighed. "I'm sorry. It was just a weird day"—I looked up, feeling quite pitiful—"and I should go home."

"That's okay. I was just making a curry, if you'd like to stay around and—"

"No. No, but thanks," I said, pushing myself up to standing. "I really need to go home." I used the back of my hand to push the tears from my eyes and swept a kiss on Will's cheek; then I rushed across the hall to my own door.

ChaCha greeted me with her usual series of Alpo-scented yips, while Vlad greeted me with his usual series of brooding vampire/annoyed teenager grunts. Suddenly he appeared over his laptop. "Are you bleeding?"

I dampened a paper towel and dabbed at the half-dried blood on my thigh. "It's nothing."

Vlad knitted his eyebrows. "You okay?"

I opened my mouth and then closed it again, staring at Vlad. I studied the sweet, concerned look on his face, the sharp ends of his fangs pressing over his bottom lip. "I'm fine," I said again.

I had the oven door open and was pawing through my earthquake stash of marshmallow pinwheels and Coke Zero—San Francisco is *thisclose* to a fault line, you know—when Nina came strutting out in a silky gown that hugged each of her marble curves. She was clipping on a gorgeous pair of Art Deco diamond drop earrings and scowling about it. Vampires can only wear clip-ons, as a piercing immediately heals itself. I found it creepily cool; Nina found it an affront to fashionistas everywhere.

"Well," she said, arcing her arms in a flourish, "how do I look?"

I crushed the package of pinwheels to my chest. "You look beautiful. Is that why you left the office at three today?"

Nina just winked at me, and I couldn't help but admire her for the easy way things slid off her back, for the way that she would never miss a meal or gain an inch. I would be satisfied with eternal life and no earrings if I could have her countenance that simply broadcast "piss me off and I'll eat you."

I shoved a whole pinwheel into my mouth and sat down at the dining table. ChaCha must have heard the rustle of the package—anything rustling must be for her, she assumed—as she came bounding up and into my lap.

"You look incredible, Nina," I said, chocolate dribbling down my chin. "Sometimes I wish I could be like you."

"Immortal?"

"That"—I popped open a warm Coke Zero and took a swig—"and uncomplicated."

Nina's eyes narrowed and the temperature in the room dropped about ten degrees. Even ChaCha started to shiver, a stripe of hair on her back standing straight up like spines.

"I didn't mean you're uncomplicated," I backpedaled.

"I just meant your life is so much fun. You know, your dad's not Satan. You can go out with whomever you want, without the fate of the world hanging in the balance." I fished out a second pinwheel. "Must be nice."

Nina was going more and more stiff; her lips held tighter and tighter.

I wasn't making any friends.

"And that's my cue," Vlad said, throwing his leather duster over his arm and beelining for the door.

She leaned over so that we were an inch apart. Both her hands lay flat on the dining table; her clip-on earrings swinging.

"Wah, wah, wah! I'm Sophie Lawson and my life is horrible because my dad abandoned me and might be the devil, and I can't figure out if I want to be with an angel or a Guardian. Wah, wah, WAH!" Nina crossed her arms, and genuine anger roiled in her eyes. "You know, some of us are damned, Sophie. That's a little bit of a pain in the ass, too. I love you, but I'm getting really tired of your world-is-ending pity parties. All of us have stuff to deal with. You're looking for your soul mate between Will and Alex? Be happy you have a soul to share."

Nina snatched her purse and keys from the peg by the door and slammed the door hard behind her. I sat at the table, openmouthed, partially pinwheeled. I felt even worse about myself, feeling a tiny warmth starting at my belly.

A beat passed and I stood up fast, rushing to the front door, throwing it open. "I'm sorry, Nina!" I called out to the empty hall. Will's doorknob rolled and he poked his head out.

"What's going on out here?" He looked at me and then frowned—with disgust or concern, I couldn't be sure. "What happened to you? It's barely been fifteen minutes and you look like you've gone from bad to worse."

I looked down mournfully at my shirtfront, now heavily flecked with bits of chocolate cookie—and dog pee.

"It's pinwheel," I said sadly. "And, apparently, dog pee."

I dragged my feet over to Will and threw my arms around him. "I suck, Will. I'm a sucky friend and a sucky Underworld protector, and I'm out of pinwheels."

Will initially arched away from me—likely in an effort to keep himself dog pee free—then held me close to him, patting my back tenderly.

"Tell me about it, love," he said, his lips nestled just above my ear.

Chapter Twenty-Four

Will took me by the hand and I stumbled behind him into his living room. "Still moving in, huh?"

Though it had been at least a year, Will still had nothing more than the two lawn chairs in the living room, a Wii console and now, an entertainment wall unit so sleek and modern, I was certain NASA was probably missing it. He shrugged, offering me that carefree, lopsided grin.

"I think the pillow there"—he pointed to a needle-point Arsenal pillow nestled on one of the chairs—"really makes the place look homey. You want to go across and change your shirt? I'll make you a cuppa."

I looked down miserably at my pee- and chocolate-soaked shirt. "I don't want to go home. I'm afraid I'll blow it up, or something will come barreling in there and kill me. Can I hang out here?"

"Sure. If anything is coming after you, it'll never find you here, right across the hall."

I felt my lower lip jut out childishly. "But you're my Guardian."

"I was just kidding, love. It's my job to protect you. But if you blow up my apartment, you're on your own." He gestured to his living space as though it were palatial or furnished. "I quite like it here now."

I nodded, looking around. "I kind of do, too."

He jerked his head toward the bedroom. "Why don't you go grab yourself a less scenty shirt, though? I've got a clean stack on the bureau. Yes"—he nodded his head modestly while patting his flat-as-a-washboard stomach—"I do laundry."

I nodded and padded into Will's room. It was smaller than mine and dim, with a tasteful bedroom set that belied the lawn furniture out front. I looked around and breathed in Will's scent—part laundry detergent, part some sort of spicy, fresh cologne. The stack of clean clothes was on the bureau, and next to that a framed photograph of an older woman, with a sweet, serene smile. Her head was slightly cocked, and her eyes were the same gold-flecked hazel as Will's. She had the same warm, playful look that I had seen so many times when I looked at Will. I knew his mother was back in England, that he talked to her often; and the thought—Will's family, his roots—struck something in my heart. No one I knew—myself included—had roots.

I turned around and grinned at Will's rumpled bed; at his nightstand, which held a half glass of water, a stack of Harlan Coben books, and a pair of eyeglasses. Nothing mysterious or mythological. Nothing magical. Nothing that said he was just passing through, only here long enough to change the fate of the world. Roots.

I slipped out of my shirt and reached for one of Will's. It smelled like laundry detergent and cleanliness.

I couldn't bear to slip into it in my dirty state. Instead, I shimmied out of all my clothes, and turned the shower on extra hot in the attached bathroom.

When enough steam filled the room, I stepped into the shower and held myself under the pounding spout. The hot water poured over my shoulders and I felt my whole body melt. I clamped my eyes shut and suddenly I couldn't tell the shower water from the tears flooding over my cheeks. I was tired. So, so tired. I didn't want to think of the Underworld or fallen angels or a father who didn't want to see me. I didn't want to piece any puzzles together or let anyone down.

I didn't want to be the Vessel of Souls.

I didn't want to protect the Underworld.

I stepped out of the shower and dried off with one of Will's ultra fluffy towels, enjoying the soothing normalcy of a bathroom stocked with all the usual stuff; and a bedroom that contained a slept-in bed and a giant picture window that could be thrown open to allow the sunlight to stream through.

I was tired.

Will's bed was welcoming with its disheveled sheets, which smelled like Will. Comforting. Clean. Simply human. I dropped my towel and snuggled under the covers for just a second, just to feel normal—like a girl who had a boyfriend. Not an angel.

Not a vampire roommate.

I was so, so tired.

When I opened my eyes, I wasn't sure where I was. The light was dim and I was comfortable; I felt alive and well rested. And then I heard the breathing next to me. It was a rhythmic rise and fall, a normal human cadence. When I rolled over, I sat up with a start.

It was Will.

And I was naked.

My heart started to thud and I rubbed my head. I had taken a shower. I had crawled into bed.

Is Will naked, too?

His chest was bare, the covers pulled just over his stomach.

I gingerly lifted up the blanket, peered underneath. He was wearing pants.

I watched his chest rise and fall in the dark, a sliver of silvery moonlight catching the perfect edge of his profile. He was handsome this way—quiet, asleep—and his lips looked lush and perfect. My heartbeat sped up and my palms were clammy damp. I leaned over, drew a breath, and pressed my lips against his.

Without a word, without a single thought, I was kissing Will and he was kissing me; his arms snaked around my waist and he pulled me close to him. My breasts crushed against his chest as I kissed him harder, pushing every other impulse out of my mind. His fingers were looped in my hair, and mine were raking across his back as we spun, kicking back covers, pulling off clothes. I felt my blood coursing through my every vein, my every artery—every single part of my body was tingling, on high alert. For the first time I could really remember, I felt alive.

Will pulled into me, holding me close. I listened to our hearts pounding, felt his breath washing over me.

There were no scars on his back—no threat of leaving when he looked at me. His skin was supple, perfect.

He knew what I knew. He saw what I saw.

He looked down and kissed me once more, and I melted into him.

Sunlight streaked through the picture window and I stirred, an ache going through my entire body. I waited for ChaCha's kibble breath, for her frenzied good-morning licks, but nothing happened. I cracked open one eye and then the other; I rolled over and took in the empty pillow.

Will.

I sat up and stared around the empty room; the unusual feeling of comfort and serenity crashing over me. I slid into one of Will's shirts and padded into the kitchen, where Will stood shirtless, staring at an egg in a frying pan as if it were an alien baby.

"Good morning," I said, trying hard to keep the sleep and sheepishness out of my voice.

"Good morning to you, love," Will said, giving me a noncommittal kiss on the forehead. "Sleep okay?"

I nodded. "What's that?"

Will frowned. "I was planning on making you breakfast in bed."

I glanced at my watch. "It's almost noon."

"Well, there is that. Also"—he poked at the egg—"I don't know how to make eggs." Will tossed the pan—milky egg and all—into the sink. "How 'bout you stay around? I'll make my famous call to Crepe Ape?"

"No, thank you. I should really get going." I gathered my clothes under one arm and carried my shoes in the other. Will and I shared an uncomfortable silence.

Do I kiss him? Thank him? Wave good-bye?

"I gotta go," I said, avoiding his gaze and slipping out the front door.

Smooth, I groaned.

And then I ran into Alex.

"Hey," he said, steadying me.

"You're back," I said, startled, but otherwise unsure how I felt.

"Yeah. Got in about an hour ago. We're done." He grinned, but his brow was furrowed. "You're sure in a hurry to get somewhere." His words slowed down as he took me in—I was in a thigh-length football T-shirt, carrying my clothes, my red-hair halo undeniably screaming, "Morning after!" I saw him swallow hard, and all my early-morning comfort crashed away.

He's not my boyfriend, I reminded myself. *So why do I feel so damn guilty?*

Alex looked down at his shoes and I shuffled my bare feet, thinking that if "Devil Dearest" cared for me at all, he'd choose this very moment to open up the mouth of Hell and call me home.

"I tried to call you, but it kept going straight to voice mail. I figured you had something going on." Alex looked as though he was working not to see my T-shirt, not to look at my naked legs. "I'm heading out again in a couple of days. Back to Buffalo, just to finish things off. I just wanted to stop in to make sure you were all right." The muscle jumped in Alex's jaw as he swallowed hard. "But I guess you're doing fine."

I opened my mouth to say . . . What?

"Um, thank you. I . . . was just . . ." I pointed to Will's door. "We were just—"

Alex shook his head; a smile that was really not a smile at all on his lips. "That's okay. You don't have to say . . . I just wanted to say good-bye."

My chest started to feel tight; my heart rose in my throat. "Because of Buffalo, right? I mean, you'll be back, right?"

Alex avoided my gaze. "Sure." He reached out, his hand landing softly on my shoulder. He patted it; then gave an awkward squeeze. "I'm glad you're okay." He didn't look at me when he said, "Good-bye, Sophie."

He turned and walked away; and every fiber of my being told me to stop him, to shout, to say something— anything—that would pull the awkward discomfort out of this moment, for something that would make everything okay with Alex, with Will—with me.

"Alex," I said to his back.

He stopped and waited a beat before turning around. "Yeah?"

I bit my lip, and words choked my throat. Alex's tender gaze; Will's comforting touch. Alex's sexy half smile; Will's sweet lopsided one. The way my name sounded in each of their mouths . . .

"Be safe," I heard myself whisper.

I stepped into my apartment, dumping my filthy clothes on the floor. ChaCha came running toward me and I scooped her up, scratching her head absently.

"Nina!" I called. "Neens, I need to talk to you."

My cheeks were hot, and my heart was crushed between walking into Will's arms—and out of Alex's.

"Nina?" I said, my voice picking up a tinny, whiny twinge, which I didn't like. "Are you here?"

I did a double knock on her bedroom door and then poked my head in. Her clothes seemed to buzz with a nervous energy and I felt my blood pressure rise. "Nina?"

I looked down into ChaCha's brown marble eyes and she cocked her head at me; then reached up on her hind legs and lapped my chin.

I gave her an extra treat from the kitchen counter, and when I reached for the paper towels (this dog is a slobber hound), I saw Nina's note stuck to the cabinet.

> *Soph—*
> *Out with H. Love this man!!!*
> *Think about what color you'd like to wear in our wedding. . . .*
>
> *XOXO,*
> *N*

I crumpled up the note and tossed it in the trash, then scoured the kitchen for breakfast food. I was halfway through a peanut butter–smeared waffle when my cell phone chirped its "you've got messages!" chirp. I shoved the waffle in my mouth and held the phone to my ear.

"You have six new messages," the unnervingly polite cell phone voice told me.

Alex had called three times; each message getting

progressively shorter and stabbing me with shards of guilt. Then there was the obligatory "this is not a sales call" message, and the last two were from Roland.

There was a pause before the message started and I could hear Roland's nervous breath in the background. I could imagine him mopping his sweaty head with that yellowed handkerchief.

"Hello, Sophie." His recorded voice sounded as weasely as his date voice. "This is Roland Townsend—Harley's agent? From the restaurant." As if he needed any more introduction. "Um, I'm calling to see if you know where your roommate is. I think she's with Harley and . . ." Roland sucked in a slightly shaky breath, which told more than his words did. "Can you just call me as soon as you get this message?" He went on to awkwardly read off his phone number.

I erased his message and his second one started immediately.

"Sophie? Roland again. Roland Townsend. Can you call me, please? Right away. I"—Roland sucked in another tentative breath—"I'm worried about your roommate. I think . . . I don't think Harley has the best intentions—the best intentions toward your friend. I think Nina might be in danger."

I sat up straight, Roland's final words slicing down my spine like a frozen blade. My stomach turned over; my peanut butter waffle felt like a hunk of raw dough rising in my gut, pressing against my chest.

I dialed Roland and he answered on the first ring.

"Aw, geez, Sophie." Roland's voice was strangled with a strange mix of tension and relief. "I'm glad you got my messages. And my calls."

I pulled the phone away from my ear and saw the frowny-faced readout: eleven missed calls.

My saliva immediately tasted bitter and my eyes started to sting. "Where's Nina?"

"She's not with you?" He breathed out a long, uncomfortable sigh. "She must be with Harley, then."

"Why do you think Harley's dangerous?"

"I don't think Harley's dangerous, Sophie. I know he is."

Chapter Twenty-Five

My heart was in my throat when I hung up with Roland. I looked down at the Post-it notes where I had scrawled the address he gave me and I barely recognized the shaky chicken scratch writing as my own. I flew into a pair of yoga pants and sneakers. On my way out the door, I glanced over my shoulder at the freezer. There, stashed in a box of Skinny Cow mint dippers, was the gun that Alex had given me a year ago; a handful of bullets rolled around in our junk drawer.

I licked my paper-dry lips and heard Roland's voice reverberating in my head. "*I don't think Harley's dangerous, Sophie. I know he is.*"

I grabbed my gun, the bullets, and went thundering out the door.

"Whoa! What's this about?" Will's eyes were big, his cheeks pushed up in a semi-surprised grin. "It wasn't that bad, was it?"

It took me a second to process what he was saying, a niggle of heat washing over my cheeks. "I need to find Harley," I croaked out finally.

Will's eyes raked over me, over the gun in my hand. "I'm going with you. And you better put that away, love, or we'll never get out the door."

I looked blankly down at the gun in my hand, its muzzle trained on the horrible industrial-grade hallway carpet. "Oh."

Will locked the door behind him and I shifted from foot to foot, worrying my bottom lip as the elevator sank down into our basement garage.

"It's going to be fine," Will said, squeezing my shoulder gently. "You'll see."

I let him lead me through the dimly lit lot, the space between us minuscule as my heart thumped solidly against my rib cage.

"Get in."

I was rolling locks of hair around my index finger—my number one nervous tic—until the tip of my finger turned cold and white while Will sped through the intersection, occasionally glancing over at the Post-it note balanced on my thigh.

"You're sure this Roland bloke is reliable?"

I nodded, unable to open my mouth lest my heart leap out onto the dashboard.

He poked at the address with an index finger. "And you're sure this is right?"

I nodded again. "I guess. This is what Roland gave me. He said Harley likes to go here."

"And you believe him?"

I shook my head, terror closing my throat. "Not exactly. But it's the only lead we have."

My eyes were locked on the road disappearing under our wheels. My hand was feeling the outline of the gun in my purse—the gun that I might have to use to kill Harley.

My heart leapt painfully again, throwing itself against my rib cage.

I had run out of the house with this gun before. I had been willing to aim it, to shoot it at unknown attackers, or attackers who were on their second, evil life. But I had never considered shooting—killing—a flesh-and-blood human being, a human being with a name and a face and a family and a life.

"*I don't think he's dangerous, Sophie. I know he is.*" Roland's words played over and over again in my mind like an ominous, horrible record. "*I know he is.*"

I gulped, trying to blink back the tears, trying to swallow back the terrified lump that clawed at my throat.

"Do you know this area?"

I snapped to the here-and-now, to Will in the car, to the ominous-looking brick buildings jutting up all around us. They were squat and industrial, lined with cracked sidewalks; little bits of weedy grass poking through the concrete. They had been trampled mercilessly.

"You're sure this is right?" Will asked again, skepticism deep in his voice.

"This is what he said," I repeated. "Besides, I suppose if"—I couldn't say his name, couldn't given him an actual human moniker—"he wanted to get Nina alone, this would be the place to do it. There!"

A bubble burst in my chest when I saw Roland, himself looking as squat as the buildings, waving his stubby arms in front of what looked like had once been a bakery.

Will slowed down, scanning the street. "Well, there's no place to park around here—"

"Let me out," I said, hands on the door. eyes held firmly on Roland, on the sweat lining his brow, on the terrified way his button eyes flashed.

"No, love—"

But I already had the door open. "Just park and come around. We'll wait for you before we go in."

Before the car even came to a complete stop, I had jumped out and was tearing across the street. My breath burned in my throat as my legs pumped.

"Oh, Sophie, thank goodness you came," Roland sputtered.

"Where's Nina?"

Roland was looking at his shoes, wringing his hands, shifting his weight. "I should have known. I should have known the way he clung to her." He looked up at me, his eyes apologetic. "I knew he had these tendencies. I knew. That's why I travel with him. Usually when I'm around, I can talk him down—"

"Where are they?"

Roland's terrier eyes rolled to the side, to the glass door of the building, the lock on it yawning open. I pushed through the door. "Nina? Nina, where are you?"

Roland was behind me. I could hear his nervous shuffle, the ragged way he sucked in those long, deep breaths.

"Oh shit," he muttered, sighing. "I hope it's not too late."

I whirled around and stared at him, feeling my eyebrows dropping into a hard V. But I was looking at

Roland's back as he fumbled with the door. I heard the lock jiggle, shake, and finally tumble into place.

My throat was dry.

"What are you doing?"

Roland looked at me, all innocence and unnecessary sweat. "I didn't want him to run out the front door."

I tried to swallow, my hand sliding down to the gun in my shoulder bag. *"O . . . kay."* I drew out the word as my hand snaked down past my hip to my thigh.

My purse.

My gun.

Forgotten.

Snuggled in Will's car's pink interior.

I looked up just in time to see Roland's button eyes glistening, lips pushed out into a rodent's smile, his small yellowed teeth bared. His fat fingers hugged a crude hunk of wood, which cracked against my skull. I felt myself wobble while I worked to focus my eyes. There was Roland. There were two Rolands. There was a sweet-looking, cupcake-shaped light fixture and graffiti on the ceiling.

My eyes were open—though they felt somehow rolled back, locked, staring at my own eyebrows. Roland started to gather me up, awkwardly, roughly, pushing me to my feet. I stumbled but stood, feeling heavy and weary. I let him gather up my hands and push them behind me before I realized what that meant. I started to fumble, to pull away, when I heard the sound of tape being ripped, when I felt the tightening as he wound it around my wrist.

"What are you doing?" I asked, the sting of my head blooming into a full-blown throb.

"I'm surprised a girl like you didn't already catch on. Guess all that time on earth didn't teach you a damn thing, did it?"

I stumbled as Roland pushed me forward. "What are you talking about? Where are you taking me?"

"Look, it's really nothing personal. We had a nice date."

"This is what that's about? The date?"

Roland snorted and continued shoving me forward. I hesitated, trying to buy some time, when I felt a swift kick to my heel and heard an exasperated groan.

"Christ. Would you walk already?"

I shuffled along, wincing, gritting my teeth against my tears, trying to listen for Will.

He knows where I am, I told myself. *He'll be here any minute.*

I heard keys jiggling in a lock and I was shoved forward again. I counted my steps—forty-one, in case that mattered—until I was spun around. I heard the click of something metal; I felt the freeing slice of a blade and suddenly my hands were free. Before I could do anything about it, I was shoved backward, and a narrow door streaked with dirt and chipping paint was slammed in my face.

"What are you doing? Why are you locking me in here?" I grabbed the doorknob and shook it, yanked it. "What are you doing?"

"I'm making it easy for you, Sophie dear. In a couple of hours the sun will pour right through that window there, and poof. End of story for all of us."

"What the hell are you talking about?"

"I know the legends. I know the rules," Roland said,

his voice creeping through the crack in the door. "One little burst of sunlight . . ." He chuckled—an eerie, grimacing laugh—and I heard his heavy footsteps as he shuffled away from the door, whistling.

The panic didn't start to set in—didn't start to creep up my neck, to reach out and strangle me—until I yanked on the surprisingly secure doorknob; then I whirled around and took in my cramped surroundings as they started to close in on me. I was in a dingy bathroom— tiny, about the size of my closet—and, apparently, untouched since the Reagan administration. The tin box spitting out paper towels was dented and rusted. The walls were filthy and laced with scrawled profanities and detailed suggestions of what I should do to myself. There was a small, high window on the back wall. It was covered with a pane of dingy glass and looked like it could be pushed open rather easily—if the whole thing hadn't been secured with a horizontal set of metal bars.

I started to feel the blood pounding in my temples. I felt beads of sweat prick out above my upper lip and at my hairline. I'm not particularly crazy about public bathrooms to begin with, so to be locked in one in the middle of . . . Oh God, where the hell was I?

I turned around and started beating the door, kicking and punching and screaming until the heels of my hands were raw and my throat felt sandpaper-achy. I gave one last wallop, one last howl.

"You don't know what you're talking about, Roland! I'm not a vampire. Let me out of here! Let me out of here and I'll prove it!"

When there was no response, I gave the door a final swift kick; then I looked for a place to slump down and cry. But being in a public restroom, I knew that seating was limited.

That made me cry harder.

Roland was trying to kill me.

Roland thought I was a vampire, so he was going to kill me.

I stopped.

Roland. Thought I was a vampire. And was going to kill me.

The idea seemed so absurd, so laughable—until I thought of Mrs. Henderson. The centaur from the dock. Bettina, and Kale.

He was going to kill me.

And I was going to die in here, and someone would find my shriveled body in a mess of single-ply toilet paper and misspelled profanities. I sniffed. There was no way I was going to let that happen, no way I would let my tombstone bear the inglorious statement: SOPHIE LAWSON: SHE DIED IN THE JOHN.

I raked the heel of my hand across my wet cheeks and wound a loop of toilet paper to blow my nose. Being locked in a public restroom did have some perks, I guess. I went to the cracked and wobbly mirror, steadying myself against the sink. I gave the mirror frame a gentle knock.

"Grandma?"

Though my grandmother was dead, she did have the uncanny ability to pop into shiny surfaces and offer help when I needed her most. I couldn't think of any other time seeing my dead grandmother's face would be more helpful. The mirror continued to reflect back my own face, extra pale in the single-bulb light. My cheeks were tear streaked and mottled red; my hair a tangled mass of ponytail and little bits of fiber left over from my sojourn on the floor.

"Grandma?" I tried again.

Again there was no answer; the wobbling glass remained smoky and plain. I felt the gurgling choke of another waft of tears. I crossed my arms in front of my chest, holding myself tightly, leaning gently against the cleanest wall I could find—which, ironically, was tagged with funky purple lettering that spelled out *O.G.s don't quit.* I'd never fancied myself an original gangster, but I considered the purple scrawl as a shiny beacon of hope—an homage to strength and Snoop Dogg, and I would follow suit.

Little redheaded girls don't quit, either.

I took several slow, deep breaths—gulping air through my mouth, trying not to imagine the multitude of bathroom-butt germs clinging to my teeth—and commanded myself to come up with a plan. I thought. I paced. I stopped.

"I've got toilet paper"—I kicked the side of the surprisingly clean toilet—"a toilet seat, which could possibly be used as a weapon. Paper towels, sink." I gave the latter a good yank, just in case it should suddenly fall away and reveal a secret passageway to the outdoors or the Four Seasons. "Um, mirror. Okay."

I nodded, slapped my thighs, and took another spin.

"Okay. Nothing overtly weapon-like or break-down-the-door–like. But that's okay. I'm a resourceful girl. I just have to think—what would MacGyver do?"

And then I realized, with a sinking heart, that I had

never seen a *MacGyver* episode full through, and I could kick myself for it.

"Not a problem," I said, bringing myself to the brink of tears but talking them back. I watched a significant amount of television; and if anything was going to spark a memory, it would be now. I didn't watch *MacGyver,* but I had my own list of television heroes, escape artists, and resourceful individuals. Right?

If only I hadn't spent an inordinate amount of time watching the Food Network.

"Okay," I said again. "Well. What would Paula Deen do?"

I felt the panic begin to stir again.

What would Paula Deen do?

She would add a stick of butter. Or a heap of pork fat. Or something slippery and slimy and . . . I looked at the small barred window on the back wall.

Then I looked at the plastic bottle filled with bubble-gum pink hand soap bolted above the sink.

That's what Paula Deen would do.

I squirmed out of my sweatshirt and yanked my yoga pants over my sneakers—there was no way I was letting my skin touch public bathroom floor. I glanced up at the window again. I sighed, then slipped my T-shirt over my head, too, and stood in the glaring light of that stupid naked lightbulb, mostly naked.

I gently tugged on the ancient faucet and a meager trickle of water began to fill the chipped basin. I loaded my dampened palm with soap, and began sudsing myself up. I chanced a glance at myself in the wobbly mirror—white soap foaming up around my neck, my arms glistening with water and tiny bubbles.

If this doesn't work, I thought, *then I hope I die.*

Once my body and underclothes were sufficiently sudsed—or greased, in Paula speak—I stood up on the toilet seat and angled an arm toward the window, giving the ancient jam a shove. To my immense relief, it opened easily and the air felt good as it washed over my damp skin.

"Here goes nothing," I said to the paper towels.

Chapter Twenty-Six

I clamped a hand around each of the bars and hauled myself up to the window a la Mary Lou Retton. Okay, Mary Lou after a few too many donuts and a couple of extra years. I stuck my head out the window first and wriggled, legs kicking, sneakers thunking against the bathroom wall, and my shoulders slipped out easily. I was out, up to my hips, when one of the bars firmly stopped my plumpish rump. The cold metal bore down hard on my lower back. I couldn't risk the leeway I'd already made by going back in for more soap, so I used the pads of my fingers to dig into the crumbling stucco outside. When I looked down, I realized that my little cell must have been nearly underground. A cement parking lot was only about a foot below me, and the realization sent a hopeful thrill through me. I gave myself a mighty wriggle and moved about a quarter inch forward, successfully scraping my chin on the wall, pushing my half-soaped panties halfway down my butt, and eking the breath out of my lungs. I rested my forehead against the concrete in an effort to regroup and cry miserably, when I was met with a pair of slowly walking, sneakered feet. They came to a rest a half inch from my nose.

"God, I *love* this country!"

I worked to turn my pancaked self over and stared up at Will. His face was upside down, but his delighted smile unmistakable.

"What are you doing back here? Weren't you ever going to come find me?" I managed to shout in breathy gasps.

"I did find you. Here. What are *you* doing here?" Will asked without breaking his stupid grin.

"Help me!" I howled. "Get me out of here!"

Will crouched down and hugged me to him; then gave my body a quick succession of gentle tugs and wriggles until I felt my butt make it under the bar. Then I felt my legs slide free.

"Oh, oh, thank God!" I said, running around the parking lot, loving the fresh air, feeling the length of my arms and legs. "It was getting so claustrophobic in there!"

"Is that why you decided to take off your clothes?"

I suddenly realized that I was running around a public parking lot that was half bathed in yellow streetlight in my underclothes.

My sudsy, wet underclothes.

I doubled over; my arms clamped in front of my boobs. "Don't look!"

"I just saved your life."

"That doesn't give you the right to see me naked."

Will's grin was sly. "Again?"

I punched Will, hard, in the shoulder. "Where the hell were you? I was being kidnapped! I was going to be singed by the sun and killed!"

Will reached out for me and I dodged him. "I'm sorry, love. I was right behind you, but the door was bloody locked. I had to find a way in."

My teeth started to chatter, the rattle going through my skull. My fingertips started to blue as an inch of breeze covered my body in gooseflesh. Will began to shrug out of his coat and I took a step toward him, shivering, my soapy arms outstretched. Will surprised me and came at me like a linebacker—deadweight that clotheslined me. We both went down hard—me on my back, the melon-like thud of my skull on the concrete as tiny pebbles needled through the bare skin on my shoulder blades. I tried to cry out, but my breath was gone. The pain behind my eyes went from a dull black to a brilliantly bright starburst.

My heart thundered against Will's forehead and I was finally able to gasp, to suck in, hungrily, huge lungfuls of the icy-cold air as he slid off me. I struggled to sit up and gaped as Will's head flopped, thumping listlessly on the ground.

Roland was hunched over, his ham-hock hands gripping Will's red-and-yellow Arsenal socks. A bubble of blood oozed from Will's hairline, leaving a two-inch-thick red smear from my collarbone to hip as Roland dragged Will's limp body down my stiffened one.

"What did you do to him?"

Roland eyed me, his lips turned up into a gruesome snarl reminiscent of a smile. He straightened, brushing his palms on his ugly dress pants and kicked at a tire iron that clanged on the ground next to Will's temple. Ice water sped through my veins and promptly froze solid when I caught sight of the smear of blood on the edge of the iron—Will's blood.

I tried desperately to moisten my lips. "What . . . Is he . . ." I couldn't form the word—wouldn't form the word.

"Dead?" Roland spat it out with a kind of horrendous glee. "No." He dropped Will's ankles and I kicked away, my damp sneakers losing traction in the parking lot.

"Don't worry about him," Roland said, giving Will's slack body a swift kick. "He went down hard, but it's really not as bad as it looks." He looked wistfully at Will's still back. "Probably. Now come on, dear." Roland crouched down, offering me a pale hand and an even paler smile.

I pitched back, staring horrified at him. "Get away from me."

Roland cocked his head in a way that was likely meant to be comforting but chilled me—damp underwear not withstanding—to the soles of my feet. "You know you can't be here, Sophie."

"Shut up." I tried to keep my voice steady as my eyes darted from left to right, taking in the empty parking lot, weighing my chances of escape.

"No," Roland said, his eyes suddenly slate gray and sharp as naked swords, "no." He straightened, holding a single pointed finger a half inch from my nose before he dove for me, his stubby fingertips digging into the flesh at the back of my arm. For a squat fire hydrant of a man, he was surprisingly strong and lithe. He had me up on my feet; my sneakers folding over each other as he dragged me toward the lone car in the parking lot.

Words—excuses, explanations, scenarios—rushed

through my head as I tried to come up with some way to stall, to keep Roland from getting me into his car. I had watched enough *48 Hours* to know that once I was in his car, I was a dead woman.

"We can't just leave Will there," I said finally, working to keep the hysteria out of my voice. "Look." I jerked my head and felt my pulse start to throb when I could see Will's shallow breath making his chest rise.

Oh, thank God.

Roland's gaze followed mine, and he must have been as stunned to see Will's body swell with breath as I was, because his fingers loosened their grip for a split second. I took off at a dead sprint; my lungs swelling with the scorching fire of desperation and fear. The streets were bare and empty; I dove toward Roland's car and yanked open the driver's-side door, pitching myself into the front seat. My feet slammed hard against the gas and the brake, my wet hands yanking on the clutch, the parking brake, anything that would make the damn thing go.

In the rearview mirror I could see Roland walking toward me, a confident saunter. I smacked at the power locks and sucked in a shaky breath, placing both hands on the steering wheel. I stared out the front windshield, as if somehow looking straight ahead would make everything on either side of the car disappear.

It didn't.

There was a quick, friendly rapping on the driver's-side window, which unleashed a torrent of pinpricks down my spine and cemented every muscle in my body. I willed myself to move my head, just enough to see Roland out the side window, his grin wide and winning.

He pinched the car keys in his fat Vienna sausage fingers and waved them triumphantly.

My heart skidded to a stop. I felt the slow smolder of terror start as our eyes met in a deadlocked gaze, and our stares held each other until they met at the door lock.

I swallowed hard, watched the pink triangle of Roland's serpentine tongue dart out from between his pressed lips. We dove for the lock at the same time. He was clutching the keys, sinking them into the outside lock; I was pushing my palm so hard against the power lock that I was certain the narrow hunk of plastic would tear through my palm. I heard the sickening squeak of metal pushing against plastic as he turned the key and the lock fought to disengage. I heard every other lock in the car pop up with a jaunty, terrifying *plink!*

When I looked up, Roland was gone, diving for the next open door. I clawed at the handle and opened it myself, kicking open the door, hearing it thunk as it hit hard. The car door swung wide, and Roland was flat out on his back. He rolled like a walrus on sand, his hands pressed against his nose. Blood streamed between his palms as he lay on the cement.

"You fucking bitch!" he managed to mutter. "You fucking broke my nose!"

But I was past response.

I launched myself from the driver's seat and had nearly cleared Roland, was feeling light and airy and Wonder Woman chic, until I felt a hand clamp around my ankle. A firm yank brought me clattering to the pavement; my knees and palms were pressing into the concrete, my delicate skin being shredded.

I felt my teeth clamp down hard on the soft flesh of

my lower lip. I felt the skin open easily and then my mouth was filled with blood so hot and viscous it was like liquid steel.

"Ooh!"

My chin went down next and then my cheek skidded across the concrete. My forehead scraped the ground and I dug the pads of my fingertips against the cement, trying to kick out of Roland's grasp. He was strong and every inch of my body cried out with stinging, searing heat. Adrenaline was pooling, weighing down each limb. He had a knee in my back and then flipped me over quickly, straddling me. His thighs were clamped hard around my hips, and I cursed Suzanne Somers and her goddamn ThighMaster as I tried to swivel uselessly underneath him.

"Forget it," he said, his hate foaming at the sides of his mouth, his saliva raining over me.

I tried again to wriggle, to move, but Roland was pinning me. My arms were clamped to my sides; my legs kicked and bucked futilely in the mocking yellow slash of streetlight.

Scream, I commanded myself. *Scream! Goddamn it!*

I opened my mouth and choked on my own breath as Roland's hands clamped down on my throat. His fat sausage thumbs dug against my windpipe.

"I've worked too damn hard with that tool Harley to let a fucking beast like you ruin everything."

In my mind I was answering him. In my mind my eyes were still open and I was still aware of the ice-cold night, the little bit of streetlight, and the furious, berserk look in his narrowed eyes. In my mind I wasn't feeling lighter and lighter. My eyelids weren't feeling heavy; the colors of the night weren't starting to fade into muted, bleeding blotches.

I tried to gasp. I tried to suck in the smallest micro inch of air through my parted lips, but the effort seared everything inside me. Suddenly there was the loudest, most sickening *thunk,* and I was drifting through the darkness. I was feeling so light, so airy.

"Sophie! Sophie!"

Will's voice was needling at me through a purple haze and I tried to turn toward him. He was dead, too.

"We're dead," I told him, my lips feeling heavy and purple; hot pools of bloody saliva dripping from my mouth. "We're both dead now, Will."

"No, we're not. Sophie, open your eyes!"

"I'll kill you both!"

I opened my eyes just in time to see Roland go for Will's wrist. Will easily turned him around and wrapped his muscular forearm around Roland's neck. I was so mesmerized I didn't hear the sound of plastic and metal sliding across the concrete until the gun hit my thigh and stopped sliding.

"Pick it up, Sophie!"

I stared blankly at the gun, then up at Will; his face was red as Roland flailed wildly, trying to bash Will in the head, trying to go for the bloody gouge that was already there.

Suddenly Will lost his footing and the pair was tumbling, limbs flailing, the sickening sound of flesh hitting flesh resounding as they fought.

"Soph—"

The sound of Roland's knuckles making contact with Will's jaw cut off my name. I wrapped my hand around the gun when Roland rolled over and had Will pinned. I closed my eyes and squeezed the trigger, the popping of the bullet roiling through my body, cracking in my brain. I opened my eyes and gawked.

Chapter Twenty-Seven

Roland bucked liked a bronco and flopped off Will, making the loudest, most terrifying sound I've ever heard. I saw the soles of Will's shoes first—flailing, kicking at the cement, then dropping silent.

Oh my God.

I heard nothing but the blood rushing in a fierce flow through my ears. My heart clanged and the tears were rolling over my cheeks before I knew I was crying. I didn't care about Roland, who was scratching the driver's-side door, trying to get into his car. I threw the gun aside and crab walked over to Will, willing myself to look at him, to see him. I would stop the bleeding; I would wait until the ambulance came; I would beg him to hold on for just a few more precious moments. I saw the police lights flashing in the distance. Could hear the mournful wail as the squad cars closed in.

"Will?" I whispered, grasping his hand. "Please hold on. Please."

I kill everyone I love, I thought. *I made love to him, and then I shot him.*

I swallowed hard and Will blinked up at me, coughing, using the back of his hand to wipe at the blood and spit on his lips.

"Will!"

"Oh, love." Will struggled to sit up. His face was scratched and bruised, and bits of rust-colored blood dried in his hair, around his nose, was liquid at the corner of his mouth. His rubbing at it only made it worse.

"I thought I shot you."

"Hands where I can see them!" someone barked.

The cop cars were on us and I shielded my eyes against the overwhelming wash of headlights and raised my hands. There were two squad cars with six cops in fighting stance, knees bent, guns drawn. Behind them came a parade of flashing-light cars—an ambulance, a fire truck, more cop cars. My heart exploded in overwhelming joy, and relief washed over me in cool waves.

"Put them up!"

My heart did a double thump and I thought about explaining, but I saw those muzzles at the ready. I raised my arms higher, until I realized all of the officers had their guns trained on Roland. He reluctantly, slowly pulled his hands from where they had been—cradling his butt—and I saw that they were covered in blood.

"She shot me!" he screamed, bits of spit flying out of his mouth as he aimed a blood-drenched index finger at me. "That crazy bitch shot me in the ass! Arrest her!"

Two officers I'd known from Bettina's crime scene rushed to me and Will, beckoning over the paramedic while another cop cuffed Roland and read him his rights.

I licked at my paper-dry lips. My tongue stung the

broken skin as I looked at the officer rushing toward us. "How did you—how did you know it was me?" I asked him.

Officer Romero draped a thick, itchy blanket over my bare shoulders as the paramedic helped me up.

"There was a disturbance reported." He looked almost sheepish. "I knew you were one of Alex's people." His sheepish look turned into a small grin. "And the one most likely to be in a disturbance. Also, someone named Athena Bushant called you in as a missing person, likely in danger."

"Who's Athena Bushant?" Will wanted to know.

I laughed—a weird, high-pitched, got-out-with-my-life laugh. "Athena Bushant, the great vampire-romance writer."

The paramedics tended to Will first, while I chanced a glance at Roland, who was being laid belly-first on a gurney. His gunshot ass faced upward, while a professional-looking paramedic cut his pants off as though he wasn't still ranting.

"Isn't it illegal to shoot someone in the ass? Isn't this America?"

"Sir, you need to calm down. You're making the blood loss worse."

I immediately made a mental note to send a donation to the San Francisco paramedics. They had rescued me on more than one occasion and I was grateful—but having to tend to Roland's butt was a whole different level of public service.

After one of the officers dropped Will and me at our apartment building, we trudged through the vestibule in companionable silence. When we came to our doors, he took my arm—still covered in six inches of industrial-grade blanket—and pulled me to him, resting his cheek on the top of my head.

"Quite a day, wasn't it, love?"

I just nodded, my head heavy with exhaustion and stinging from the paramedic's Mercurochrome. Will looked down at me and slid one bandaged hand underneath my chin, raising my lips toward his. He kissed me softly and I kissed back—briefly. When I pulled away, tears were stinging my eyes.

"I should get inside," I said without looking back.

"Oh my God!" Nina screamed when I let myself in. "I was so worried about you!" She gave me a brief once-over before smashing me to her. Her eyes filled with tears. "We're so, so sorry."

I stiffened and pulled back. "We?"

Nina looked over her shoulder, heart-shaped lips pursed in a modest pink smile. "Harley and I."

I felt anger roil through me. "Nina, Harley's the reason—"

Harley held up a hand. "I'm so sorry, Sophie. I should have known. Roland had become really controlling and paranoid in the last few cities. He would disappear for hours and mutter about how he was going to 'clean things up.' He said he saw things—ridiculous things—demons, gremlins. I just thought he was drinking. I never imagined he would—would peg you for a vampire."

A little breath of hysterical laughter passed my lips.

"Vampire?" I said, feeling the laughter rise in my

throat. "That's why Roland came after me?" I said, playing along.

Harley nodded solemnly. "He got this idea that there were all sorts of demons and monsters roaming around. He said he had to kill them, or the book would be a flop. I didn't think he was serious. I thought it was more of a stress thing."

"Vampire," I said again, feeling my shoulders ache as the laughter shot through my whole body.

"Wow," Nina said, her eyes intent on mine. "Imagine our little Sophie, mistaken for a vampire."

Harley laughed, too, now; and Nina followed suit, her small fangs catching the light. Harley was oblivious and slung an arm around his girlfriend, pulling her to his side. "Can you imagine? He actually thought vampires existed!"

"Can't imagine at all," Nina said, one eyebrow raised, mischievous lips curling over her fangs. She trailed her fingers down Harley's arm and laced her fingers with his.

"Oh, honey, your fingers are always so cold." He brought her pale fingers, entwined with his, to his lips and kissed them. "I told her she should see a doctor about her circulation problem."

I nodded while Nina pulled Harley behind her. "I'm going to say good-bye to Harley, Soph. He's leaving for Seattle in the morning. You going to be okay for a little bit, or should I call Vlad to stay with you?"

Vlad—that reminded me.

"Hey, Neens, there was a pipe in the back of your car. Do you know what that was for?"

Nina's brow furrowed. "A pipe?" Then she brightened. "You mean the long silver bar."

I nodded.

"It's a closet extender. Vlad is helping me add a little closet space. So, should I call him?"

"I'll be fine," I told Nina, glad for a little peace of mind, quiet, and clothes.

"That nephew of yours is a really odd kid," Harley was saying as they walked out the door. "All the dark clothes and nail polish. Is that what they call 'Emo'?"

I slipped out of the paramedic's blanket and dropped it on the bathroom floor, pulled off my underclothes, which had now stiffened with dried soap and blood, and lowered myself into a hot bath loaded with peach-scented bubbles. I felt everything—Will, Alex, Roland—slide off me and drown in the sweet-scented water. I stopped counting the scratches and bruises and instead washed my hair and luxuriated until my skin was puckered and pink. Eventually I got out, wrapping myself up in my fluffiest chenille bathrobe and pushed my feet into soft pink slippers, which Nina had gotten me.

I was making myself a nice evening plate of grapes and peanut butter crackers, when there was a stiff, clipped knock on the door. I considered ignoring it and pretending that I was *Sophie Lawson, Normal Girl,* spending a quiet Saturday night at home after a trip to the farmer's market or something. I imagined anything other than what I had done—anything that didn't include a public restroom—but the knock sounded again.

I pulled my robe tighter over my chest and yanked

open the door, about to tell Will that I wasn't interested in company.

But it wasn't Will.

The air was silent, like the entire building was holding its breath. I could hear the electric buzz of the overhead lights, could hear each straining pump of my heart. I swallowed and willed myself to snap the door closed, but my hand was melted to the knob.

My fingers in a solid death grip.

"It's been a long time, Sophie."

Please turn the page for an exciting sneak peek of Hannah Jayne's next Sophie Lawson novel, coming soon from Kensington Publishing!

He stood in my doorway looking remarkably comfortable, without the faintest glow of otherworldly aura or the oozing, fetid sores I had come to know on those who returned from the dead.

"Sophie."

He said my name and my hackles went up; I was all at once intrigued, delighted, and horrified.

I opened my mouth and then closed it again, willing the words that tumbled through my brain to form some coherent, cohesive thought, something great and all encompassing enough to explain what I was feeling.

"I see dead people," I mumbled.

Without conscious thought my arm snapped back and the door clamped shut. I ran backward into my apartment, falling over the arm of the couch and landing with a thump on the pillows, ending in an inelegant heap on the carpet. My pup ChaCha trotted over to me, sniffed, and walked away. *It's happening, it's happening, it's happening . . .*

I was shaking, the mantra rolling through my head as I curled in on my chest, rocking gently. I knew it was only a matter of time before I developed some sort of mystical powers—red hair and an insatiable appetite for chocolate or anything in a take-out box couldn't be the only things I inherited from my mother and grandmother, who both had been powerful mystics with the ability to tell the future.

"I'm getting my powers." I licked my lips, terror and joy bounding through me.

That was it.

This was my power.

"I see dead people."

I felt the words in my mouth, the exhilaration of finally belonging and finally feeling a connection to my paranormal family chipping away at the terror that sat like an iceberg at the bottom of my gut.

The jiggling of the ancient hardware on my front door brought me crashing back to the reality of a doorknob turning in front of me. I stared at it as it moved horror-movie slow, and my blood pounded in my ears. The person on the other end of the door knocked again. This time it was a quick, warning rap and when he pressed the door open, the air that I had gulped in a greedy, terrified frenzy whooshed out.

"What are you doing here?"

He grinned. "I thought you'd be happier to see me."

I rolled over onto my back and pushed myself up, my eyes still trained on the man—*the apparition?*—that stood in my foyer, smile wide, welcoming, and corporeal looking.

"Mr. Sampson?" His name was a breathy whisper that made my bottom lip quiver. "You need me to help you cross over," I said.

I took a tentative step toward the man whom I had known so well—who had been more like a father than a boss to me for so many years, who had given me my start at the Underworld Detection Agency—whom I had watched being tortured until he finally disappeared, news of his death reaching me months later.

I reached out in front of me, fingers shaking and outstretched, willing myself to touch him, knowing that all I would feel would be a cold burst of nothingness of the displaced molecules that should have been a living, breathing human form.

I stuck my index finger in his right nostril, my thumb brushing his bottom lip.

"Oh, gross!"

"Sophie! What the hell?" he snapped.

My hand recoiled back in near-boogered terror. "Oh my God! Mr. Sampson! You're alive!"

My heart threw itself against my ribcage and every fiber of my being seemed to expand with joy. I crushed myself against Pete Sampson, feeling his wonderful heart thudding against my chest, relishing the human feeling of his tender, warm skin against my own.

He shrugged me off—gently—and held me at arm's length. "You look wonderful."

"You're alive . . . You're alive." I mumbled it dumbly again and again until my eyes could focus on the stiff reality under my fingers. I massaged Mr. Sampson's arms, feeling the ropey muscles flinch underneath his soft flannel shirt, my fingertips working down his fore-arms until I found his bare skin, his pulse point. I paused, counted.

"You're not dead at all. You're really, really alive."

A smile cut across Sampson's face—a smile that went up to his milk-chocolate eyes that crinkled at the corners and warmed me from tip to tail. I stiffened, shook his hands off and slapped him across his chest, anger and betrayal walloping me.

"How are you alive? You're dead. You *were* dead! I mourned for you! And Alex," I huffed, a sob choking in my throat, "and Will." I sniffed, "And I'm the Vessel . . ." Tears flooded over my cheeks and dripped from my chin as I hiccupped and quaked. "Will's my Guardian."

Sympathy, with just the slightest tinge of amusement, flitted across Mr. Sampson's face as he took me by the wrist and offered me a stiffly starched hankie. I held it in my hand, my fingers working the burgundy stitching— the letters *P* and *S* embroidered elegantly against the white cloth.

"You look so different."

The Mr. Sampson whom I had known was always freshly shaven and dressed impeccably in tailored suits that highlighted his powerful build. He kept his dark hair close-cropped and slicked back. This man sported a three-day beard peppered with gray stubble and looked unkempt and disheveled in a wrinkled un-buttoned flannel shirt over a plain white T-shirt. He wore a pair of jeans that were a combination of broken-in and over-worn, but as I held the handkerchief to my nose I smelled the faint scent of the Mr. Sampson I used to know—a scent that was spicy, familiar, with just the slightest hint of salt and pine.

Sampson pulled me to the couch and I sat down next to him, leaving just enough space to let him know that de-spite his heavenly return from death, all was not forgiven.

"What happened to you?" I managed to whisper.

It was then that I noticed the easy laugh lines that had

sat like commas on either side of Sampson's mouth were hard etched now; it was only then that I noticed the latticework of worry lines between his eyes, the thick frown line that cut across his dark brow and the thin streak of gray that sprouted at his hairline, peppering his deep brown hair with a washed out sheen.

"I'm sorry I never contacted you." Sampson shook his head and stared at his hands in his lap. "I wanted to; the last thing I wanted was to have you—you and everyone else at the UDA—worry about me. But if you knew I was alive, that's what would have happened. You would have worried."

He offered me what I assumed was to be his appeasing smile but it only served to stir up a hot seed of anger in my belly.

"You could have let us decide whether or not we worried about you," I spat. "I thought that the Chief killed you. That's what Alex said—"

I stopped, the words going heavy and bitter in my mouth. I felt my eyes narrow, and knew that I was holding my mouth in a hard snarl. "Did Alex know? Did he know this whole time?"

Sampson pushed himself off the couch, avoiding my gaze. "Sophie, Alex—"

I launched myself up then, too, hands on hips. "Alex knew this whole time, didn't he?"

"Not the whole time, Sophie. I had to hide. I had to make it look like I was dead or they would keep coming after me and no one at the Agency would be safe. I wasn't going to do that to the Underworld, Sophie. I needed to know when it would be safe to come back again. And the only way I could do that—the only way

I could do that and still even have the slightest hope of coming back was to have eyes out here."

"Alex's."

"He helped me, Sophie."

I thought of Alex, of his ice blue eyes and that cocky half smile, of the two-inch scars above each shoulder blade that had grown silvery with age after years of wandering the earth without his wings.

Alex was a fallen angel, earthbound but determined to do good, to one day be restored back to grace. He had been my protector, my lover, my friend; and he had lied to me.

"Does he know you're back now?" I wanted to know.

Sampson made a show of looking around my apartment, his silence a clear answer. I made a mental note to Google "ways to kick a fallen angel's ass" on the Internet.

"So, where were you?" I asked.

Sampson cocked his head. "Everywhere. Nowhere. After that night—"

An involuntary shudder wracked my body. The memory of being chained with Sampson in an underground basement while a madman sharpened the sword he was going to use to pierce my flesh was still as cold and as fresh in my mind as it was two years ago. Sampson slid a comforting arm across my shoulders and I slumped against him, my body relying on muscle memory because my brain was still calculating, figuring, tying to make sense of Pete Sampson, alive, in my living room.

"I was rescued—or so I thought—from that damn little kennel."

Sampson clapped a hand over his chin and rubbed where the salt and pepper stubble littered the firm set of his clenched jaw. He looked at me and I could see the smallest flitter of embarrassment cross his face; his shoulders seemed to sag under the weight, under the memory of being chained, being beaten—being treated like an animal by a man whom he had once considered a friend.

"There were people; they said they knew about the Underworld. I didn't have a choice. I got in the car and immediately passed out. I must have been drugged. Then I was crated, moved. I woke up in a shipping yard, somewhere. I knew it was woodsy, or forested, but that's all I knew. Nothing was familiar."

"They dropped you in the woods? In the middle of nowhere? That's awful!"

Sampson wagged his head, the hand that was stroking his chin now raking across his ragged curls and over eyes that were tired, heavy. "I was starving, naked, in the middle of nowhere and by the time I came fully to, so did they."

I gulped, the sour state of my own saliva catching in my throat. "Who were they?"

"The werewolf hunters." He licked his lips. "Trackers. It's an ancient calling . . ."

I nodded. "I know what trackers are, Sampson."

I knew all too well. It had only been a couple of weeks since Will—Will, the man charged with keeping me and all my Vessel of Souls-filled self safe—had had a run in with Xian and Feng Du, Werewolf Hunters. And although werewolf hunters sound incredibly elegant and Van Helsing-esque, you should know that werewolf hunters these days have come out of the silver-bullet forging days of ancient, dusty castles and now took up residence in more urban environments—like in the back of a retro delicatessen in San Francisco's Chinatown.

You should also know that werewolves are not the drooling, shirtless mongrels that modern cinema would like us to believe, changing each time the moon becomes full. First of all, it's not just the moon that brings on the hairy changes in werewolves. If it was, I might have never gotten my first job at the Underworld Detection Agency under Pete Sampson. What edged out the other applicants—a fairly well-put together zombie woman with melon-shaped boobs and a vampire so newly formed that his fangs were still short—was my ability to chain up a grown man in thirty-four seconds flat.

I licked my lips, choosing my words carefully. "So why now? Why did you come back now?"

Sampson swallowed slowly, his eyes flicking quickly over mine, then working hard to avoid my questioning stare.

"Hey, who's this?" He patted ChaCha who popped up on her popsicle-stick back legs and danced around like the ferocious ball of three-pound fur that she was. I snatched her from under his hand and held her to me.

"Why now?" I asked again.

"I couldn't run anymore." Sampson's lips were set in a hard, thin line. "I would have to spend my whole life running. The trackers weren't going to back down."

"How do you know that?"

"They sent me a message."

He paused and I sucked in an anxious breath.

"There was a den—about six of us, werewolves that had been driven from our previous lives. We were living off the grid in a nothing town north of Anchorage. The townspeople were good to us, didn't ask questions, but," he cocked his head, "they knew."

I put ChaCha down, hugged my elbows. "What happened?"

"A few of us went out, decided to check in with one of the satellite UDA offices. When we got back," Sampson swallowed slowly, his Adam's apple bobbing with the effort, "the whole den had been slaughtered."

"That's awful."

Sampson nodded. "They didn't stop there. The town had been ravaged, too."

I felt myself recoil, felt the ice water race through my veins. "They went after the townspeople? I thought the trackers were only after werewolves."

Sampson looked at me, his warm eyes full and wide. "It used to be that way. But this new breed of trackers," he looked away, breathing out a sigh that seemed to dwarf his shoulders, seemed to carry the weight of the years in it. "They're relentless. They attack werewolves . . . and anyone who helps us."

I looked over my shoulder, the hair on my arms standing on end. Sampson reached out to touch my shoulder, then seemed to think better of it, his arm falling listlessly to his side. "I don't want to put you in any danger, Sophie. I'm only here to warn you and Alex. I couldn't stand it if I knew that this—" Sampson turned his hands palms up, "that I—was responsible for anything bad happening to you. I'm leaving tonight. I just needed you to be aware."

"You can't keep running. You said so yourself. They're just going to keep coming after you."

Sampson shrugged. "It's nothing I'm not used to."

"No." I clamped my hand around Sampson's arm. "I want to help you." I paused. "I'm going to help you. Me and Alex—and Will, and Nina—"

Sampson's jaw clenched, fire blazing in his eyes. "I don't want to get any one of you involved in this. It's my fight."

"You said they were coming after the Underworld. It's our fight now, too."

"You don't understand, Sophie. It's bad out there." He gestured absently over his shoulder, toward the San Francisco Bay or the entire world, I couldn't be sure.

I sucked in a breath and forced a smile. "I'm okay with bad. I mean, how bad is bad? Werewolf hunters. Silver bullets, right? Heh, that's nothing. I was almost blown up. And I was kidnapped. Held hostage in a restroom. A *public restroom*." I raised my eyebrows, "beat that!" style.

"After they attacked our den, they decapitated all the townspeople."

My stomach lurched and bile tickled the back of my throat. "That's nothing," I whispered hoarsely, the smile on my face painted on. "So it's settled. You'll stay here."

I looked around my apartment, feeling suddenly hopeful. "Yeah. Yeah, you could stay here. They wouldn't come looking for you here, no one would. And Nina wouldn't mind—you could probably even stay in her room. And Vlad—Vlad and Nina could probably track the trackers before they tracked you. You know," I patted my nose with my index finger, "vampires and their sense of smell."

Sampson shook his head, a smile that held no joy on his lips. "It doesn't work like that, Sophie. They won't stop. If they can't come after me directly, they'll go after the things that are closest to me. That would be you, Nina, the whole Underworld. They'll try and smoke me out by destroying the things that I care about."

"Like the townspeople." The weight of what Sampson was saying, the actual *meaning* set over me, crushing my heart, squeezing what little hope I had managed to summon. "You came back to warn us." I hugged my shoulders. "Because they're already coming here. After us."

"They're coming after the Underworld Detection Agency." Sampson's eyes were fixed on mine. "They're going to come after you."

I crossed my living room in two short strides and had my hand on the phone. "We've got to call Dixon. He's running the UDA now. We need to put him on high alert, tell him you're back. He'll know what to do. He'll know how to protect you. That's what we do," I told Sampson, uselessly, as he knew exactly what the Underworld Detection Agency was about. "We protect our own."

Sampson put his hand on my arm and I held the receiver, limp.

"No one can know I'm here, Sophie. No one can know I'm alive. Especially not anyone at the Underworld Detection Agency."

I hung up the phone, the click of the receiver like the ominous cock of a gun. "So what do we do? How do we outrun them?"

"We don't outrun them, Sophie. We have to fight them."